The
Paradox Initiative

Alydia Rackham

"Alydia Rackham's latest book <u>The Paradox Initiative</u> is a heart-stopping journey through time and space. It combines romance – impeded by a rendezvous with a woman 600 years dead – with time travel, and a breathless chase through a sinister clinic on a strange planet. Rackham's skills in developing character, narrating action, and building a suspenseful plot are all on display here. Much recommended!"
-Dr. Kim Stanley

www.alydiarackham.webs.com
alydia.rackham@facebook.com
Twitter: @AlydiaRackham

For those of you who know who you are.

ONE

Kansas City, Kansas, 2510 A.D.

The alarm beeped. Sharp, ear-splitting pulses.

Kestrel Evans jerked awake.

She groped in the dark and slapped the top of the clock. The alarm stopped. She peered toward the foot of her bed. Light seeped through the little gap between her windowsill and the room-darkening screen. Kestrel groaned, flopped over and threw her blanket over her head.

"I don't want to," she muttered to her pillow. The accusing blue light of her clock just glared at her through her thin blanket.

The soothing sleep music coming from her overhead speakers switched to a quicker, more up-beat tune. Kestrel gritted her teeth.

A lower beep sounded. She huffed, pushed her covers off herself and glanced over to her desk where her little Gramcom sat. She dragged herself out of bed, and set her bare feet on the wooden floor. Swiping her long brown hair out of her face, she yanked her rectangular communicator off its stand. The screen lit up and she squinted down at it.

1 Message.

She punched the picture with her thumb and bit her lip. The message opened, and a bright red-and-green hologram hopped up from the output, making her blink. A vivid 3D image of a rose rapidly bloomed in front of her, and a puff of rose scent drifted into the air. Curly words then blipped into existence and Kestrel half smiled as she read.

So sorry that your job at the museum fell through. They're idiots for not hiring the best intern they had. Hope you feel better soon. ~Anny

Kestrel sighed, closed the message, and snapped her fingers. Her four mushroom lamps came on, which hung in the corners of her ceiling. She tossed her Gramcom down on her bed and stepped up to her set of gray drawers. The bottom one slid open as her feet touched the floor near it. She folded her arms as she considered the clothes inside.

"No." She said. The drawer slipped shut, and the next one hissed open. She bit her lip. "No." The next one opened. "Nope, nope, nope." She glanced up. "Weather report?"

"*Partly cloudy—*" the male-toned computer boomed.

"*Sshhh!*" Kestrel scolded, wincing and throwing up a hand. "Morning voice!"

"*Partly cloudy,*" the computer began again, much quieter. "*Current temperature: sixty-five. The high today: seventy-five. Wind speed: twenty miles per hour.*"

Kestrel tapped the top dresser drawer with her knuckle and it opened. She yanked out a pair of calf-length black pants and a short-sleeved black shirt that came down to mid-thigh. She peeled off her sleeping clothes, tossed them on the bed, put on her undergarments, pulled on the pants and shrugged into the shirt, then laced up the front. She tugged on a pair of closed-toed riding shoes, then dragged to her bedroom door, rubbing her eyes—

And banged her forehead into the door.

She jerked back, her hand flying to her head.

"Ajax!" she snapped at the computer. Nothing happened. She heaved a sigh and slammed her palm against the door. "Wake up, stupid."

The door buzzed open. Her music stopped. Kestrel rolled her eyes and stumped out into the dark hall. "Worthless computer..." She swung around a corner stepped through the door of the white kitchen.

She stopped and blinked against the bright light. Her mother, pulling a protein shake out of the refrigerator, straightened and slid the door shut.

"Good morning, Sis," she smiled. She wore a black, sharp suit, her blonde hair done up in a bun. She always looked so tall and dignified—and beautiful, of course. Her blue eyes sparkled at her daughter.

"How did you sleep?"

"Meh," Kestrel shrugged, and started toward the refrigerator as well. To her left, she glimpsed her dad sitting at the kitchen table, also dressed in a black suit, chewing a bite of toast as he watched the business reports that blinked across his pad screen. He had graying black hair and a short beard.

Across from him sat her two younger brothers, twins, who had the same complexion as their mother, and curly blonde hair. Each of them wolfed down his scrambled-egg substitute with one hand and held a beeping pad screen in the other.

"Are you two cramming for your bio-stellar exam?" Kestrel arched an eyebrow at them as she passed.

"I'm not cramming," Marcus, the elder, said around a mouthful of food. "I'm playing *Ortheus.*"

"Then you're an idiot," Aidus, the younger, remarked, narrowing his eyes at his own screen. "You're going to fail."

"I looked over everything last night," Marcus protested. "I know it all."

"That had better be true," their dad warned, glancing up at them. "Since you two probably spent at least three hours playing games last night."

The two teenage boys launched into a hearty self-defense while Kestrel drew up next to her mom, faced the refrigerator and stared at the glowing screen on its stainless-steel front.

"Feeling okay?" her mom asked, pulling her into a side hug and kissing the side of her head. Kestrel sighed.

"I guess. Still not too happy."

"That whole situation just makes me mad," her dad muttered, finishing off his toast. "The museum tells you that they're going to *hire* you after you finish your internship, so you should go ahead and get an apartment downtown and plan on quitting your job—and then *nothing.* They hire the owner's *nephew.*" He shook his head. "I'm just glad you were able to get out of that apartment lease."

"*I'm* glad to have you around again," her mom winked at her and crossed to the cupboard. "I was lonesome without you."

Kestrel smiled a little in spite of herself. She flicked her fingertip across the images on the front of the refrigerator, biting her lip, then pointed to one of a fried egg. The stove and refrigerator revved up, and she headed to the bathroom across the hall.

She untied and sleepily combed out her chestnut, waist-length hair with the straightening comb, eliminating every wave and stray curl.

"How do those dark streaks look?" her mother called from the kitchen. "Have they faded at all?"

Kestrel glowered, holding up a strand.

"No. I'm not using that dying program again." Swiftly, she bound all her hair up in a high ponytail so her tresses fell across her shoulders. After washing her face, she glanced at herself in the reflecting screen, then glared. Her skin was smooth, but she looked slightly colorless.

"Why don't you wear that new sparkly purple eye-shadow I got you?" her mom suggested. "It looks so pretty with your big brown eyes."

"I don't feel like it," Kestrel admitted, glaring back into the gaze of the identical young woman. She headed back into to the kitchen, retrieved her now-fried egg along with a glass of juice, sat down at the table on the other side of her dad and made herself eat. She only half listened to her brothers' banter and her dad's comments about the stock market, and her mother's concerns about the case she would be trying that day. Kestrel gazed out the window at the birds fluttering on the green lawn, her heart heavy, and finished her meal. After putting her clattering dishes in the washer and brushing her teeth, she grabbed her satchel and pushed the front door open.

"Bye, sweetie," her dad called. "Try to have some fun anyway, okay?"

"Okay," she managed. "Bye."

A warm breeze greeted her. She drew a slow breath of the scent of apple blossoms. She kicked a rock down the cement path that cut through the lawn, adjusting her pack on her shoulder. Robins chirped madly all around her, and she caught sight of several white butterflies. Bright sunlight flickered through the new leaves of the maple in her front yard, glinting against the white and chrome of her racing blastbike parked in the drive.

She reached out and patted the soft, leather saddle, then slung her leg over the bike, grabbed the handlebars and pressed the buttons with her thumbs.

"*Good morning, Kestrel Evans,*" a calm female voice greeted her from the console.

"Hi, Thrix. Let's go."

The engine rumbled to life and revved. Heavy-beat driving music blared from the speakers. Kestrel turned it down two clicks, then kicked off.

The light, slender, two-wheeled vehicle zipped down the driveway, then swung around and darted off down the narrow paved road. Trees and houses whipped past, lit by the golden morning. The finely-tuned engine sang. Wind whipped Kestrel's hair. She squinted.

"Sparks," she muttered.

"*Is there a problem?*" Thrix voice asked.

"Forgot my shades," she answered over the wind. "Put up the shield and call Anny for me, will you?"

"As you wish."

With a zap, the invisible, protective force field popped up around Kestrel, shutting out the wind, humidity and road noise. The bike phone trilled. Kestrel kept her eyes on the road as she swept out of the narrow residential street and up an on-ramp, leaning hard to one side, her engine howling into a new gear. Cool air blew at her from the console.

She clicked on her turn signal and merged into a broad, busy four lane highway. But even though hundreds of flashing liftcars and bikes sped along all around her on their morning commute, the only engine she could hear was that of her own bike.

"Hi, Sweetflower," Anny's clear voice came through the small vox speaker.

"Hello."

"Sleep any last night?" Anny wondered.

"Not much," Kestrel confessed, swerving around a puttering, rusty family wagon and settling back in the saddle. "I still can't believe I didn't get it."

"I told you, girl. They're idiots. You'll find another job soon—a better one. But I understand if you need chocolate."

Kestrel smiled crookedly as she eyed the upcoming traffic light hovering over her lane.

"That's a definite possibility."

"I'll get some for you," Anny stated. "And, as a bonus, I'll send my personal ninjas after the museum manager. Wahahaha!"

Kestrel grinned, her heart lifting.

"Thanks. You're the best."

"Message me if you need to. And if you want, I can come by and we can get lunch—I'm just down the terminal, remember. It isn't the season to travel to ice planets, so selling thermal gear hasn't really kept me that busy."

"Okay—sounds good," Kestrel said. "I'm almost there. Talk to you later."

"Ciao."

The call ended just as a massive, heavy growl pressed down on her. She grimaced and glanced up.

A huge, sleek, silver ship glided through the air, glittering in the towering light, leaving three graceful jet streams behind in the crystal blue sky. Kestrel watched its trajectory, for she and the ship now headed the same direction.

Ahead of them, leaping up against the skyline like a mountain, waited a vast, city-sized structure resembling a titanic stadium. Ten miles wide and two miles high, its outer walls flashed with thousands of moving advertisements and signs, and in the towering sky above it, hundreds of glittering, multi-colored spacecraft circled and wove, waiting their turn to land.

Kestrel kicked her bike into the highest gear and sped through the last intersection, blasting past two older bikes to sweep down the exit ramp.

"I hate Mondays," she sighed as the shadow of the spaceship fell across her, and she pulled into the crowded, noisy, seething parking lot of the Kansas City Space Port.

"I'm sorry I'm late," Kestrel said before the door shut behind her. "They put in a fifth security gate and it held everybody up."

Her boss, a black-haired, middle-aged woman in a blue suit, glanced up from behind the counter at the other end of the room.

"You forgot to put the M68's back on the rack after you polished them last night," her boss said before returning her attention to the portable screen before her. Kestrel winced.

"Sorry. I'll program a reminder." Kestrel hurriedly checked the rest of the shop, hoping she hadn't forgotten anything else. All of the weaponry, both small and large *Blitz* technology guns, and hunting staves and knives, hung in neat, gleaming rows to her right—pristine and sharp against the white walls. On her left, all the thermal bags, travel bottles and coolers lay stacked or hung, and behind the counter, all of the non-perishable food packages and ammunition remained locked in their clear cases. Kestrel's heels clicked on the white tile floor as she quickly maneuvered around the counter—and her boss—and entered the more dimly-lit back room, which was stuffed with black boxes of merchandise.

"*Good morning, Kestrel Evans,*" the time-clock computer

acknowledged.

"Hi, Diva."

"*You are late this morning, Kestrel Evans.*"

"I *know*, Diva," Kestrel sighed. "I have a clock, too."

"*Perhaps you need a new one, Kestrel Evans,*" Diva replied.

"Oh, ha ha," Kestrel shot an ugly look up at the lights. "So now you've grown a humor chip?"

"*I do not understand the question,*" Diva stated.

"Good," Kestrel muttered, set her satchel down on the narrow table and went back out into the shop.

"I am going up to the office to order more ammunition for the 85X's, since we're running low," her boss stated as Kestrel entered, still studying the screen of her computer. "If you could stock the non-perishable green-beans and the prunes, that would be good—though I have no idea why we're low on those. They're disgusting."

"I guess they last the longest," Kestrel assumed as her boss stepped past her and headed toward the elevator to their right.

"Yuck," the boss replied. "But if people want to buy them, I'll stock them. Call me if you need anything."

"Okay," Kestrel nodded as the other woman entered the lift and the door shut behind her. Kestrel sighed, glanced down at the food rack, then at the guns.

"Cheap guns or disgusting space food first?" she murmured—and her heart sank. She took a deep breath, swallowed, and drew herself up. "Okay, okay. Guns first."

"So which one is more efficient, energy-wise?"

Kestrel folded her arms and looked up and down the wall of guns, then glanced at the middle-aged tourist who stood beside her, dressed in too-tight pants and a too-loose white shirt, both made out of fine material. He had all the marks of a businessman, freshly retired, who was out trying adventurous things for the first time but didn't have a clue what he was shopping for.

"Well, the K95 is pretty good about conserving *blitz*volts," Kestrel said. "But aren't you going hunting?"

The graying man nodded.

"Yeah, on Yeshin, in the mountains. Just a group of friends."

Kestrel's eyebrows went up.

"So you're hunting bear and wildcat and stuff like that."

He grinned at her.

"You bet."

"Then the K95 is not what you want. That's for a hand weapon, self-defense stuff. You want the C12 up there."

"The long one up there?" he pointed.

"Well, it's long*er*," Kestrel shrugged. "Longer than the K95 but shorter range than the C10. The C10 is *really* long, and built for hunting on the flatlands. The C12 is designed specifically for hunting large game in the mountains. There are three regular scopes, plus an infrared scope and an internal conditioner that keeps your power source from freezing or creating condensation."

"How much is it?" the customer asked.

"Four hundred. And the ammunition is fifty."

He winced.

"That eats up a third of what I'd decided to spend on this stuff."

Kestrel shrugged.

"That's the gun you've got to have. And I promise, you won't find it cheaper in this spaceport."

He let out a puff of air.

"Can I try it out in a simulator?"

"Sure. Training Mode C12 to ground level," Kestrel called. The C12, a glimmering silver and black shoulder gun, ejected from its spot at the very top, and the robotic arm holding it extended down with a hum, passed over the other guns, and handed the weapon to Kestrel. She took the gun down and flipped it around, its light weight clicking in her hands. She lifted her chin and faced the customer, holding it out to him with a smile.

"The target screens are straight through there," she pointed to a black door to her right. "Take as long as you need."

"Thanks," he nodded, and took the gun from her as if it might break. Kestrel put her hands on her hips as she watched him head through the door, then faced the wall of countless guns. She patted the nearest one, then headed back behind the counter to sit down and work on inventory while she waited.

Not ten minutes later, the man emerged.

"Well, how did you like it?" she asked brightly, looking up from her list.

He shook his head.

"I didn't. I want the K95."

Kestrel frowned.

"But—"

"I don't enjoy long guns, and I can't afford this one, anyway." He set it down on the counter in front of her. It clacked loudly.

"Oh. Okay," Kestrel managed, got up from her stool, walked back out and called down the operational K95. She hefted the much-smaller in both hands, checked it quickly, and then came back to the counter. She hesitated, then glanced up at him.

"You want to try this in the simulator too, or—"

"No," he looked down at the time-piece on his wrist. "I don't have time. Thank you."

"All right. There's a security device I have to remove," she said, turning around to the workbench. "And then I can check your ID and license and take your card."

"You seem to know a lot about this stuff," the customer commented.

"I've worked here on and off for two years," Kestrel answered, picking up the small deactivator and running it three times across the butt of the gun. It beeped.

"How old are you? You go to school?"

"I'm twenty-four. And I graduated."

"From where?"

"Missouri University for Linguistics and Literature," Kestrel answered, snapping the gun into its case, turning back to him and holding out his purchase. The man chuckled and assessed the room.

"And you're working *here?*"

Kestrel froze. Then, she looked down and activated the register. She pulled in a tight breath and forced a smile.

"Yep. Working in the hometown for a while, making some money, building up the bank account."

"Sure, sure," he nodded, picking up the gun. "That's good."

He handed her his card. She took it and swiped it across the reader. Then she checked to make sure he had the right ammo, exchanged parting pleasantries, and watched his back as he strolled out of the shop and into the port. The door clicked shut, and Kestrel was left alone. For a long moment, she didn't move. Finally, she leaned her hands on the counter and closed her eyes.

The floor trembled.

The cases rattled.

Her eyes flew open.

The walls heaved. Guns clattered to the floor.

Kestrel whirled around.

A deafening *BASH* crashed through the back room. Kestrel grabbed hold of the counter and held on.

It stopped.

The shop fell silent. She waited.

But nothing else happened.

She started breathing again.

Her heel squeaked as she took one step toward the door of the back room. Another. Then another. She bit her cheek, and crossed the threshold.

Diva said nothing. The whole room sat in darkness. Kestrel stopped.

Sparks snapped across the room.

She flinched. Everything went black again.

A sound.

A low, steady hiss. Like pressure releasing.

"Hello?" she called.

No one answered. She bent down and felt for the small cabinet to her right. Her fingers bumped it. She tapped the door, and it slid open. She groped inside. Her fingers closed around the rubber handle of a small flashlight. Straightening, she clicked it on.

She gasped.

In the middle of her wrecked storage room, boxes crushed and sundered all around it, stood an eight-foot-tall silver cylinder. Steam simmered out from under it, covering the floor.

She snatched her Gramcom out of her pocket and lifted it to her mouth.

The cylinder clicked.

She jumped.

With a grating grind, a formerly-invisible door eased open. White light spilled out.

Kestrel dove for a broken box. She shoved the lid off, dropped her Gramcom and grabbed the heavy handgun inside. She straightened up and leveled the gun at the machine. Her hands shook.

A figure stood inside.

A tall black silhouette, cut sharply against the shining white.

Broad-shouldered. Windblown hair.

He stood very still.

An ember breathed to life near his face. Smoke curled against his shadow and rose into the air.

And then, the white light glinted against the barrel of some sort of weapon.

Kestrel's gut clenched.

"What are you doing with that?"

He had spoken. His voice rasped low, deep—and sounded as if he held something between his lips. Kestrel's cold fingers shivered.

"Who are you?" she demanded. "What happened? How did you get in here?"

"Put that down," he said, his tone deathly calm, like ice frozen to the depths. "You don't know how to use it, anyway."

"You think I don't?" Kestrel snapped, lifting it higher. "Want to put money on that?"

"It's not loaded."

Kestrel stopped. Slowly, his shadowed head tilted. The ember glowed to life again, then faded. He reached up with his left hand and took whatever-it-was out of his mouth, and sighed. A gust of smoke clouded around his hair.

"I don't want to shoot you," he said. "But I will if you keep pointing that thing at me."

Kestrel's body shuddered.

His whole bearing turned hard.

"Put it down."

Kestrel's mouth went dry. Slowly, she lowered the gun, and set it on top of the cabinet. It clicked against the surface. She let go of it.

He moved.

He strode right toward her—she leaped to the side, crashing noisily into a fallen box and barely catching herself.

He stepped into the light of the doorway, then halted, gazing out into the shop.

He loomed over her—taller than her father. He wore a beaten black leather jacket and scorched jeans. His light-brown, unkempt hair gave him a sharp, wild profile, and barely hid a long scar on his forehead. He was young—just a few years older than her. Handsome even. Stubble marked his jaw and upper lip, as if he hadn't shaved in a day or two. Strong, keen features—rugged and intent—a set mouth and a scowling brow.

He lifted his left hand and brought a short white stick to his lips. He pulled in a long breath—the ember glowed. He sighed again, and gray fume issued with his breath. It smelled like poison. He lowered the white stick, and turned his head toward her.

Gray eyes. Striking, shadowed gray eyes, like the sky over the prairie before a storm. His knitted brow eased—dark eyebrows raised in a softer, wry expression. He studied her face.

"It *wasn't* loaded, was it?" he said.

Kestrel stared at him. She swallowed.

He almost smiled, then gave her a look.

"You've got to work on that poker face, Brown Eyes."

Kestrel's lips parted—she couldn't say anything.

And then she twitched back when he hefted his weapon.

He hooked the long, metal barrel over his right elbow, stuck the white stick in his mouth again and, frowning, snapped the barrel open and stared down the tubes. He pulled two little cylinders out of the tubes, glanced at them, then rammed them into his coat pocket.

"What..." Kestrel choked. "What kind of gun is that?"

He didn't answer. He snapped the barrel shut, took one last pull on the white stick, then dropped it on the hard floor and stepped on it.

"Where am I?" he asked.

"Uh..." Kestrel stammered. "The...The KCSP."

"The *city* would be helpful," he muttered, stepping heavily down out of the back room and into the shop. His attention caught on the wall of weapons, and he slowed down.

"Kansas City...Space Port," Kestrel managed. "What—Where did you come from?"

"*Transmission sent and received. System failure. Self-destruct initiated.*"

Kestrel spun around. A computer had spoken. And it *wasn't* Diva.

The cylinder's door slid shut. And all at once, the air turned hot.

A shoulder thudded against hers. Kestrel staggered sideways.

The stranger leaped through the door, his gun in one hand. He skidded to a stop and stared at the cylinder. For an instant, neither of them moved.

The cylinder quivered.

He barked one word in another language.

He threw down his gun—it clattered on the floor. He grabbed Kestrel's arm and yanked her out of the back room. She tripped. He jerked her up.

"What is going on?" she yelped. He didn't answer. They raced through the shop, he shoved the front door open and threw her down onto the outside floor. She crashed onto her side, pain jarring her knee and shoulder—

He leaped on top of her, smashing her, wrapping his arms around her head and shoulders and pressing his forehead to her temple. Leather, smoke and the smell of fireworks smothered her—

BOOM!

Kestrel screamed.

A concussion slapped into them, crushing them into the laminated floor.

Pressure mounted—the skylight burst.

Bits of rock and shards of metal and glass pelted them like hailstones, shattering all around them and beating against his back.

Blistering heat rolled over them.

And then a thick, choking cloud of dust swallowed them.

The thunder of the explosion yammered through the wings and levels of the spaceport, then gradually faded.

Kestrel's ears rang. Her head spun. Her breathing rattled around in her skull, too loudly—she couldn't hear anything else.

He pulled up and off of her—his jacket slipped loose of her fingers. He sat back on his heels and, wincing, glanced back toward the door of the shop, but the brown dust billowed like fog. It settled over him, coating him. Sunlight spilled down through the now-open ceiling, flooding through the clouds and casting him in an eerie, distant light. He looked like a ghost.

His throat convulsed. He took a deep breath, then coughed, hard. He covered his mouth—his brow knotted. Kestrel sat up, shook her head, tugged on her right ear...

Her hearing cleared.

He coughed again. The sound tangled through his chest, like pneumonia. He gasped sharply, swallowed, then coughed again, and staggered to his feet. Dust washed across him, almost hiding him.

Kestrel stood up. She stumbled sideways. Her skull buzzed. She closed her eyes, shook her head, and opened her eyes again.

"You..." she started, and winced. Her thoughts skittered away. She squinted at him—he faded into the cloud. She opened her mouth. No sound came out.

Her knees went weak.

Everything turned black.

TWO

Five Days Later

Kestrel leaned her head against the window of the family flier. Absently, she watched the cityscape and other vehicles speed by outside, lit by the midday sun, as she rubbed one thumb against the back of the other. The engine hummed, lulling her, and the cool gray interior soothed her headache. Much better than white, *white* everywhere...

"You feeling all right?" her dad asked from the driver's seat—she sensed him turn his head and glance at her.

"I've been feeling completely *fine* all week," Kestrel answered. "But I still spent all week in the hospital."

"You had a *head injury*," he reminded her. "They had to watch you."

"Yeah," she sighed.

"Listen," her dad said, shifting in his seat. "Mom's having your favorite made for supper, and then all of us can play a round of *Ortheus* together. You don't have to start job or apartment searching until tomorrow, okay?"

Kestrel smiled at him.

"Okay. Sounds good."

Her dad smiled back—deepening the affectionate lines around his dark eyes—and he let go of the steering with one hand. His warm fingers reached hers, wrapped around and squeezed. She squeezed back as his grip on her tightened, and she turned toward the window again.

A head injury. That's what *everyone* thought—and she let them think it. She had told them she couldn't remember anything that had happened.

She set her jaw.

Striking gray eyes, like the prairie sky before a storm...

As soon as she had regained consciousness, the law-enforcement had plied her with questions. Then the doctors had their turn, then the nurses, then her family, then Anny, then the detectives, then the law-enforcement again...

No.

No one would believe her if she told the truth. And she would *not* take the risk of anyone rushing her back to the hospital—it felt too good to be back in her form-hugging black clothes instead of those almost-sheer medical robes.

She would keep everything to herself, just as she had all week. And she would try to forget about it.

Kestrel sat down on the soft white chair in the courtyard behind her house. She settled and leaned back, letting out a deep sigh. The cool evening air rustled the topmost leaves of the single cottonwood sapling in the center, evoking a sound like distant tumbling water. She absently glanced around at the shadowed yard as she laid her head back against the canvas pillow. Her mother had designed the small space so that every surface had been lined out with white stones—the walls and the floor—and various pots of shrubbery and bright red geraniums stood in corners or huddled around the base of the cottonwood. Kestrel tapped her boot once against the flagstone, listening as the quiet *slap* resounded. She did it again—but this time, laser shots, cries of triumph and a simulated explosion from back inside the house interrupted the echo.

She glanced back at the reflective sliding door, then faced the yard again. Her family was still playing *Ortheus*—they'd been at it for three hours. Kestrel had joined them at first, but finally had complained of a headache and retreated outside.

Now, she tilted her head back, facing the sky. The whole vast canvas, brushed through with high, wispy clouds, had faded to pink and light purple. Traffic rumbled in the distance. She could faintly hear the neighbors' 4D entertainment system emitting a steady, musical beat, and she could almost taste the scent of grilling steak from the restaurant two blocks away.

The back door slid open.

"Hey, Kes."

"Hm?" Kestrel didn't turn around. She knew it was Marcus. Her brother leaned on the doorframe—it creaked.

"Wanna come in and play another round?"

"What, and get beat again?" Kestrel laughed.

"I'll let you win," Marcus allowed. "I'll play with my other hand. Aidus will too."

"Like *that* will help."

"You're a good shot!" Marcus said. Kestrel kicked against the ground and spun her chair around to face him. Her tall, blonde brother raised his eyebrows at her.

"I can shoot better than you with my eyes closed," she declared, and pointed at him. "But I can't fly worth anything and you *know that.*"

He grinned at her.

"Yeah, you're pretty bad..."

"Shut up."

Marcus chuckled.

"Oh, come on. Don't be a coward."

"Okay," Kestrel huffed, leaning back and spinning around again. "In ten minutes I'll come in."

"You'd better," Marcus warned, stepped back inside and shut the door.

Quiet fell again. The muted sound-effects of *Ortheus* resumed.

Kestrel studied the sky. A single star had come out to twinkle while she had been talking with her brother—very high, very soft. She bit her lip as her heart grew heavy. Today was almost over. Tomorrow, she would begin another long search, another quest to find a career, a purpose, a goal...

The sky gradually darkened. More stars winked into being. The shadows of the courtyard deepened.

Something flickered.

Thud.

She blinked. Sat up.

Looked toward the far corner of the yard.

A form crouched on the ground. He stood.

Kestrel's chest locked. She grabbed the sides of the chair.

He walked toward her. Long, swift strides.

Then, light from one of her house windows washed across part of him.

Heavy boots. Jeans. A leather jacket and faded shirt. Broad shoulders; dark, wild hair. Striking, rugged, handsome face and limitless, piercing gray eyes.

Eyes that instantly found hers.

"Miss Evans?" he asked—cutting and quiet. "Miss Kestrel Evans?"

"I...What?" Kestrel stammered.

"Is that your name?" he demanded, drawing up and standing in front of her, his gaze pinning her.

"Yes," she said, heart pounding. "What—Who are you? What are you doing here?"

"You don't remember me?" he frowned.

"I—Yes, I do," she admitted, eyes wide. "What do you want?"

"I need to ask you something," he answered. He glanced past her at the back door, then addressed her again. "Have you ever heard of a man named William Jakiv?"

Kestrel's mouth fell open.

"Yes, he's...He's a scientist," she managed. He watched her.

"What kind of scientist?"

"Um..." Kestrel's mind flew. "The last time I heard anything about him, he was working on something very controversial. The...I think it's called the Paradox Initiative."

His eyes narrowed.

"What's that?"

"Exploring time travel," Kestrel said. "Self-replication, the interference principle...But it's illegal to experiment."

He turned his head, his attention shifting away—distancing. His jaw tightened. Kestrel risked a breath.

"Who are you?"

He glanced back at her.

"My name is Jack Wolfe," he said.

"Why did you...I mean, why are you here?" Kestrel asked, her heart pounding so fast it was hard to breathe.

"You owe me a debt," he said, keenly surveying the tops of the courtyard walls. "And you've got no reason to tell me stories." He dug in his pocket, pulled out a little rattling box and glanced down into it. His mouth tightened. He pulled out a short, white stick and put it between his lips, then stuffed the box back in his pocket. Then, he withdrew a small device and cupped one hand around the end of the white stick. He struck a flame. The light flashed across his face, illuminating the long scar across his forehead, and another one on his cheekbone that Kestrel hadn't noticed before. He lit the end of the white stick, put the lighter away, and puffed delicate gray smoke through his lips.

"Who are you *really*?" Kestrel whispered.

He looked right at her. For a long moment, he didn't move.

Then, something sharp and unreadable crossed his face.

The air vibrated.

A deep, sub-sonic disturbance thudded through Kestrel's bones.

She jumped to her feet and spun around.

"What—" she gasped, searching the dark sky.

Harsh white lights flashed up through her front yard, splintered by the leaves of the trees. The pulsing *thud-thud-thud* shook the ground. It lowered, settled—

Wolfe touched her elbow.

Something on the front of her house—a window, a door—bashed open and shattered.

Wolfe grabbed her.

"*Mom!*" Kestrel screamed. Wolfe yanked her backward, clapping a hand over her mouth. Kestrel lashed out, twisting to strike him in the neck, the face. He caught her other hand, wrenched her arms behind her, turned her and drove her out in front of him.

Something else smashed. Startled voices darted through her house. First her mom, then Marcus—then Aidus and her dad.

"Dad! *Dad!*" Kestrel shrieked. Wolfe spat the white stick onto the ground.

"Shut up," he snarled in her ear as he shoved his shoulder against the side gate. "Shut up or you'll be dead."

Kestrel's throat closed. They stumbled through the metal gate—it clanged shut after they passed through. Then, Wolfe leaned back and kicked the control panel of the garage. The side door hissed open. It was black in there. Wolfe threw her inside. Instantly, the smell of must, engine parts and paint filled her lungs. She couldn't see anything.

Her shins barked against Thrix. Wolfe shoved her down on her knees on the cement—he landed right behind her. He wrapped one arm all the way around her, binding her arms to her sides, and the other hand pressed over her mouth. He pulled her tightly back into his chest—she could feel him breathing, feel his heartbeat staggering against her spine. Kestrel's eyes flashed.

He was afraid.

Kestrel tried to take a breath—he crushed her to him even tighter. She almost gagged on the stench of that dirty smoke.

Voices out front. Men yelling.

Her mother and father protesting—desperate.

Kestrel twitched.

"*Sh*," Wolfe said through his teeth, the fingers of his left hand clenching the sleeve of her right arm. Then, she caught some of the shouted words.

"Where is your daughter?"

The tones sounded electronic—spoken through a distorting vox mask.

"I don't know—What do you want?" her mother demanded. "You can't come in here and—"

"We are authorized to take whatever measures are necessary," the strange voice answered. "Where is she?"

"You come here and attack my house and expect me to tell you where my daughter is?" her dad raged. "Under *no* circumstances will I—"

"Then, sir, you're all coming with us," said another voice.

Kestrel writhed. Wolfe tightened down so hard her ribs felt like they were about to crack.

"You *can't*—" her mom tried again—and then a chaos of shouting and howling erupted from every member of her family. Kestrel's brow knotted. She swallowed repeatedly, but couldn't move.

The voices shifted location—moved out from the house and onto the lawn, toward the deep thudding and the lights. They faded—silenced.

Kestrel's heart stopped.

Then—

"Search the house," the machine-like voice ordered. "And open this garage."

Wolfe, his hand still over her mouth, turned Kestrel's head to the right—he pressed the bridge of his nose to her temple and his lips moved against her ear.

"Is this a bike in front of us?" he breathed. "Nod if so."

She gulped—managed a short nod.

"As soon as the door cracks open, jump on it and turn it on. Then lay flat on the console and keep your head down."

Kestrel didn't move. He shook her.

"Do you understand?"

She nodded again.

Many footsteps rang on the paving right outside the garage door. Keys beeped on the control panel. The overhead engine moaned.

A sliver of light sliced underneath the door.

Wolfe's arms abruptly released her—he shoved her up and forward.

Kestrel fumbled for the saddle—her hands slipped across the smooth leather. She clambered on and straddled the bike, and slapped her hands down on the handlebars.

The garage door swept up and open.

Five men waited outside, silhouetted sharply against the white light.

They had guns.

"*Good evening, Kestrel Evans,*" Thrix purred—and the powerful blastbike thrummed to life.

Wolfe leaped on behind her. He shoved her head down onto the console and pushed her hands off the bars. His whole chest pressed down on her back—he wrapped his legs around hers and planted his heels on the footrests. Kestrel craned her neck to see out front...

"There!" one of the men cried, pointing.

Kestrel gasped.

Wolfe gunned it.

Thrix shot forward. Kestrel frantically grabbed the control board to keep from slipping off. The men threw themselves out of the way.

The bike blazed out into the night, wind whipping through their clothes and hair. Kestrel managed to lift her head...

A sleek black ship hovered just twenty feet above her front lawn. Spotlights mounted on its side blared stark illumination straight at her house. Wolfe headed right for it.

Laserfire cracked behind them.

Green beams flashed past their heads. Kestrel yelped and ducked.

Wolfe steered Thrix out over the grass, straight toward the ship—

They swept into its black shadow—and passed beneath the whole ship.

The pounding thrusters shuddered against them. Kestrel gritted her teeth...

They bumped down the curb and burst out on the other side.

Wolfe shifted gears—Thrix leaped forward, tearing down the street, engine howling. Following gunfire ripped the air behind and in front of them.

Fighting the g-force, Kestrel reached out, slid her hand across the buttons and clicked one switch.

Bzzt!

The protective shield snapped up around them.

The bike twitched—Kestrel grabbed Wolfe's wrists.

"What was that?" he barked.

A green bolt *pinged* off the shield.

Wolfe and Kestrel jerked their heads around—the men kept firing at them.

"You'd rather get shot?" Kestrel panted.

"No, thank you," he muttered. He leaned hard to the left. The engine whined as he wheeled around a corner and sped off down a dark street. Tall lamps blurred together on either side.

The air throbbed again. Kestrel couldn't breathe.

And the blinding searchlight of the ship cascaded over them.

Kestrel, gripping the bars right next to Wolfe's hands, tried to glance up over his shoulder—

"Keep your head down," he ordered. Then, he swerved to the right, into an unlit alley, and kicked up a fury of dust as he shifted into the *next* gear.

The throbbing lessened. The beam of light broadened. Kestrel felt the ship lift higher into the air.

The alley turned. Wolfe ignored it. He plowed through gravel, clipped between three tall trash bins, flattened an empty carton, hopped down a curb and screamed down a ramp and onto the highway.

The wide road flooded with lamplight. Kestrel clenched her jaw hard as Wolfe recklessly wove back and forth through the noisy traffic, threading the bike like a needle between bulky, towering cargo transports and low, mean-looking sports fliers. Thrix shivered tightly with every turn and dip and swing. Kestrel glanced down at the glowing speedometer. Wolfe was breaking the speed limitation by thirty miles an hour. Kestrel had *never* driven Thrix this fast.

The distant spotlight still surrounded them in a jarring halo that cut through the other lights—and Kestrel could still sense that low *thud-thud-thud.*

And then it grew louder.

The blaring light glinted against every metal surface of the bike. It turned their skin white.

The ship was coming down *on top* of them.

Kestrel's breath caught. She turned—her eyes instantly dazzled—

Wolfe braked.

Kestrel lurched forward.

The spotlight darted ahead.

Wolfe jerked the bars. Thrix reeled to the right, flashed dangerously close to the front end of a low flier, and plunged down an exit ramp.

No sooner had they reached the bottom than Wolfe wheeled to the *left* and darted underneath the overpass. He screeched to a halt and killed the engine. The shield snapped off. Panting, Wolfe leaned slowly to the side and put one foot on the ground.

Kestrel froze, her heart pounding, her fingers shaking on the handlebars. She blinked, trying to clear her eyes of the spot of white light. Wolfe's labored breathing pressed rhythmically against her back, disturbing her hair.

Kestrel gulped. Out ahead of them, an empty, narrow, dimly-lit street waited. Trash blew across the cracked paving. An orange sign blinked, half burnt out, on a low rooftop.

Wolfe drew in a low breath, then eased back off of her.

Kestrel sat up, pulled her left knee up and turned around on the saddle, sitting on her leg and facing Wolfe directly. He leaned back and raised his eyebrows at her. She could see most of his hard features in the dingy light.

" *What...*" she hissed, her voice and fists quivering. "...is *going on?*"

"We don't have a whole lot of time—" he started.

"Talk fast, then," Kestrel countered. He sighed, glanced away and put his hands on his legs.

"William Jakiv," he muttered. "The scientist I was asking about." Wolfe looked at her. "He's after you."

"What?" Kestrel cried. "Why?"

"Because the machine landed in your shop. And then it self-destructed."

"But that didn't have anything to do with me!" Kestrel protested.

"He doesn't know that," Wolfe shook his head. "He thinks he can use you."

"For what?" she demanded. He gazed at her.

"To get to me."

Kestrel hesitated.

"You?" she paused. "Why?"

Wolfe shrugged one shoulder.

"I know a couple things about him," he answered, scooting back and glancing past her. "Things he'd rather nobody knew."

"Like what?" Kestrel pressed, watching him.

Wolfe returned his attention to her.

"The less *you* know, the better," he said. "Because right now, your folks are the ones he's got."

Kestrel's whole gut tightened.

"What will he do to them?"

"No idea," he confessed quietly. "But I wouldn't trade places with them."

Kestrel shuddered, her body going weak. She pressed her hand to her lips—her fingertips shook. Wolfe's voice softened.

"Do you have any idea where Jakiv lives?"

"Most scientists live in the Triple Star System," Kestrel answered faintly.

"The Triple *Star* System..." Wolfe repeated, his tone suddenly distant. He stayed silent for a second, then shifted in his seat. "Where, specifically, in the...Triple Star System?"

"The Gain Station," Kestrel murmured, unfocused.

"How long does it take to get there?"

"I don't know," Kestrel shook her head. "Maybe two weeks, by public transport." She swallowed. "At least, that's how long it took when I went with my dad..."

Neither of them said anything for a minute. Then, Wolfe leaned toward her. The leather squeaked.

"Listen, Brown Eyes," he said, lowering his head so he could see her face. "I've been hunting for this man for years. He has something that I want, and I *will* get it. But right at the moment, as I'm taking a look around..." he sighed, and shot a glance up the street again. "I think I'm going to need a navigator."

Kestrel's head came up. He regarded her plainly, his grey eyes looking straight into hers.

"I don't like women as traveling companions because I don't appreciate having to take care of them all the time," he said. His voice firmed. "But if you'll help me, I give you my word that I'll help you get your family back."

Kestrel's heart leaped—then tightened as she stared back at him. She lowered her hand from her mouth.

"And I'm...I'm just supposed to trust you."

He shrugged.

"Don't have much of a choice. Unless of course you want to try and find them all by yourself."

"But—But this could be a setup!" Kestrel realized. "You could be kidnapping me to get...Or tricking me into—"

He raised his eyebrows at her.

"Why, Brown Eyes?" he asked. "Are you rich?"

"Um...No..."

"Related to someone important?"

"Not that I know of—"

"Work for the government? Know something top-secret?"

"No—"

"Do you have some special ability? Like computer hacking or code breaking or walking through walls?"

Kestrel hesitated. He waited.

"No," she murmured. He smirked.

"I *do* need you, but just to navigate. I don't know this area very well. And I'll return the favor—I don't imagine you've had much experience breaking in and out of places."

"No," she whispered.

"Well then," he said, and watched her.

And all at once, she answered.

"All right."

It sounded like someone else's voice. Kestrel paused, weighed the words, and said them again. "All right." She held out her hand.

He studied it for a moment. Then, he grasped her fingers firmly.

"Okay, turn around," he said, letting go of her and scooting forward again. His tone darkened. "And from now on, it'd probably be a good idea for you to keep your opinions to yourself."

Kestrel faced the front again and straddled the bike, her pulse jiggering.

Wolfe leaned over her back and gripped the handlebars. He pressed the starter. The engine ignited, and with a jolt, they pulled out from under the overpass and into the middle of the dim, grungy street.

THREE

"Should I turn on the headlight?" Kestrel asked.

"No," Wolfe muttered, swerving around a fallen trash can. He didn't say anything else. They passed one more block, then Wolfe steered sharply up a drive and right into an abandoned garage. Light filtered through a dirty window from a streetlamp outside. Wolfe cut the power, leaned the bike to the side and slid off. His boots hit smooth cement.

"Come on," he urged. "We have to ditch it."

"Ditch…" Kestrel straightened, her hands closing around the warm handlebars. Wolfe stood still. Kestrel stared down at the lightless control board, unable to move.

"Leave her here?" she whispered.

"We don't have time," Wolfe warned.

Kestrel's throat closed. She ran her fingers across the console.

"But…"

"He's still trying to find us," Wolfe interrupted. "We have to keep moving."

"I'm…I'm so sorry, Thrix," Kestrel managed. She slid off and stood on her feet, her gaze lingering across the bike's smooth lines…

"Come on," Wolfe said again, turned and walked toward the door.

Kestrel pulled back, turned and strode after him, closing her hands into fists. A deep ache started in her chest and throbbed all the way through her body, and she bit her lip. Her vision clouded. She didn't say anything.

Wolfe waited for her, then strode on ahead across the street, and onto the cracked, deserted sidewalk. Kestrel ironed out her steps, keeping up with him. His tall form stayed to her left, near the street, and a little in front of her. Shivers raced across her skin as their feet tapped on the paving. Trash rustled in the gutters. They passed beneath a drooping street lamp, through its sickly light, and turned to the right.

A low, rectangular building waited at the end of the street. Completely dark, except for a single blue light inside that glared through the tall windows. Kestrel glanced up. At the top of the building perched a leaning, extinguished sign: " *The Half-Mask.*"

Wolfe headed right up to the entrance. Kestrel got colder with every step. The front door looked like it was made of wood, but all the paint had peeled off. Wolfe hopped up the stoop and shoved the door open. The hinge creaked. He glanced back at her, then past her.

"Stick close," he muttered. He turned back and stepped through. She eased in after him.

Their boots immediately crunched on the broken black-and-white tile floor. They entered a small, square room, shadowed and lit by that one bulb hanging in the far corner. A dingy bar with a long, cracked mirror behind it stood in front of them, and up-ended metal tables and chairs lay scattered from one end of the room to the other. Wolfe stopped.

"Huh," he commented. "He's let this place go to the dogs..."

"What is it?" Kestrel whispered. Wolfe didn't answer. He just maneuvered around the bar and toward a narrow back door. As he passed, he slid his palm absently over the bar top, his feet scraping against shattered glass. Kestrel stayed. Wolfe lifted one hand and pushed on the flaking red paint of the door. The hinges squealed. It opened. He stepped over the threshold and disappeared. The door drifted shut.

Kestrel locked in place. She looked behind her at the broad windows— the dark, empty street outside...

Silence fell.

Kestrel spun around—strained for any sound Wolfe made.

Heard nothing.

Kestrel charged around the bar, hopped over the glass and knocked through the door.

"Shh!" The voice snapped like a match in the dark, right in front of her face. The door banged shut. She jerked to a stop. She smelled Wolfe again, directly in front of her.

"Quiet," Wolfe ordered.

"Sorry," she whispered, her heartbeat thundering.

He said nothing. Kestrel wrapped her arms around herself. Then, as she listened, she heard what sounded like distant voices, deep down—like the ground itself was whispering. Then, Wolfe's knuckles rapped on a thin, hollow metal surface.

Tap, tap-tap-tap-tap. Tap, tap.

The voices silenced. Now Kestrel heard Wolfe's breathing—low, measured. Then, shuffling issued from the other side of the door.

"What's the occasion?" a deep, gravelly voice grunted through the metal.

"A game of chance and a ha'penny in my pocket," Wolfe answered, just as low.

A long pause stretched between both sides of the door.

"Naw, it isn't..." the other voice mumbled. There was more shuffling, and an odd shout from further away. Grumbling, spitting. Fingers fumbled at a lock. Buttons beeped. Then—

The bolt flew. The door screeched open. Thin light leaked out, silhouetting a short, fat man with fuzzy cropped hair, leather clothes—and holding a glinting gun.

Pointed right at them.

Kestrel's heart collapsed. Wolfe didn't move.

"Doesn't seem polite to greet an old friend that way," Wolfe canted his head.

"I never seen you before in my life. No idea who you are," the fat man grunted, then pulled in a raspy breath—and the tip of a thin white stick of his own lit with a bright orange ember.

"Then why did you open the door?" Wolfe countered. The fat man took another pull, then took the stick from his mouth with his meaty right hand. Kestrel ducked behind Wolfe's shoulder and gulped painfully.

"Mr. Conrad wants me to ask you what you call yourself," the fat man answered. Wolfe remained quiet for a long while. Kestrel watched the back of his head. Finally, Wolfe drew himself up.

"Tell Mr. Conrad the Lieutenant is here to call in his favor."

The fat man went still. A curling column of smoke from his stick trailed upward, caught in the beam of foggy light behind. Then, he stepped back, and lowered his gun.

"Come in, Lieutenant," he growled. "I'll tell him you're here."

Wolfe stepped down the last two stairs. Kestrel followed. For just a second, she glimpsed the fat man's face: bearded with dark stubble, his right eye replaced by a robotic one, and a deep scar running across his right cheek.

Then his gun jerked up and aimed at her face.

Kestrel's hand clamped down on Wolfe's arm.

Wolfe lashed out and grabbed the barrel, knocking it away from her. The fat man's attention darted to him, jaw tight. Kestrel reflexively pressed her forehead into Wolfe's sleeve, trying not to strangle. Wolfe's fingers tensed around the gun.

"Who's she?" the fat man snapped.

"She's with me," Wolfe said—his deep tone deadly-calm. The fat man's unnerving gaze flicked back and forth between Kestrel and Wolfe, his jaw working, then he nodded. Wolfe let go of the barrel.

Kestrel sucked in a shaking breath, then eased her fingers off of Wolfe's jacket.

The fat man jerked his head, turned and waddled down the dim, dripping, tunnel-like hallway. Wolfe turned his head minutely back toward Kestrel, then followed the man. Kestrel, her insides trembling, tried to keep up with him.

Along the right hand wall every fifty meters, a weak, flickering square light hung, casting heavy, stark shadows. Pipes and wires crisscrossed the ceiling like a network of blood vessels.

"You're being watched from at least five angles," the fat man warned without turning back to them. His voice reverberated down the corridor. "So go ahead and try something if you want—it'd be funny."

Kestrel shivered. All of their booted feet slapped against the wet stone. They turned right, then left, then right again, then left twice, and after that, Kestrel lost track. Which made her sick to her stomach.

But she did notice one thing: the walls on either side started to look cleaner, whiter, and the floors seemed drier. Then, when they rounded a corner, semi-bright overhead lights illuminated a colorfully-painted hallway and a single tall door that didn't have a handle. A little control panel hung beside it on the wall. The fat man stopped in front of that door, turned and faced them.

Footsteps echoed from behind. Kestrel spun. Three giant, narrow-eyed, broad-jawed men, all clothed in sharp black and each wearing six weapons, emerged from the shadows and halted.

The fat man raised his hand to his ear and tapped a communicator. "Sir? Yeah, I brought 'em."

Kestrel crept closer to Wolfe, glancing back and forth between the bouncers and the door. Wolfe stared straight at the fat man and waited. The fat man eyed the two of them, a low, crooked smile on his face.

"Yes, sir," the fat man said again, running his eyes from Wolfe's head to his shoes. "He did, sir. He says he's called the Lieutenant."

Everyone held his breath. Silence fell. Kestrel felt the guards lean in.

The smug smile faded from the fat man's face. His eyebrows lifted.

"Yes, sir," he said hoarsely, now meeting Wolfe's gaze. "I will bring them both in right away."

The fat man dropped his hand, and leaned his head back, looking at Wolfe down his nose.

"Mr. Conrad says he will see you," he said. "But if you try anything, you'll be dead before you hit the ground."

"Don't worry about me," Wolfe answered. The fat man's jaw flexed, but he didn't reply. He turned and put his hand to the control panel, and his flying fingers tapped in a ten-digit code. The door released, hissed open—

Thudding, metallic music pumped out into the hall. Flashing beams of green, red and silver lasers blinded Kestrel, cutting through the dark room ahead. The fat man strode straight in. Wolfe followed him. Bracing herself, Kestrel kept on his heels—

The seething crowd swallowed her. Kestrel halted. The men— handsome, young, and slick, with serious faces and piercing eyes. The women— gorgeous, hard, fierce, their elaborate hairstyles immovable, and their ears, necks, wrists and fingers dripping with jewels. Kestrel recognized the clothes the men wore: top-of-the-line, designer suits and shoes—all black or white, and slender-cut. The women's necklines plunged, and the fabric of their dresses glimmered and sparkled in countless brilliant shades. Those nearest Kestrel turned and watched her over their glowing drinks. Their eyes, necklaces and earrings glittered in the erratic light. Some of the men and women swayed back and forth on a center dance floor, many gathered in little groups, talking—but the loud music drowned out their words. Kestrel caught the edge of a sweetly-rotten smell, and that poisonous smoke again.

And now, she could only see the top of Wolfe's head in the middle of this crowd of night crawlers. Her mouth opened—but there was no use yelling to him. She darted forward, weaving between two Amazonian women, then pressed as close behind Wolfe as she could, throwing backward glances at the sparkling mob.

Up ahead, the crowd thinned, and Kestrel glimpsed a brighter area—a clear glass bar, lit from within by rotating yellow and orange lights. The fat man drew closer to it, turned and roughly motioned Wolfe up to the bar. Wolfe paused, then stepped forward and eased down onto a stool, turned and faced a man already seated. Kestrel shifted nearer, and stopped behind Wolfe's shoulder.

"Mr. Conrad," the fat man leaned in to the stranger at the bar. "This is the man who calls himself The Lieutenant."

The new stranger did not move. The noise of the club faded to the back of Kestrel's attention. Then, Mr. Conrad straightened, and turned his face toward them.

He was good-looking. Perfectly so. He had brilliant, warm blue eyes, sandy-colored hair casually and neatly combed; cultured features; a wry and careful mouth, and quietly furrowed dark eyebrows. He wore all black—a spotless suit with a high collar. He half smiled at Wolfe, shifted his shoulders toward him, and slowly laid an uncalloused right hand down on the smooth bar. A simple silver ring glittered on his little finger. His other hand came to rest on his own knee, elbow turned out. For a long while, he just gazed at Wolfe's face. Wolfe said nothing. Mr. Conrad took a breath.

"So," he said, his voice soft and calm, his eyes unwavering. "You're supposed to be the one my grandfather told me so much about."

Wolfe still didn't answer. Kestrel cautiously glanced at the side of Wolfe's face. His expression betrayed nothing. Conrad's smile broadened.

"I have to say...You look the part."

"So do you," Wolfe answered. "But I actually think you take after your grandmother."

Conrad's smile faltered. Wolfe raised his eyebrows—and half smiled.

"Interesting," Conrad murmured. "Would you like a cigarette? Something to drink?"

Kestrel jolted, then bit it back. Wolfe nodded.

"I'll have a cigarette, thanks."

Conrad glanced at the fat man. The fat man scowled, but came around the bar, reached underneath it and pulled out a small metal box. He flipped it open with a click, and held it out to Wolfe. Wolfe plucked a short white stick out of it—a *cigarette!*—stuck the cigarette in his mouth, and waited, watching the fat man. The fat man made another face, then flipped a switch on the top of the metal box. A flame lit—he held the box toward Wolfe, and lit the end of the cigarette. Wolfe drew in a deep breath, took the cigarette out of his mouth and exhaled the smoke. He regarded Conrad, and nodded again.

Conrad's eyes narrowed.

"Who put you up to this?"

"Nobody," Wolfe answered, puffing on the cigarette again. He took it down and rested his hand on his knee. "I'm just here to call in that favor."

"What favor?" Conrad asked.

"Don't play games with me, Conrad," Wolfe warned. "You know what favor, and you know you have no choice."

Kestrel blinked—clamped her fists, and stared at him. The fingers of Conrad's right hand opened and closed.

"You're right, I don't have a choice," Conrad said. "And when the real Lieutenant comes, I'll fulfill my grandfather's promise." His gaze turned icy. "But don't take me for a fool. Plenty of other men have." He drew himself up. "It hasn't gone well for them."

Kestrel swallowed. Out of the corner of her eye, she caught several patrons of the club turning to watch them.

Wolfe's jaw tensed.

"What do you need to see?" he asked.

Conrad folded his arms and sneered.

"Now, you shouldn't need to ask that, should you?"

Wolfe took a short breath.

"All right," he glanced down briefly, then around the room. "But in a back room someplace."

"Oh, I don't mind if they see," Conrad countered, not moving. "And I'm comfortable right here, thanks."

Wolfe regarded him. He sat perched on the edge of his stool. For a second, Kestrel thought he was about to stand—

He set his cigarette down on the bar, sat up straight, shrugged out of his leather jacket and pulled it off, revealing a tighter, short-sleeved gray shirt beneath. He tossed the jacket onto the bar, and held out his muscled arms toward Conrad. He turned his hands palms up, exposing his wrists and inner arms.

Kestrel's eyes fixed. Deep black tattoos marked the insides of Wolfe's arms. The skin of his left bore plain, stark letters spelling the word **JUSTITIA**. On his right was written, in the same lettering, **ULTIO ULTIONIS**.

Conrad's features lost all humor. He stared at the tattoos. Wolfe stared at *him*. Then, Conrad met Wolfe's eyes—and waited.

Wolfe drew a breath. He stood up.

Kestrel took half a step back, confused...

Wolfe grabbed the hem of his shirt and pulled it up, baring his toned right side and back...

And a ghastly scar running from the tip of his right shoulder blade, down across his ribs to the front corner of his right hip bone.

Conrad jumped to his feet. He turned pale. Wolfe pushed his shirt back down.

Conrad looked up at Wolfe's face again, his expression stark and solemn.

"Come with me," he urged, picking up Wolfe's jacket and handing it to him. "Hurry."

He about-faced, swept around the bar toward a rear door and walked straight through it as it opened. Wolfe tugged his jacket back on as he followed, and Kestrel hurriedly kept stride with him. The fat man trailed after. They entered the room and the door shut.

Kestrel slowed down and blinked, trying to adjust. Much brighter, cleaner light filled this room. Lit wooden shelves lined the walls—shelves covered with rusted antiques, old-fashioned framed photographs, battered signs and cases of weapons, medals and trophies. An intricate iron-wrought lamp hung from the ceiling. She tread on smooth wood. At the far end of the room stood a carved desk surrounded by three chairs. The whole place smelled like dust and furniture polish. Wolfe paused, assessing—and the edges of his unyielding expression softened. He nodded once more.

"I remember this."

Conrad crossed the wood floor, stepped around the desk and seated himself.

"Please sit down," he invited, waving to the two plain blue chairs in front of the desk. Wolfe passed the lines of shelves and took a seat in the left hand chair, leaning back and propping his elbow on one of the armrests. Kestrel hesitated, sensing the fat man take up a position directly behind her, in front of the only door. She gritted her teeth and made herself sit down on the remaining chair. Conrad appraised her for just a second, then returned his attention to Wolfe.

"So," he said. "My name's Ian Conrad—and I think I can guess what you want."

Wolfe's jaw tightened. Conrad regarded him.

41

"You're still looking for someone."

"Yes," Wolfe answered.

"Do you know his name yet?" Conrad wondered. Wolfe took a careful breath.

"Yes," he said. "William Jakiv."

Conrad blinked.

"The scientist?"

"What do you know about him?" Wolfe wondered, leaning back as his eyes narrowed. Conrad's aspect darkened. He rested his forearms on the desk and interlaced his fingers.

"He's extremely famous. Well, *infamous*," Conrad said. "At the beginning of his career he made huge advancements in healing technology, but during the last few years he's been dabbling in projects that most people aren't...*comfortable* with."

"Such as?" Wolfe arched an eyebrow.

"Human cloning," Conrad said flatly. "*And* Paradox Theory—time travel. But he's been stymied at every juncture by legislation, and by an underground resistance that picks up the government's slack," Conrad smiled. "I'm proud to take some of that credit."

Wolfe answered with a mirthless smile of his own.

"Your granddad would be happy," he told Conrad. "But why keep up with the club and the black market business?" He jerked his thumb over his shoulder. "Sounds like you're more of a humanitarian than a crime lord like Peter."

Conrad shrugged.

"Gotta keep the lights on somehow." He grinned crookedly. "Especially when you're helping fund an underground resistance."

"Ha. And all the talk used to be that energy would be cheap by now," Wolfe remarked wryly.

Conrad chuckled.

"Don't believe everything you hear."

"I never do," Wolfe assured him, shaking his head once. Conrad's amusement subsided, and he studied Wolfe.

"So what can I do for you, Lieutenant?"

Wolfe lowered his arm, his smile fading. He gazed at Conrad a moment.

"I've heard Jakiv's on the Gain Station in the Triple Star System," he finally said. "I need you to get us there."

"Us?" Conrad repeated.

"This lady owes me a favor," Wolfe explained without looking at Kestrel. "And I need a navigator."

Conrad sat for a moment, thoughtful. Finally, he nodded.

"Okay, makes sense." He drew himself up. "I don't suppose you have any Travel Permissions on you?"

"No."

"Money?"

"No."

"Anything at all that might get you through security and onto an intergalactic transport vessel?"

"What do you think, Conrad?" Wolfe sighed.

"Well, good sir," Conrad smirked. "You're in luck. You've come to precisely the right place."

"All right," Conrad sat back, sweeping his attention across the multitude of hovering, green-glowing holographic documents in front of him. "I used some of your existing information, Miss Evans, and tweaked it a little. It's best not to change too much if you don't have to. Your name is now April Johnson. Wolfe, I had to dig into some old records of my grandfather's, but they worked out just fine. You get to keep your first name, but your last name is Johnson as well—thought it would be easier if you travel as a married couple. You both are now fully equipped with identification disc forgeries, forged digital Travel Permissions, forged authorization to cross the Liquor Line, a meal plan, a limited line of credit, luggage marks, and booking in a first class suite on board the *Exception*—a luxury cruise liner renowned for both its speed and amenities. The ship boards no later than 12:13 this morning. It launches at 1:13. Once it hits space, you should get to the Triple Star System in..." Conrad squinted at one of the documents. "...a little over two weeks."

"And there's no way to get there faster?" Wolfe cut in. Kestrel opened her mouth, but Conrad answered plainly.

"Sure. If you want to buy a private transport, hire somebody to fly it for you, fuel it, run it through ten more levels of spaceport security—"

Wolfe rolled his eyes and waved it off.

"I've kept some suitcases in a back cabinet for just such an occasion," Conrad got up and re-buttoned his coat. Wolfe immediately stood up, too—so Kestrel did the same, trying not to twist her hands together. Instead, she clenched them at her sides.

"While we've been arranging things here," Conrad went on, addressing both of them. "My people have been loading them up with clothes and supplies so you can be on your way. Your best bet is to catch the Rail to the Hub, then get on a train to the port."

"Where can we catch the Rail?" Wolfe asked.

"It's right on the north corner here. There's a flashing sign, you can't miss it," Conrad waved vaguely. Then, he drew himself up and smiled at Wolfe with an air of finality. His tone quieted, and he gazed at Wolfe. "Well, I hope that's what my granddad had in mind—because that's the best I can do."

Wolfe held out his hand to him.

"That's all I can ask."

Conrad considered his hand, then took it. The two men shook firmly, watching each other's faces. Then, Wolfe let go and straightened.

"Lead the way."

"No, I need to be heading back to my patrons. They'll wonder where I am," Conrad said, striding around the desk. "But Epski here has your things."

He waved toward the door, and Kestrel turned to see the fat man bearing two medium sized, square, black, nondescript travel bags, and wearing a scowl.

"IDs and passes are in satchels inside," Epski grunted. Conrad stopped and faced them as he stood in the doorway. He tipped his hand to Kestrel, then nodded at Wolfe.

"Happy trails," he bid them, as if saying that was a little funny. He turned and strode through the door as it opened. It hissed shut behind them. Kestrel's gut clamped.

"Here," Epski shoved one bag at Wolfe, and the other at Kestrel. Kestrel automatically reached for it—

Wolfe snatched it from Epski, tugging it sharply out of his grasp. Wolfe glared at him.

"Were you born in a barn?" Wolfe muttered, shifting his grip on both bags. "Which way out of here?"

Epski's lip curled.

"The back way."

"What back way?" Wolfe demanded. Epski just shook his head, lumbered past them, then slipped his fingers behind one of the cases. A latch clicked.

The case slid out of the way, revealing a door—and dark, cement steps heading upward.

"Now get out of here before somebody finally decides to just kill you," Epski advised.

"My pleasure," Wolfe answered. "C'mon, Brown Eyes." And he marched loudly up the staircase and disappeared into the dark.

FOUR

Kestrel almost ran into his back. She raced up the steps—and then the cabinet door shut behind her, plunging the whole stairwell into blackness. Her hand met the leather of his coat. She instantly halted, but he kept climbing, much slower. Gulping, and blinking in vain, Kestrel kept shuffling her feet up the steps, running her right hand up the rough, cold banister. Their breathing and their steps echoed in the little space.

"Okay," Wolfe grunted, and she felt him turn around. "Hold these." His fumbling hands found hers, and slipped the handles of the luggage into her grip. She caught them up, trying not to trip backward.

A loud *click* snapped right in front of her face. Metallic and dangerous.

"What—"

"Sh."

Bang.

He threw his shoulder against a sheet of metal. It flew open. Wolfe leaped out, pointing a gleaming handgun, his boots sliding on gravel. Kestrel stayed put.

Wolfe's steps settled as he glanced around at the uneven parking space. The neon lights on the side of the building cut his figure sideways. He lowered his gun, then stuffed it back inside his coat.

"Well, look at that. A man of his word," he said to himself. "For the time being, anyway." He faced Kestrel and motioned. "C'mon. Let's go find this Rail."

Kestrel shakily emerged from the doorway, her jaw locked. He stepped quickly toward her, his attention downward.

Kestrel flinched back.

He stopped, seeing her face.

"Woah, woah!" he said, instantly holding up his hands. "It's okay—I'm not gonna hurt you." His eyebrows came together. "Did you think I was going to hurt you?"

Kestrel's fingers clenched on the handles of the luggage. Her brow knitted.

"Hey," Wolfe said carefully, watching her. "It's gonna be okay, Brown Eyes. You just have to breathe, and stick with me. Stick right with me, and it'll all be fine. Promise."

Kestrel swallowed hard. Wolfe slowly reached out with his left hand and took light hold of the handle of one bag. He rested it there, giving her an earnest look. Kestrel couldn't breathe with him standing so close to her, towering over her, but she couldn't find the strength to back up, either.

"I need to tell you something important, and you need to listen to me," Wolfe said, his tone low. "You listening?"

Kestrel managed a nod.

"I've never been to a spaceport before. Well, not counting the other day," he amended. "Never gone through security, never boarded a ship."

Kestrel blinked.

"You haven't?"

"No," he shook his head. "So I need you to take over from here. You sound like you've done a fair bit of traveling, right?"

She nodded again.

"Okay," he nodded too. "So I need you to get us to the Rail, and then to the spaceport, and to our ship. Think you can do that?"

Kestrel stared up at him for a long moment. Her throat spasmed, and her hand twitched on the bag he was touching.

"Yeah," she said. "I'll try."

"Good," he pulled the bag out of her hand, much more gently than he had with Epski, then waved toward the shadowy sidewalk. "After you."

Kestrel's mind reeled. She squeezed her eyes shut for a second—then forced them open and gritted her teeth.

"Okay," she took a deep breath. "Okay...Did he...Did he say there was a Rail station on the north corner?"

"Yep," Wolfe answered.

"All right," she said again, her head clearing. "I think I see the sign."

P

The little station stood abandoned. One buzzing blue light hanging from the center of the ceiling was the only thing illuminating the tile floors, benches bolted to one wall, and the broken glass front of the other wall. Graffiti marred the once-white paint of almost every surface, and trash huddled in the corners. It stank.

"Cheerful place," Wolfe remarked, casting around. "How long are we stuck here?"

"What time is it?" Kestrel asked.

"Don't know."

Kestrel hefted her bag up and set it on the bench, and clicked open the latches.

"Let's see if he gave us a watch." She opened the lid. A little lamp blinked to life underneath that lid, showing her the contents.

Neatly-folded men's shirts and pants, a toiletry kit and a small, hard, round clear case filled with five flat pieces of metal half the size of playing cards. Wolfe stepped close to her as she straightened, and he looked down over her shoulder.

"Looks like you've got my bag," he noted. "What's this here?"

"This," Kestrel picked up the clear case and pointing at the cards inside. "Is everything—your whole life, if you're traveling. The blue card is your ID, the red one is your Travel Permission, the purple one is your Liquor Line Passport, the orange one is the meal plan and the gold one is your credit. All very important and easy to lose." Kestrel carefully pushed it back into place in his bag. "It'll be easier when the Implant legislation goes through."

"Implant?" Wolfe repeated.

"Yeah, you know—where they put a microchip in the back of your skull or something and it carries all your information," Kestrel told him as she felt around in the bag for a timepiece. "Either that or they'll have DNA identification."

"That sounds great," Wolfe commented darkly. "Until the

government turns around and bites you."

Kestrel paused, then turned and looked up at him, the frost of that thought settling over her.

"I suppose so," she murmured. He set his bag down with a clunk and put his hands on his hips, glancing out through the shattered glass.

"Any watch?"

Kestrel turned back to the open bag, then shook her head.

"No. But trains are supposed to come every ten minutes, so—"

"Shh," Wolfe held up a hand and faced the south. Kestrel shut the bag and latched it, then peered that same direction.

A rattling noise rose out of the silence—and then a bright white light glared around a corner and made straight for them. The train, speeding along on one rail, blazed right up to the front of the station before lurching to a stop, hissing and groaning. Wolfe stayed where he was, eyeing the side of it.

"This is it?" he said.

"Yeah," Kestrel nodded, picking up the bag and holding it tight.

"Hm," he growled. Kestrel couldn't argue. The train's sides were rusted and also covered in graffiti, and a few of the back-most windows were cracked. The whole vehicle had once been smooth and aerodynamic. A long time ago.

"The trains in this part of town tend to look like this," Kestrel said, stepping out the station door and approaching it. "That's what people tell me, anyway."

She heard Wolfe pick up the other bag and follow her. The door of the first car clattered open.

"Where do we pay?" Wolfe asked.

"We don't," Kestrel said, stepping aboard. "Public transport."

"*Now* it makes sense," Wolfe muttered, coming on after her. The door shut again. Kestrel faced the rest of the long, empty car. Narrow, dingy lights overhead. Three poles in the center, for the use of standing passengers, and more benches off to the sides. All of it dirty.

Kestrel stepped around one of the poles and sat down onto a bench, bent down and stuffed the bag under her chair, then sat up and tucked her heels against the bag to keep it in place.

Wolfe eased down in the seat on her left, and he did the exact same thing with the bag that she had. He sat back, coughed into his elbow, then folded his arms. His shoulder brushed hers.

"So, it's 10:05," Wolfe swallowed and nodded toward the red numbers hovering over the door. The car lurched again, then rolled forward. Kestrel watched the little station whizz off into the darkness.

"You need at least an hour to get through security for an interstellar flight," Kestrel said, worriedly checking the clock. "And we'll have to change trains at the Hub."

"How long will *this* trip take?" Wolfe pointed at the floor.

"Don't know," Kestrel murmured. "I have no idea where we are."

Wolfe shifted, but didn't answer.

They sat in silence, Kestrel counting the lamps that flicked past outside the opposite windows. Every breath she took smelled of must, and the smoke on Wolfe's jacket.

"So," Kestrel ventured. "How did you know that Conrad?"

Wolfe shifted again.

"I didn't."

"Then...how did he know who *you* were?" Kestrel wondered, turning to watch his profile.

"I knew his grandfather," Wolfe replied, resting his left ankle on his right knee. "Saved his life."

Kestrel's lips parted, but her questions blundered into each other instead of lining up so she could say them. So she closed her mouth, and stared resolutely out the window again.

In fifteen minutes, the train slowed, and the clock blinked to the words: STATION 6.

"Is this us?" Wolfe straightened.

"No," Kestrel said. "It'll say 'The Hub'—it isn't called anything else."

"'Kay," Wolfe said as the sign clicked back to the clock, which now read 10:20.

The train screeched, then drew to a halt. The door opened...

And four men filed in.

Kestrel bit down on the inside of her cheek.

The men wore long black coats decked in jingling chains. Two of them had shaved heads. One wore a hoop earring in his right ear. All wore colorful motion tattoos that writhed across their foreheads and ears. They muttered to each other, and all of them glanced across Wolfe and Kestrel. Two of them smiled, showing all-metal teeth.

Wolfe set both feet down on the floor, then leaned toward Kestrel and casually draped his arm across the back of the chair behind her shoulders. Kestrel didn't move—and as soon as she could, she fixed her gaze on nothing but the red numbers of the clock.

Ten more minutes dragged by. Kestrel counted each minute, clasping her hands tightly in her lap, her heart fluttering. The men muttered to each other. Kestrel could feel them constantly throwing looks at her. Wolfe's fingers settled on her arm.

The train jiggled, and the clock blinked.

THE HUB

They slowed down. Kestrel fought inertia, but still leaned a little into Wolfe. The train halted. Wolfe reached underneath and grabbed a bag, then waited for her to do the same. Then, he stood up alongside her and pressed his hand to the small of her back as they stepped toward the door. It opened, and they emerged into the curved, stone tunnel. Wolfe kept his hand where it was.

He urged her along the walkway, past the windows of the train, toward a bright EXIT sign ahead to their left. They didn't say anything. Kestrel didn't dare look back.

And then four sets of quick, purposeful footsteps loomed up behind them.

"Nice piece of meat you've got here," a stranger's voice purred right between Kestrel and Wolfe's shoulders. "Mind if we have a taste?"

Kestrel's chest locked in horror. Wolfe's arm tensed across her back.

The voice materialized into the man with the earring—and he cut right between them. He shoved Wolfe's arm out of the way and grabbed Kestrel by the neck. She yelped. He whirled and threw her backward—she slammed into the stone wall. Her vision blurred. He clamped down on her throat. Her whole body screaming, she clawed at his grimy hand. He grinned. Metallic teeth gleamed.

Something flashed.

The man howled. His head jerked to the right. He doubled over and grabbed his ear. Blood leaked between his fingers.

Wolfe stood there, the man's hoop earring looped around his forefinger. His eyes burned. He stepped in and delivered a savage blow to the side of the man's head. The man collapsed, writhing. Wolfe threw down the earring. It jangled on the stone.

The other three stared at him, their eyes wide, their fists closing. Wolfe waited. Kestrel put a hand to her throat. Her heart stalled.

One man charged.

Wolfe stepped aside and slapped the man's face. The man's hands flew up—

Wolfe spun and kicked him, knocking him sideways, then grabbed his arm and wrenched it.

Snap.

His wrist broke.

Kestrel jumped.

The man screamed and fell to the floor. Wolfe turned back around and advanced with long strides straight back toward the other two. They backpedaled. One of them reached inside his coat.

Wolfe drew his silver gun faster than Kestrel could track—aimed at the man's feet and fired.

Kestrel jolted back and threw her hands up to cover her ears. Thunder careened through the tunnel—but she hadn't seen any bolt!

The man's boot toe burst open. He shrieked and fell down, fumbling around his ankle. Wolfe stopped, lifted his gun and pointed at the last man—

Who turned and pelted the other way as fast as he could.

Kestrel gasped in a breath. Wolfe took hold of his gun in both hands, spun the center cylindrical part of it, then popped that open.

"Out of bullets," he whispered. He gazed at his weapon for a moment, as if he couldn't hear the muffled moans of the three men lying on the ground.

His attention remained on the gun for almost a minute. Then, he fondly rubbed the handle. With a short sigh, he turned around and let go of it, letting it fall into a brown garbage bin. Finally, he met Kestrel's eyes.

"I'm guessing I wouldn't be able to take that through security."

Kestrel was only able to shake her head once. Wolfe nodded, picked up the bag he had dropped, hurried to her, took her by the arm and pulled her around the corner and up the stairs.

She heard distant shouts behind her, and running—probably the police. Bracing herself for the thousandth time, Kestrel did nothing but try her best not to trip.

The soft bustle of a crowd descended on them before they emerged from the wide staircase into the station. Kestrel had to blink to readjust her eyes.

Wheat-colored marble flooring with wide, black designs intersecting it. Tall, Romanesque walls with arched windows of paned glass. At the far end across from them, a towering window bearing an old-fashioned, gold-faced clock. A clock which now read 10:40. Several groups of people milled around throughout the room. The lights of passing trains flashed outside all the windows.

Wolfe tilted his head back, studying the huge chamber.

"I've been here before," he murmured. He cast a glance at the milling crowds. "It wasn't this busy, though."

"This historical part hasn't been open very long," Kestrel answered, trying to keep herself from shaking. "It's probably more than five-hundred years old."

"Was it always called The Hub?" Wolfe asked.

"Um, no. Union Station," Kestrel answered, hurriedly scanning the terminal signs. "But it's gotten so big lately that if you ride a train, you *have* to go through here, whether you want to or not."

"Hm," was all Wolfe said.

"There it is," Kestrel pointed, starting toward one of the widest, busiest terminals. More than thirty people, all carrying baggage, waited outside its doors. Up above it, in gold, digital letters, it said: KANSAS CITY SPACE PORT—TRANSIT TIME: 30 MINUTES.

"This is *really* cutting it close..." Kestrel winced.

A ruckus issued from behind. Kestrel spun—

Four black-clad policemen darted out of the stairwell, their hands on their weapons belts, frantically searching through the crowds.

"C'mon," Wolfe whispered, then nudged her further into the mass of people waiting, most of whom were now watching the police.

Beep.

The sliding door in the wall opened, and then the door of the train outside did the same. Wolfe slipped Kestrel right through first and followed, then guided her toward a corner seat.

"*The train to the Kansas City Space Port is now boarding,*" a pleasant computer voice said. *"Please seat yourself quickly. If you are standing, please use hand rails. Thank you."*

Kestrel sat down and stuffed her bag under her chair again. Wolfe sat down directly beside her and did the same, again. All the rest of the thirty-some people filed in, some half-heartedly glancing back to watch the police. Finally, the doors closed, and the train powered out of the station, picking up speed every second. And Kestrel felt Wolfe let out a low sigh.

FIVE

This car did not rattle or jiggle. The inside smelled fresher, and most of the passengers had dressed for travel—comfortable, clean clothes, and carrying baggage. Nobody talked. They studied the floor, or gazed out the windows as they leaned back and forth with the movement of the speed train.

Kestrel's attention drifted out the window to her right. The city lights blinked past, and sometimes blacked out altogether as they passed through a brief tunnel. The engine hummed all around them.

"There it is," a woman said to her little daughter, and pointed. Kestrel leaned forward to see...

The spaceport, its unfathomable walls alight with colorful dancing advertisements, shining like a sun through the blackness. Flashing tower lights stood atop its circumference, giving it the appearance of wearing a crown. Far above it, in an endless line stretching off into the distance, hovering spacecraft waited to land, their running lights creating a highway in the cloudy sky.

"That's somethin'," Wolfe murmured. Kestrel didn't answer. Instead, she turned and considered him.

"Those guys..." she said quietly. "They were just...Just muggers, right?"

Wolfe focused on her face. Said nothing.

"Or—did they work for Conrad?" Kestrel whispered. Wolfe shrugged, looked out the window.

"Don't know. Don't think so."

"Or, do they work for..." Kestrel trailed off. Wolfe's jaw tightened. He didn't answer. Kestrel fell silent.

Five minutes later, they plunged into a terminal and halted. The doors *beeped* open, and everyone jostled out. Kestrel snatched up her bag as Wolfe hustled her through the door—

And they stepped into the grand entryway of the KCSP.

Wolfe stopped.

Loudspeakers in every corner announced flight cancellations, baggage claims, terminal changes, warnings about suspicious activity, and personal calls.

Thousands of travelers walked noisily and with great purpose every which way, crossing the elaborate tile design on the floor, ducking in and out of the hundreds of inviting shops that lined the circumference of this huge level, or stepping aboard elevators. Directly ahead of them waited a vast staircase, which held ten rows of up and down escalators. On either side of this staircase hung suspended pools of water—water that then cascaded straight down into the floor and vanished. The sound of the rushing falls muffled the foot traffic, and filled the whole chamber to its height.

"Come on," Kestrel said, and together they left the tunnel of the train terminal and stepped out into the majestic space. The floor, a black-and-royal-blue mosaic of Orion, reacted to their footsteps—the white tiles flashed, and the blue tiles lit up with sparkles. But after a few strides, Kestrel couldn't help but look up—even though she'd seen it hundreds of times before.

The skylight—the entire ceiling—through which everyone could see all of the blinking starships waiting to land; and the clouds above, which glowed as they reflected the running lights and the lights of the spaceport itself.

Kestrel adjusted her grip on her luggage and faced the staircase—now, she could see the over-arching, banner-like sign hanging from end to end of the chamber, its letters twinkling like diamonds.

THE KCSP: YOUR GATEWAY TO THE STARS

"Watch your step," Kestrel advised as she hopped onto an escalator and started to rise. Wolfe nimbly followed her.

"Gatway to the Stars," he mused, slapping his hand down on the rail.

"St. Louis always got to be called 'Gateway to the West," Kestrel said, keeping her eyes ahead of her. "Kansas City wanted to go one better."

"Might as well."

Seconds later, they got off the escalator...

And stopped in front of a black wall with a single door, above which a severe blue sign blinked.

SECURITY

"Okay," Kestrel took a deep breath. "We have to get our cards out now." She set her bag down on a metal bench off to the side and opened it, then pulled out the clear container. "Here, this is yours—I need mine."

Wolfe quickly set his bag down, took what she handed him, and pulled out her case.

"And you need to carry your own luggage, and I need to have mine," Kestrel said, impatiently shoving a strand of hair out of her face as she took her IDs from him. She shut his case and faced him as people strode off the escalators behind him and passed into security. She met Wolfe's eyes. He stood completely still, brow furrowed.

"We'll get separated in here," she told him quietly. "And separated from our bags. We'll have to meet up after we're all the way through."

"Fine," he nodded.

"Just..." Kestrel made herself keep breathing. "Stay very calm, and do whatever they say. You don't...have any more weapons on you, do you?"

He smiled crookedly.

"Fresh out."

Kestrel frowned.

"No, Brown Eyes," he said. "That means no."

"Fine," she said, irritated. She opened her case and pulled out the blue card and the red card. "You need to have these first. They'll want the others later, when we actually board."

"How long does this process usually take?" Wolfe asked, pulling out his own cards and snapping the case shut.

"About an hour."

"And it's...eleven-ten right now," Wolfe observed, pointing to a clock across the way. "And we're supposed to board at—"

"Twelve-thirteen," Kestrel finished. "We're going to have to run."

"Then let's go," Wolfe decided, picking up his bag and striding toward the door. Kestrel immediately followed him, stepping through the intimidating entrance and up to one of the dozen security androids—a tall, silver, bulky robot with no facial features except red eyes.

"*That way, please,*" it pointed to its right. Kestrel bit her lip as she watched Wolfe get sorted off in the other direction. He didn't look back. Kestrel started walking.

In about ten paces, she stopped in front of a shut door. On the wall off to the right of it, a computer blipped.

"*Please insert your identification card and your Travel Permission card into the slot indicated by the green light,*" a female computer overhead commanded. Kestrel stepped forward and slid them in, in the order specified.

"*Please remove all sun-shades and hats, and stand as still as possible in front of full body scanner.*"

Kestrel's heart hammered. If her cards didn't work, if the scan didn't match up with the info *on* the card...

The door glowed, then flashed at her. An exact replica of her image transferred onto the door, and a red line traveled up and down its length, lingering especially on her face...

She held her breath.

"*Welcome to the KCSP, April Johnson. Please proceed,*" the computer instructed. Her chest loosened. The door hissed open. She stepped through. It hissed shut behind her. Now, she stood in a low, narrow, black tunnel, with walls and ceilings of gleaming, one-way mirrors.

"*Please place all luggage in the slot to your right.*"

Kestrel lifted her bag, careful to keep her little clear case in her left hand, and set it inside the wide opening. She let go. Her bag instantly disappeared.

"*Your safety is our concern. As you proceed onto the conveyor belt, please watch your step.*"

Kestrel kept her attention on her feet as she climbed aboard the conveyor belt, feeling her palms start to sweat. The belt picked up speed—to about walking pace. Slower, in fact. She ironed out her expression. When she was little, this part had been kind of fun. Now her skin crawled at the idea of all the androids, cameras, technicians and armed guards watching her through that one-way glass.

A green archway appeared up ahead labeled BODY SCAN TWO.

"*Please close your eyes.*"

Kestrel did. She passed through the archway, and a bone-buzzing *thrum* vibrated her entire frame. She opened her eyes, unclenching her jaw and rubbing her tongue on the roof of her mouth. That one always made her whole face itch. However, the sensation had only just passed when another arch came into view.

BODY SCAN THREE.

"Ugh," Kestrel groaned, but kept her balance.

During the next twenty minutes, she passed under seventeen more body scans, each of which buzzed, beeped, tingled or shivered through her whole frame. Finally, she could see ahead of her that the conveyor belt ended in a small room.

"Please wait for a probing android to inspect you."

Kestrel gritted her teeth as the conveyor stopped.

"Please stand with your feet apart and your arms out to the sides."

Kestrel obeyed, staring at the door ahead of her. A trash-can shaped android shot out from a slot in the wall to her right and whirled all around her, rapidly raising and lowering, waving glowing blue wands. It swept them over every surface of her body, then extended upward to eye level and glared a light in her face.

"Open your mouth, please," it monotoned. Kestrel did. It rammed one of the wands into her mouth. Her whole skull vibrated.

"Open your eyes, please."

Kestrel forced them open, and the android scanned both of them.

"Thank you." It withdrew, and darted back into its little slot. The door opened, and Kestrel walked through.

A woman wearing a blue jumpsuit stood behind a podium. She smiled at Kestrel, and held out a gloved hand.

"May I see your other travel cards?"

"Yes, ma'am," Kestrel said, handing her clear case to her. The woman swiftly opened it, then pulled all her cards out and inserted them into her desktop. She watched the screen. Kestrel fought not to fidget.

"Authorization to cross the Liquor Line—check. Meal plan—check. Sufficient credit—check." She looked at Kestrel and smiled again. "Proceed past me and down that hallway," she pointed. "Turn to your right and wait for the search of your baggage to be completed. You'll pick up your ID and your Travel Permission card there as well."

"Thank you," Kestrel nodded as the woman handed her cards back. Kestrel immediately slipped the cards back in the clear case, then followed the glowing arrows in the floor down the straight corridor to the turn.

She rounded the corner. Four stoic, armed men in blue uniforms stood against one wall. Two more men wearing gloves had Kestrel's bag open on a table, and they shuffled through the clothes, pressed against the lining, examined the hinges and clips, and felt all its edges. Kestrel waited at a respectful distance, saying nothing.

A man snapped the bag shut, turned and held it out to her.

"Here you are, ma'am. And here are your ID and Permissions cards back. Have a safe trip."

"Thank you." She gave them all a smile and took her bag and cards.

"The terminal is just that way," the man pointed. She nodded, turned around and hurried out of the room, hoping Wolfe had not proceeded too far without her...

She walked through a set of clear doors and came out into a well-lit white lobby filled with benches and people re-arranging their possessions after having them tousled by security. Kestrel slowed down, sweeping the crowd, her body tensing...

"Come on," a voice snapped in her ear. She whirled to see a scowling Wolfe towering over her right side. He didn't pause—he plunged ahead, toward the door of the lobby. "Like you said, we've gotta run."

"What time is it?" Kestrel asked as she trotted up next to him. The doors in front of them whooshed open and they rushed into a long, brightly-lit, crowded white lobby that would force them to turn either right or left.

"That clock says 12:05." Wolfe pointed to one hanging overhead.

"Oh, no—" Kestrel gasped.

"Which way do we go?" Wolfe demanded.

"Um...Um..." Kestrel spun around, searching the hovering signs toward the extremities of the hallways. "*The Effervescent, The Exhilaration, The Entertainment, The Elation...*"

"*The Exception,*" Wolfe pointed far down the wide corridor to their right. "That sign there, see it?"

"Yes—!"

"Go, go, go." Wolfe broke into a run. Kestrel leaped after him.

They pounded down the concourse, weaving in and out of the crowd, hopping over resting luggage and dodging around fake trees.

"Excuse me, sorry, sorry—excuse me!" Kestrel tried as she shoved people's shoulders. Wolfe didn't offer any apology—he just plowed ahead of her, running as fast as possible with all these people in the way.

Kestrel glanced up. A broad, dark hallway stood open in front of them, and above it in golden letters gleamed the words:

THE EXCEPTION—NOW BOARDING

A gate stood between them and the hallway—a gate and a security android. Wolfe skidded to a halt, and Kestrel huffed up next to him.

"*Identification, please,*" the droid held out a square hand with a slot in it.

"Oh, —" Wolfe bit out another expletive Kestrel didn't recognize, dumped his bag on the floor and threw it open. He yanked out his clear case and dug out his ID.

"*Insert the card here, please,*" the droid said. Wolfe rammed the card into the android's scanner and pulled it out.

"*Welcome, Jack Johnson,*" the android said. "*Travel Permission card, please.*"

Wolfe bared his teeth, but stuffed that card in as well.

The android processed. Kestrel, panting, glanced at the clock.

12:12.

"*Welcome aboard The Exception, Jack Johnson. You may proceed.*"

The gate clicked open. Jack grabbed his things and shoved through — and kept walking. Kestrel's heart jolted.

"Here," she gasped, shoving her ID into the android's reader.

"*Welcome, April Johnson—*"

"Here, here!" she cried impatiently, shoving in her Travel Permission.

"*Welcome to The Exception, April Johnson. You may proceed—*"

She didn't wait for it to finish. With her bag in one hand and her ID case in the other, she raced into the wide, dark hall—

And almost ran into Wolfe.

"Wh—Why did you leave me there?" she demanded, catching herself.

"I didn't leave you there," he countered, sounding out of breath. "Why would I do that? Your job's not done yet."

Startled, she threw him a look—but despite his labored breathing, he charged ahead, up a slight incline toward another wide door in a red wall.

A young blonde woman in a red ship's uniform stood beside it. She beamed at them.

"Welcome aboard *The Exception*," she greeted them warmly. "You've just made it."

"Thank you," Wolfe answered, and walked right in, Kestrel at his heels.

SIX

The narrow, metal passage almost instantly opened up into the widest hallway yet. Shimmering silver ceiling, flawless white flooring, and dazzling walls covered in moving, colorful, speaking advertisements. Adventurous, mechanized music swelled against Kestrel's hearing. A few passengers strode away from Kestrel and Wolfe and further into the ship.

Kestrel and Wolfe's hurried feet thudded against the white tiles. Huge, elegant red letters leaped to life across the floor, unfurling before them like a carpet.

The Exception—A Luxury Liner
Unlike Any Other

Wolfe instantly hopped off of the letters, glaring at them like they were snakes. They faded back to white. He marched onward, Kestrel struggling to keep up. They passed over a black line in the floor—

A holographic wall leaped up in front of them.

Wolfe threw his arm out in front of Kestrel. A giant, red-headed woman's face blipped into view—she winked at them and held up a green bottle of liquor.

"*Don't forget O'Donnel's Pub once you've crossed the Liquor Line,*" she quipped. "*All the best spirits served twenty-four hours a day!*"

"What is this?" Wolfe demanded—and Kestrel noticed he was still breathing hard.

"Just an ad," Kestrel told him, slipping past his arm and stepping right through the hologram. It buzzed and faded. Wolfe caught up with her, glowering over his shoulder, then faced front again and measured his strides.

"They pop up about every fifty meters," Kestrel explained. "They sense your body heat. They'll have bracelets in the lobby we can rent that'll keep them from popping up as often."

He only made a snorting noise in reply, frowning blackly. They paced further down the hall, overtaking several more passengers who strolled along, chatting with each other. Kestrel caught sight of a sign reading LOBBY, with an arrow, so they followed it—

Into yet another mind-boggling room.

A circular chamber the size of a stadium, ringed by levels of silver balconies leading to all the decks. The ceiling was a brilliant orange-and-red replica-stained-glass of a bursting sun. The main level, where Kestrel and Wolfe walked, rang with the laughter of children, for right in the middle stood an enormous, shimmering turquoise swimming pool. In the center of the pool towered a platform, and from it branched a dozen intertwining waterslides. Despite the late hour, several kids zipped and whizzed down the slides, screeching with excitement before splashing spectacularly into the water. All around the pool, vendors in classy, brightly-colored carts camped, beckoning passengers closer to show their wares—jewelry, toys, hand-games and food. Faux palm trees leaned over these carts, and mechanical birds chirped and flapped in their branches. The moving, talking advertisements persisted here, too—running along the balcony railings, speeding beneath people's feet, spinning through the pool water and crawling up the sides of the water slides.

"Over here," Kestrel said, and they approached a desk off to the side labeled RECEPTION. Forty other people stood in line ahead of them. Kestrel rubbed her neck, feeling hints of a headache. Wolfe let out a low breath. Kestrel regarded him.

"You look pale," she realized. "Are you all right?"

"I'm fine," he answered, and turned to watch the kids going down the slides.

It took half an hour for the line to wane, but finally they stepped up to the man in a black coat with brass buttons.

"April and Jack Johnson," Wolfe sighed, slapping his ID card down on top of the metal desk. "I think we booked a suite."

"Just a moment, sir." The man inserted Wolfe's card and glanced at a screen. He smiled, and looked up at Wolfe. "Yes, sir, level three, room 301. Just go down that hallway, take a left, then take the lift to your level. It should be the first room to your right. Your ID card opens the door. Welcome aboard *The Exception*." He handed it back to Wolfe.

"Thanks," Wolfe muttered, and took it, then strode past him toward the hall indicated. Kestrel, her head really pounding now, dragged after him.

They had barely stepped into the hallway before a wall-ad jumped up. A teenage boy in a jumpsuit holding a glowing gun.

"Get to the Galactic Arcade and test your fighting skills!" He fired a green laser right at them.

Wolfe ducked, then cursed and swatted at the hologram, banishing it.

Two more ads hopped up as they walked—both for restaurants. Kestrel tried to listen to them, but Wolfe barged through them before they could finish their pitches.

"This the lift?" he motioned.

"Yeah," Kestrel nodded, coming up to stand beside him in front of a closed door. It opened right away into a dark blue room entirely covered with slowly dancing stars. They got in, the doors shut. Nothing happened.

"Level three," Kestrel sighed.

"Level three," the lift computer repeated—

And the lift shot upward. Three seconds later, the doors opened and they stepped out.

"There shouldn't be any more ads up here," Kestrel said. "They're too noisy."

Wolfe didn't say anything. He strode across the black carpet to the room marked 301 and held his ID card in front of the lock. It beeped, and the door slipped open. Wolfe went in. Kestrel trailed after.

The hidden lights came on, though not to their full brightness. Black carpet, blue walls. A sitting area took up most of the space right in front of her: four soft-but-blocky black chairs circled around a shiny multi-entertainment console. Another chair sat against the wall straight across from her, near the space window, which was shut. Off to her left, tucked in the far corner, sat a plain single bed with a standing lamp keeping it company. Directly to her left, a kitchenette occupied that corner, as did a floor-to-ceiling dry-washing machine. Between the foot of the bed and the dry-washing machine stood a doorway, probably to a bathroom. Kestrel turned to the right. Up a single step, another door—a wide one— opened to another bedroom. She could see a queen-sized bed in there, and guessed that this bedroom had its own bathroom.

The front door snapped shut. She jumped. Wolfe didn't break stride. He headed straight for the single bed and tossed his bag down on it.

"Go ahead and get some rest," he half-heartedly gestured to the other bedroom as he tugged his leather jacket off. "Nothing more we can do tonight."

Kestrel only nodded, then started toward the bedroom. He looked at her over his shoulder.

"The front door stays locked when it shuts, right?"

"I think so," Kestrel said.

"Good," he said, and sat heavily down on the bed and pulled off one boot. Kestrel hesitated, her stomach tightening to a painful degree. Then, she labored up that single step, went in the bedroom, paused, then waved her hand in front of the sensor. The door closed.

The great big bed right in front of her, its head against the other wall, had soft gold sheets and pillows and a fluffy comforter. The rest of the room...

Thin carpet, a lamp, a temperature regulator—and yes, a bathroom to her right.

And deep, penetrating silence.

Silence she could feel in her bones. Silence that almost caused a soft static in her hearing.

Then...

A low, sub-sonic, almost undetectable *thrum*, far down in the bowels of the ship.

The launch prep.

They were leaving.

Slowly, Kestrel set her bag down on the floor. She straightened, closed her eyes, and put a hand over her mouth to stifle her tears.

Kestrel stared at the black ceiling. Off to her left somewhere, toward the bathroom, a night-light glowed. But it didn't do any more than outline the short posts at the foot of the bed, and the edges of the door beyond them.

It was so quiet. She'd never been anywhere so quiet, ever. After the low reverberation of the launch, everything had fallen still. Now she could hear every breath she took. She turned over. The sheets rustled with an inordinate amount of noise. She winced. Could he hear her thrashing around in here?

She punched at her crisp pillow, then squeezed it against her. There had to be sound-deadening technology in the walls. There was no way everyone else on this ship was tucked in his bed, asleep. She bit her lip.

She'd never gone to bed without some type of music playing. As far back as she could remember, her mother had set some soothing lullaby going in the same movement as turning out the lights...

A sharp pang shot through Kestrel's chest. She clenched her pillow and choked. Desperately, she turned her face into the pillow, holding her breath and squeezing her eyes shut, battling back the feeling of jagged glass tearing at the inside of her ribs.

She gasped, threw off her covers and sat up. She raked her hands through her hair, then took fistfuls of it, her whole body breaking out in an icy sweat.

These weren't her pajamas. This wasn't her bed. This wasn't her room. The soap in the shower hadn't smelled anything *like* her soap, and her mom and dad and brothers weren't...

"Where is your daughter?"

"I don't know—What do you want? You can't come in here and—"

"We are authorized to take whatever measures are necessary. Where is she?"

"You come here and attack my house and expect me to tell you where my daughter is? Under no circumstances will I—"

"Then, sir, you're all coming with us."

"Stop, stop," Kestrel ordered herself, shakily swiping away the tears that spilled down her cheeks. "Stop it, calm down. *Calm* down." She clasped her hands in front of her and sucked in deep, purposeful breaths through her mouth. Her heart fluttered and banged against her sternum like a caged bird.

"Stop it," she said again. "Calm down."

She wiped her face off with her long sleeve, took three more breaths, then grabbed the edge of her blankets and shook them out. She folded them back away from her, turned and pushed her pillow into the right position, plumping it as she did. Then, she lay down, tugged her covers over herself and made herself shut her eyes.

DAY ONE

She didn't sleep. Not more than a couple hours. She was staring at the numbers that hovered in the air just over the surface of the bedside table when they clicked from "6:29" to "6:30."

She sighed. Then she shoved her covers off, sat up and set her feet on the floor. Chills raced over her skin.

Wincing, she grabbed the top layer of blankets, tugged it loose of the mattress, then wrapped it around her shoulders and got up. She trailed across the carpet to the door, and hazily watched it hiss open. She blinked slowly, and looked out across the room.

Wolfe lay on top of his covers on his bed, gazing at the ceiling. The standing lamp beside him glowed at about a quarter of its full brightness, leaving a good deal of his form in shadow. He wore his jeans and gray short-sleeved shirt. His leather jacket sprawled at the foot of the bed. One bare forearm lay across his forehead, turned so she could clearly see the black tattoo. Something rested on his chest: a piece of folded leather, open and face-down. Kestrel considered it. It looked like there were pieces of thin, worn plastic between the leather halves. *Was* it plastic...? He breathed steadily, evenly, as if he were counting.

Kestrel sank to the floor, curling her feet up underneath her, and leaned sideways against the doorframe. She tucked the blanket around her, sighed, then let her head fall against the doorframe, too.

Minutes ticked by. Hours, maybe. She lost track, after a while. Her eyes started to drift shut as her hands relaxed...

Wolfe pulled in a sharp breath. Kestrel's eyes opened.

He sat up, groaning and running a hand through his hair. He rubbed his face.

"What time is it?" He cleared his throat.

"Um..." Kestrel croaked, startled, then glanced back over her shoulder. "Seven."

"Okay," he sighed, shutting his folded leather piece and stuffing it inside his jacket. "Get ready. We'll go find something to eat."

Kestrel tied her hair up in its usual ponytail and looked at herself in the full-length mirror of her stainless steel bathroom. She'd showered, washed her face, brushed her teeth and put on the little bit of makeup she could find the sparse kit she'd dug out of her bag. The no-nonsense, form-hugging zipped gray jacket and pants fit her pretty well, but the slipper-like shoes she'd found in the bottom of the suitcase felt a little too soft, so she had tugged on her beat-up boots. She sighed, tilting her head as she studied her reflection, and then ran her fingertips across her cheeks. She looked tired. She rolled her eyes.

"Gee, why would I look tired?" she muttered, tightening her ponytail again. Kestrel turned, snagged her card case and pulled out all her cards, then zipped them securely into a side pocket of her jacket. Taking another breath, she left the bathroom, crossed through her bedroom and out into the main room.

Wolfe stood waiting for her, hands in his jeans pockets. Absently, she noticed he wore a different shirt, he was clean shaven, and his hair was damp and half-combed. He had put on his jacket again. He met her eyes.

"Ready?"

She nodded. He didn't say any more, just walked straight through the entrance and out into the hall. Kestrel lowered her head and followed him for the hundredth time.

"So where would be the closest place to find food?" Wolfe asked her as they stepped aboard the lift.

"This early in the morning?" Kestrel thought about it. "Well, cruisers usually have a sun deck, where it's simulated daytime all the time..."

"There's food there?" Wolfe said as the doors slid shut. Kestrel shrugged.

"Probably."

"Okay, so..."

Kestrel raised her voice.

"Sun deck."

"*The Sun Deck*," the computer said back, and they shot off. Wolfe reached out and gripped the rail on the wall, steadying himself. Kestrel took hold of the rail on the opposite wall, her stomach flipping as the little vehicle shot upward, sideways, then forward. In ten seconds, it slowed, and the doors opened.

Kestrel flinched, then squinted, pausing a second to let her eyes adjust. Wolfe was out of the lift already. She quickly stepped out too, scanning the place, her first breath filled with the scent of bacon, coffee and toast.

A huge circular room opened up in front of them, ringed with food stalls, the center filled with white chairs and tables. Umbrella-like, clear tinted shades hovered over the tables, offering just enough protection to those who sat from the golden "sunlight" that streamed from the center of the ceiling and flooded the whole chamber.

The dark green floor under Kestrel's feet felt like rubber—their steps didn't make any noise. She caught sight of only one other group of people, a family of four, seated all the way across the room. Clanking, buzzing and hissing issued from all of the food stalls as the businesses opened up and started up.

"Okay," Wolfe said again, pausing on the edge of the seating area and turning to scan the vendors. "Pick one."

"Me?" Kestrel's eyebrows went up.

"Yeah, go ahead," he nodded. "I'll have whatever you have."

"Okay..." Kestrel said uncertainly, glancing at the options. "There's a...A regular breakfast place. *The Biscuit*—it's got eggs and toast and—"

"Fine. Go," he nodded to it. Kestrel glanced at him, then crossed the room to the vendor.

"Good morning." A white-clad man adjusting a screw on the side of the machine smiled at them.

"Good morning," Kestrel answered, then faced the tall machine, which was made up of several large blocks, each one containing a touch screen. She moved forward and tapped one, dismissing the welcome screen, then tapped twice on a picture of a plate of eggs and bacon with a glass of orange juice. It beeped at her. She dug out her orange meal plan card and stuck it in the slot next to the screen.

Your order should be ready thirty seconds. Thank you.

"What—food comes out of a tin box now?" Wolfe remarked from behind her. She turned around.

"Um..."

He heaved a sigh, pulled out his own card and stepped up to a different screen.

"Why am I surprised anymore?" he muttered, flicking through his options. Seconds later, he had ordered and paid, and they stood waiting in silence. Then, a large drawer opened beneath Kestrel's screen—her steaming plate lay on it. Her cup of orange juice appeared in the grasp of a claw hand out from the side of the machine. She picked them both up, then waited for Wolfe to do the same.

"Where do you want to sit?" Kestrel asked.

"Doesn't matter," he said, walked over and seated himself at the nearest table, adjusting his jacket and then picking up his silverware. Kestrel hesitated, then moved around and set her plate across from him and sat down.

Wolfe set his forearms on the table and began to eat. Methodically, taking a drink between every fifth bite, staring at his food, or at nothing.

Kestrel sipped her orange juice, watching him, then took a few bites of eggs. After several moments of silence, she took another drink, swallowed, and spoke.

"So. What's the plan?"

"What plan?" he asked, scooping his over-easy egg onto a half piece of toast.

"Once we get to the Triple Star System," Kestrel clarified. "What are we going to do?"

He glanced at her, then took a bite.

"Find William Jakiv," he said.

"Why?" Kestrel wanted to know, folding her arms and setting them on the table. "You told me that you know things that he'd rather you didn't know, and we ran *away* from him. And now we're running *toward* him."

"I also told you that the less *you* know, the better," he reminded her.

"Why?" Kestrel demanded again. "How is keeping me uninformed going to help me make decisions?"

"You aren't going to be *making* any decisions," Wolfe growled, finishing off the last bit of his food. Kestrel's eyes flashed.

"So now I'm your prisoner?"

"No," he said scornfully "But I've been tracking this man for three years. What we do in the end will be my call, not yours."

"You're forgetting that he's holding *my* family hostage," Kestrel snapped, leaning forward. "*My* family, who never had a *thing* to do with this scientist until *you* came along."

He sighed, and when he met her gaze this time, he seemed tired. "Look, Brown Eyes—"

"*Attention passengers on levels one through three: please proceed to the Star Deck. Mandatory escape drills for your decks will be conducted at eight-thirty this morning, Kansas time. If you do not arrive promptly at eight-thirty for your roll call, an attendant will come to your cabin to assist you.*"

The announcer's pleasant voice made Kestrel grind her teeth.

"You'd better finish that," Wolfe pointed at her plate. "That clock over there says we've got ten minutes."

Kestrel scowled, stuffed her bacon in her mouth and swallowed her questions.

"Star Deck," Kestrel said to the elevator after the doors shut.

"*The Star Deck.*" And it buzzed straight upward.

"What's the Star Deck?" Wolfe asked, holding onto the railing again.

"The front half of the very top level of a star cruiser is always transparent," Kestrel explained. "It's a huge room just for looking at the view. The escape pods are usually all around the edges of it." She shot him a narrow look. "So when are you going to tell me what I asked?"

The doors opened. Wolfe stared out.

A small, black hall waited before them—and at the end of it, something shimmered. His brow furrowing, his eyes intent, he stepped out. Kestrel followed him, watching. They strode down the corridor toward the low opening...

And out onto the deck.

Wolfe drew to a stop.

High over their heads arched a limitless dome—a dome so broad it looked like the sky itself, stretching from horizon to horizon. Except this sky had no atmosphere, no clouds, no city lights to pollute or disguise the endless heaven above it.

It was just there. *Right* there. The cold, fathomless depth of blackest space, pierced through by millions and millions of diamond-like stars—like pinprick facets caught in the full sunlight, flashing and twinkling. All of the stretching cosmos hovered just above them, as if they could simply reach up and run their fingers along the spine of the galaxy...

And at the same time, it plunged to an infinite distance up and away from them, looming dark and bright and full and utterly empty all at once.

Kestrel had been on star decks before. But this view never failed to stop her in her tracks, and erase everything she had been thinking about. It made her feel like the smallest, most insignificant speck of dust in existence—and yet, somehow, it put a thrill through her blood that she could never explain.

Out of the corner of her eye, she caught sight of Wolfe, gazing upward, hardly breathing. She risked a glance at him...

His face, silvery in the starlight. His eyes brilliant and vivid, his lips slightly parted. Then, he let out a shaking sigh, his eyebrows drew together...

And he almost smiled.

"'Canst thou bind the sweet influences of the Pleiades,'" he quoted, quiet and hoarse. "'Or loose the bands of Orion?'"

Kestrel stared at him—but he seemed to have forgotten she was there. Slowly, he wandered forward, never taking his attention from the stars, until he stood in the center of the vast, dark deck. Kestrel absently noticed other travelers filtering in, but none of them spoke loudly. A deep, awesome hush settled over each one of them as soon as he entered.

For a long while, Kestrel watched Wolfe's tall, solitary form, then let her attention drift back to the stars. Only when the Escape Pod Assistant emerged and commanded that they listen to him did she or Wolfe move at all, or think of anything but the towering skies.

Kestrel stood with her hands on her hips, assessing the contents of her luggage. She had spread everything out on her bed, and had just finished counting it all. She had sufficient shirts, pants, socks and undergarments to last a week, and enough toiletries to last a month, if she was careful. She made a face. All her clothes were either black or gray, except for the one blue shirt she'd worn aboard. Sighing and massaging her temples, Kestrel stepped over to the silver bureau and tapped the top drawer. It opened. She stacked her clean clothes inside the drawers, shut them, then put her toiletry bag on the counter in the shiny bathroom. She returned, then picked up her dirty clothes and headed to the door.

Before the doors had even opened all the way, she heard coughing. She stopped on the threshold. Wolfe stood at the kitchenette sink, one hand braced on the counter. He'd taken off his jacket, so Kestrel could see his back shuddering. He coughed hard, gulped, then coughed again as he pushed the cabinet door open. He snatched a plastic glass and shoved it under the water dispenser in the sink. Water splashed over the edges and only half-filled the glass before he pulled it to his lips and took several careful swallows.

He put the glass down and gasped a long breath, wiping his mouth and then his forehead with the back of his hand.

"Are you...sick?" Kestrel wondered, stepping down and crossing closer to him. His head tilted toward her, but he didn't look.

"Chest cold," he muttered. "Can't seem to shake it." He took another drink. Carefully, Kestrel walked behind him to the other side of the kitchenette.

"I'm going to drywash some of my clothes," she mentioned, opening the machine's large door with a snap. "Do you have anything to wash?"

He shook his head, resting both hands on the counter now.

"What about your jacket?" Kestrel pressed.

"What about it?"

"It might get the...The smoke smell off," she ventured. He glanced at her over his shoulder and frowned.

"Why would I care about that?"

"Smoking is illegal this side of the Vice Line," Kestrel said, holding her clothes in front of her but looking at him steadily. "If anybody smells it on you, you could get into trouble."

He sniffed, cleared his throat, then turned back toward his bed and snatched up the jacket.

"Do I have to do anything to it—turn it inside out or something?" he asked. "It won't fall apart, will it?"

"Fall apart?" Kestrel lifted an eyebrow. "No, the machine can handle any sort of fabric. You don't want to have anything in your pockets, though."

"Oh," he murmured, stopped and dug into an inside pocket. He pulled out the folded leather square and tossed it onto the bed, then tugged out two jingling bits with short ribbons trailing from them. He stuffed those in his jeans pocket, then handed her the coat.

Kestrel set her clothes down on the floor, then laid the jacket out on the first tray of the cleaner. She put her own clothes on the lower trays, shut the door, and punched the button for *Medium/Gentle* clean.

"How long will that take?" Wolfe asked, picking up the leather piece and sitting down on his bed.

"Mine will probably take fifteen minutes," Kestrel answered. "It might want to work on your coat a little longer."

He just grunted, leaned back against the wall and opened the folded leather, flipping through the thin pieces inside. Kestrel paused.

"What is that?"

"What's what?" he asked.

"That," she pointed at it. A shadow of a smirk crossed the edges of his mouth.

"A book."

"A book?" she breathed. "Does it have...*paper* inside?"

"Yes," he said, turning one more leaf.

"I've never seen one except in a museum," Kestrel realized, holding out her hand. "May I look at it?"

"No," he answered. Kestrel stood there for a moment, then dropped her hand. She turned and started toward her room. Halfway there, she halted. Her fists closed. She spun on her heel and marched toward the door.

"I'm going out," she announced, and before he could say anything, the door had opened to let her through, and shut behind her.

Loud, upbeat music swam around her head as she walked, hands in her pockets, down a long, wide, gradually-curving white hallway. Dozens of other passengers strolled back and forth all around her, diddling on their hand-held devices, talking into their communicators, stopping to marvel at the wall-adverts, or darting into the fantastically-lit shops and restaurants on either side.

Kestrel flinched as yet another ad for the shooting arcade bounced up in front of her. She charged through it and it blipped off. She looked up, found another elevator and boarded it along with five other people.

After making several stops, the doors opened to the main deck—the stained-glass sun overhead blazed down on the noisy swimming pool and slide. Kestrel maneuvered around a crowd of passengers standing at the reception desk—they probably were having problems with their cabin doors—and found the desk labeled *Ad-Links*.

"Hi," Kestrel smiled at the young, blonde woman behind the counter.

"Good morning, ma'am," the woman answered brightly. "What level of Ad-Link are you interested in renting today?"

"What are my options?" Kestrel asked, folding her arms. The woman pressed a button, and the surface of the side counter slid back to reveal three bracelets on a white surface: one red, one yellow, one green.

"The red one here is our Basic Link," the woman pointed. "Completely water-proof. Deactivates fifty percent of the pop-up wall ads. The yellow one is the Enhanced Link, also waterproof, which deactivates seventy-five percent. And then of course we have our Maximum Link, which eliminates them all for you. Of course, prices vary according to deactivation percentage."

"I'll take the Enhanced link," Kestrel decided, remembering how expensive the Maximum always was.

"Just one?" the woman activated the purchase screen on her desk.

"No, um..." Kestrel closed her hands, then lifted her chin. "Two of them, please."

P

Kestrel sat on a high bar stool, a neon-blue soda on the counter between her fingers, watching the activity of the main hallway through the glass wall in front of her. Her eyes unfocused. She barely heard the noises of the other customers in the restaurant, or the pulse of the music.

The Ad-Link bracelet worked. With it firmly clasped around her right wrist, she'd marched across several sensors all across the level and only three walls had popped up.

And now she had nothing to do.

After two laps of the whole commerce section, she'd meandered into a café she'd passed four times before, ordered a drink and sat down...

Only to feel her skin steadily go icy.

Listlessly, she stirred her drink, watching the bubbles rise to the surface. A pain had started behind her breastbone as she sat—she fought it back, and any thoughts that tried to intrude with it.

Movement caught her eye. Rather, *lack* of movement.

Someone had stopped outside, right in the middle of the busy corridor. Kestrel blinked, and lifted her head.

He wore a long, camel-colored dress coat, his hands casually resting in its pockets. He was fairly tall and slender, had curly golden hair and a handsome, flawless, cultured face.

And he was looking at her.

His dark brows drew together as their eyes met. He had very blue eyes. Penetrating, yet soft.

He smiled. A mysterious, quiet expression. He inclined his head to her...

And then promptly walked away.

Kestrel started breathing again. She pressed her hand to her chest. Why had she stopped?

She took a bracing drink and swallowed the cold, fizzy liquid, but couldn't make herself move from that spot for a long time.

SEVEN

DAY FOUR

Kestrel sat at the end of her bed, thoughtlessly rubbing her fingers back and forth, back and forth, across her yellow Ad-Link bracelet. No sound came from anyplace in her room—the sound system had a glitch. Once, she'd managed to get it to play some fast, metallic music, but that was no good to sleep to. And she wasn't in the mood to bug the management about it.

The crisp *flick* of a page turning issued from the other room. She didn't lift her head to look, though the door was open. It was just Wolfe, leafing through his book again.

Three days. Three days had gone by, and they'd barely spoken ten words to each other. Each morning, they ventured out to get breakfast, but Wolfe was never inclined to engage in any sort of conversation. He ate as if it were his job, he walked as if he were going somewhere important, and never said anything to her except to get expedient information. The rest of the morning he would read or write in his book as he sat on his bed or in one of the chairs. These past days he had foregone lunch, letting her go alone, and when she came back she always found him asleep. Or feigning sleep. Then, later in the evening he would get up, clean up, and they would head out to eat dinner. Never anything different—always the food court on the Sun Deck. Then they would return, and he would read some more, and go to bed.

So during the days, Kestrel wandered. Not far—but she couldn't stand to just sit in the room. Once, she'd made a move to turn on the entertainment console in the sitting area, but Wolfe had given her such a severe look she'd backed away instantly. So, she had meandered through the deck, half-heartedly exploring each one of the shops and restaurants.

Now, something blinked. She glanced over at the clock.

6:30

She got up and walked out into the sitting room. Wolfe sat on his bed beneath the light of the lamp, leaning against the wall and frowning down at his book. Kestrel took a breath.

"Dinner?"

"No," he said absently. "Go ahead."

Her brow furrowed.

"You're not hungry?"

He didn't answer.

Kestrel swallowed hard, looked down at her feet, then hopped down the step and swept out the door.

She couldn't see straight for several paces, but her feet worked on autopilot, taking her straight down the hallway and toward the noise and light of the level's main commerce section. She emerged into the big, white, busy hallway, taking a breath of the scent of all the cooking food. She walked with long strides, fighting to leave her thoughts behind her, scanning the options for her evening meal.

She'd made two laps before she realized that she'd seen everything already. There were only three dining places on this level. Everything else was either desserts, coffees and teas, or novelty shops.

Kestrel stopped in the middle of the floor. Other passengers wove around her, talking happily as if she wasn't there. She hung her head, then shuffled toward the closest restaurant and asked for a table for one.

Kestrel made herself eat her sesame chicken and steamed vegetables. She had no appetite, but her mother had always told her...

She stopped. Her stomach turned over. She closed her eyes, took a deep breath, then another, and pulled down a drink of milk.

She sat back against the cushy seat, glancing at her half-full plate, and folded her arms.

They'd put her in a booth by herself, which gave her a small amount of relief. She didn't feel so exposed, the way she had several other times when she'd been sitting at a little table in the middle of a busy dining room. She glanced around at the red walls, the sparkling oriental décor, and the clusters of families laughing all around her. Aidus and Marcus loved Chinese food. It was their favorite. And her dad liked it because it was usually cheap...

Kestrel shoved her plate away. She couldn't eat any more.

The staff android came by a while later and took her plate and glass. But she didn't go anywhere. She sat there alone until the restaurant emptied and fell quiet, and the chef had to come and politely ask her to leave.

She crossed the threshold of the suite, paused, and sighed. Her breath hurt her.

It was dark in here, except for a light on in her room. He'd gone to sleep already. Tugging her ponytail loose and tiredly braiding her hair, she stepped up the stair and went into her room. The door shut behind her. Quietly, she put on her soft night clothes, washed her face, brushed her teeth, and came out and stared at her bed.

She choked, then clapped a hand over her mouth.

"Stop," she insisted, calming her shaking. She threw her covers back and climbed in, snuggling down before she turned out the light.

Dead silence and complete blackness descended on her. Her breathing shuddered. A tear trickled down her temple. She dashed it away. Her forehead twisted.

She couldn't stand it anymore.

She threw off her covers, stumbled over to the closet and pulled out the complimentary bathrobe. She tugged it on and tied the sash, then groped her way to the bedroom door. It hissed open just as her hand hit the wall next to it. Carefully, though her legs trembled, she slid her feet forward until she found the edge of the stair, then stepped down. She crossed the carpet, moving to her right, until her hands bumped against the plush softness of the chair next to the wall, right by the star window.

She maneuvered around its arm and sat down, tucking her feet under her and stuffing her hands in the soft pockets of the robe. Then, she closed her eyes, and listened.

It took a few minutes of straining—and she had to hold perfectly still for a long time—but finally, she heard it.

Wolfe's breathing.

Steady, deep. And just across the room, on the bed.

She listened, her eyebrows drawing together, as the sound of him filled her consciousness. Until her breathing joined with his. She opened her eyes.

Carefully, she reached up, and pushed open the sliding star window.

Light spilled in. White, soft light. Billions of stars waited just outside, not seeming to move at all, even though she knew the ship was racing along at a speed she could never comprehend. Her brow tense, she kept listening, as the stars out there twinkled coldly.

"What are you doing up?"

His voice jolted her. Her head twitched around, but she couldn't see anything but dark.

"I...can't sleep," she answered.

"Hm," he grunted. He didn't say any more. Kestrel swallowed, wrapping her arms around herself again and turning to the window.

"Something bothering you?"

His voice startled her again. Kestrel shifted, that pain in her chest coming back.

"Oh, no, just..." She swallowed again. "My bike."

"Your bike?"

"Yeah," Kestrel said tightly, staring out the window. "The one we left in that shed."

"What about it?"

She almost looked toward him. His voice sounded different. Not irritated or indifferent this time...

"My brothers found it for me," she said. "Marcus and Aidus—they're twins. They found it in a junk heap outside of where they work in the summertime. They brought it home and surprised me. I'd always wanted one." She shook her head. "But it wouldn't run. Not at all. So...My dad and I worked on her every night in the garage, buying parts one at a time, picking out the right color to paint her, giving her a little personality." Kestrel smiled. That hurt, too. She fiddled with the end of her sash. "I named her Thrix. Dad gave me the idea. Told me it was the name of a famous racehorse he'd watched when he was a kid." She shrugged one shoulder. "And since he put down about half

81

the money fixing her up, he told me I'd better be careful with her, or I'd be in more trouble than I knew what to do with." Kestrel smiled again, her vision clouding. She swiped at her face, then did it again. Her lower lip trembled, and she stared resolutely out the window, even though she could hardly see it.

Quiet reigned for a moment. Then, a soft rustling made her shift in her seat.

Footsteps across the carpet.

Then, he stood in front of her. Loomed over her, his left half caught in the starlight, his other half in complete blackness. He looked down at her—one of his gray eyes appeared silver.

"It *was* a pretty bike," he said. "Handled like a dream."

Kestrel, meeting his gaze, managed a nod. He stood for a second, put his hands in his pockets, and glanced out the window too.

Then, as if something occurred to him, he turned away from the window, searching. He moved and grabbed one of the other chairs, then dragged it over so it faced her. Then he snatched up a small, stool-like coffee table and set it between them.

"Not enough light," Wolfe commented under his breath, then crossed back over toward his bed, picked up the standing lamp and brought it back over, setting it down to Kestrel's left. He turned it on—it glowed at half power, illuminating them both but not blocking the view of the stars.

He wore his jeans still, and a long-sleeved gray shirt rolled up to the elbows. His hair looked like he'd just run his hands through it. Kestrel could see the scars on his face clearly, and the tattoos on his arms. But she also caught a glimpse of a softening around his eyes and mouth. She gazed at him a moment, uncertain.

"Well, since we seem to be in the same boat," he said, scooting his chair closer to the table. "Have you ever played checkers?"

"What?" Kestrel said, surprised.

"It's easy," he said, pulling out his leather book and flipping through it. "Okay, here's the board. Kinda...makeshift, but it works." He opened the book and laid it out, pages up. Both pages together formed rows of checked squares, colored with some sort of ink. The leather was limp enough that the book stayed open. "Here's the pieces." He pulled out an envelope from between the pages, opened it, and dumped out twenty-four little paper circles—half of them colored black, the others blank. "You can be black," he said, quickly sorting those pieces out from the others and pushing them toward her. Kestrel leaned forward, trying to pay attention to his movements.

"All right, put those pieces of yours on the line of dark squares closest to you," he instructed. Kestrel did, being very careful with her fingertips as she touched the little bits.

"It's paper, Brown Eyes. Not glass," he said. "A lot rougher hands have touched it than yours, trust me."

She glanced up at him, but he was busy setting out his own pieces. She did the same as he did, attempting not to be so cautious.

"All right," he said, glancing over the board. "Black goes first, then we take turns. Now, you can only move your pieces to dark squares, so you always have to go diagonally, like this," he put his finger down on one of her pieces and slid it toward him, then put it back. "And you can't go back toward your base line there. You have to keep moving forward, always. Make sense?"

"So far," Kestrel said, putting a finger to her lip as she narrowed her eyes at the board.

"In a normal move, you can only move a piece forward one square," Wolfe went on. "If you find one of *my* pieces in your way, then you jump over it and take it off the board. And if you find a whole row of mine there, with spaces in the middle, you can jump over them and take them until you can't anymore. But if you can make a jump, you have to. No option."

"Is that the point of the game?" Kestrel asked. "To make jumps?"

"Yeah," he nodded. "And take my pieces. *And* get to my back row, here. Once you do that, we put another piece on top of yours and crown it 'king,'—that way it can move backward or forward, whatever you want."

"How do you win?"

"By getting me into a position where I can't move without being taken," Wolfe said. "Usually that works by taking all my pieces, but it doesn't have to."

"So we're basically trying to corner each other," Kestrel realized, looking up at him. "But whoever does it first wins."

"Right," he nodded. "You start. I'll go easy on you."

He *did* go easy on her. The first game, he coached her along, his voice deep and precise, advising her every move, pointing at the pieces. She listened, eyes fixed on the board, considering everything he said. Then, before she realized it, she'd won.

"Ha," she cried softly, sitting up. "I...Wait, you can't move that one, can you?"

"No," he shook his head. "And I can't move that one, or that one either."

"I won!" she realized. "And I don't even know how to play!"

"Good job," he said. "Let's reset."

They did, Kestrel quite eager this time. They began...

And he beat her soundly.

"Wait..." She frowned sharply at the pieces. "What just happened?"

He sat back and folded his arms.

"I can't move," she said, pointing. "How did you...?"

"You got cocky..." he sighed, shaking his head in mock regret as he sat forward again and brushed the pieces off the board.

"I did not get cocky," Kestrel objected. "Put those back—we're going again."

The edge of his mouth curled up as he counted out the pieces.

"If you say so."

They played again. He beat her again. And again, and again, and again.

And then it came to a draw.

And then *she* beat *him*.

"I let you win that time," he said, flicking her kinged pieces off of his back row, then crossing his arms and resting them on the table.

"You did not!" Kestrel objected, leaning forward to pick up her scattered bits. "I made three jumps in a row. You had no idea that was coming—"

He shrugged.

"You must have been hallucinating."

"No, I *saw* your face—"

He gestured to the board, chuckling.

"Look, I was just being a gentleman—"

"Oh, excuses," Kestrel scoffed. "You just don't want to admit that the person who didn't know how to play this at *all* about an hour ago can now *beat* you—"

"Truth be told, I refuse to be beaten by a girl," he said frankly—and suddenly gave her a warm, unguarded grin. His eyebrows lifted with a hint of teasing. It startled Kestrel—she burst out laughing.

And he laughed, too.

He ducked his head for an instant to hide it, but he couldn't help it. It sounded deep and rusty, but genuine. It rang through the room and lit up his whole face. Kestrel covered her mouth, trying unsuccessfully to stifle herself.

"Okay, okay, fine," she finally decided, blinking her watery eyes and mussing the pieces. "We'll go again." She tried to send him a pointed look. "See if you can rescue your pride somehow."

"You're really a glutton for punishment," he observed.

"Says the guy who is about to *lose*," she countered. "C'mon, set up your pieces."

And he did. And they played and played, long into the night.

EIGHT
DAY FIVE

Kestrel woke up in the chair. She sat up, groaning and rubbing her neck, and squinted around to the rest of the room.

All the lights were on. Wolfe's book no longer lay on the table. His bathroom door was shut, and she could hear water running inside. Reflexively, she glanced out the window...

To see stars. She smirked.

"Remember where you are, Kes." She got up, her legs stiff, and headed back to her bedroom. She took a hot shower, which woke her up, and as she dried off and dressed she realized that she felt a lot better than she had since getting on this ship. She tied her hair up, put on some makeup, then re-entered the sitting room.

Wolfe stood waiting for her, in a shirt, jeans, boots and leather jacket, as always. But today, instead of just walking out the door, he met her eyes.

"Good morning."

She blinked.

"Good morning." She stepped down the stair.

"Hungry?" he asked. She nodded, watching him curiously.

"Yes."

He nodded, then started to the door—but didn't charge out ahead of her. As they walked down the hall toward the lift, he shortened his strides to match hers. Then, right before the lift door, he stopped, and sighed.

"I'm tired of bacon and eggs," he said. "Is there someplace else we could try?"

"Um," Kestrel said, startled, then thought. "There's a little coffee and pastry place on this level."

"Coffee's good," Wolfe nodded. "Lead the way."

"Okay." Kestrel nearly smiled, then turned and strode the other direction, toward the bright commerce hall.

"I don't understand why you would want to put all of that in your coffee," Wolfe said, taking a bite out of his pastry and pointing at her cup. "All that cream and sugar and chocolate and everything just ruins the taste. It's not even coffee anymore. It's dessert."

"Exactly," Kestrel sighed, and took a sip of her hot mocha. He just shook his head and chewed, looking out the front window.

They sat at a white, two-person table up against the front window of the café. Outside, passengers of all ages headed to and from breakfast, and inside they crowded, chatted, played on their devices, or ordered loudly. The staff and stainless-steel androids behind the counters barked and beeped commands back and forth, the dispensers steamed and hummed, and the air flooded with the scents of coffee and sweets.

Kestrel set her cup down and studied Wolfe as he took a drink of his own coffee—black—and folded her hands in her lap.

"So..." she said quietly. "Are you going to tell me what the plan is?"

"I told you, that's none of your business," he answered, wiping his fingers off on a napkin. He leveled a look at her. "I'll take care of it, okay? Stop worrying."

"Stop worrying," she repeated indignantly, but keeping her voice down. "How can I *stop* worrying?"

He sighed again, and glanced at her.

"That's not what I meant."

She just looked at him.

He crumpled up his napkin and stuck it in his empty coffee cup.

"Look, I *will* tell you," he said. "Just not yet."

"Why not?"

"Because," he said pointedly. "Just trust me."

Kestrel gritted her teeth and turned away. Wolfe scooted his chair back and stood up.

"Now," He pulled his jacket off the back of his chair and shrugged into it. "Let's go find something to do."

"What?" Kestrel's head came up.

"I'm going stir-crazy in that room," he admitted. "Any ideas?"

"How about..." Kestrel started, then hesitated. "Well, you might not..."

"What?" he waited.

"The arcade?" she ventured.

"What, that ridiculous ad?" he growled. "Do we have to go to the main level where all those flashing walls are? Because if that's the case, then I don't—"

"Actually," Kestrel said, putting her hand into her pocket. "I got you this." She pulled out the other yellow Ad-Link.

"What is it?" he asked, taking it from her.

"If you wear it, it eliminates about seventy-five percent of the wall ads," Kestrel told him, getting up too.

"Not all of them?" he asked, turning it in his fingers.

"That option is really expensive," Kestrel shrugged. "I decided we could put up with a few ads if it meant we still had enough money for things like, oh, food."

He laughed softly.

"Right. Priorities." He opened the bracelet and snapped it onto his left wrist. "It doesn't have to be showing, does it?"

"No," Kestrel shook her head. "It's wireless and remote."

"Good," he said, tugging his jacket cuff over it. "Because it looks silly."

"Wha—It does not," Kestrel protested.

"Yes, it does," he countered, heading to the door. "Especially on you."

The door ahead of them gaped. A wide archway stood at the end of the hall, and above it in striking, glowing green letters stretched a sign:

GALACTIC ARCADE

Inside, the huge room looked mostly dark, interrupted by neon space designs on the floor, and pinging simulated lasers dancing off the walls. Music rolled out—fast-paced and energetic. Wolfe winced.

"Loud," he commented. Kestrel lifted one shoulder.

"That's so that when you miss the target or crash your fighter, you can curse and the little kids won't hear you."

Wolfe grinned again, kicking his head back. Kestrel, more eager than she ever had been to enter an arcade, strode right up to the front counter.

"How many?" the black-clad girl asked.

"Two," Kestrel said, laying down her gold credit line card.

"Would you like the complete package? It includes the obstacle courses, virtual battle courses, target shooting and piloting. Or, you can just cut that in half—do the obstacle and battle courses, or the shooting and piloting."

"Hm," Kestrel thought for a moment. "Just the shooting and piloting for now, thanks."

"Okay," the woman took the card and Kestrel paid, and the girl gave them each another bracelet to wear—neon purple this time.

"Great," Wolfe said as he strapped his on. " *This* one glows in the dark."

Kestrel chuckled, then sensed him follow her as they moved further in.

All around them, shrieking kids darted between blinking, beeping machines, their bracelets waving like beacons to their parents, who hurriedly trailed after. Glowing pictures of colorful planets, comets and stars moved slowly across the black floor, giving Kestrel the odd feeling that she was walking on air. Overhead hung dozens of life-size star-fighters, their edges flashing with lights. She glimpsed several wide-eyed people in each cockpit, working the controls and howling their way through the simulations. Six-armed androids trundled about on their large, single wheels, maintaining the games and keeping the waiting lines in order. Moving ads occasionally blipped to life on the walls, happily suggesting that they take a break to go get a Fizzy-Wizzy drink at the nearby snack counter.

"So, where do we go?" Wolfe asked, stepping closer to her and frowning all around them.

"Looks like...over there," Kestrel pointed. "If you want to practice marksmanship."

"Is it quieter in there?"

"Probably," Kestrel said, starting toward that door. It opened for them, and shut behind.

It *was* quieter, and the music pulsed with cool focus. To their left stood a whole wall virtually covered in firearms. To their right stood the range, divided up into stalls and long corridors. Four other sets of people were already there, taking up the furthest four rows. Wolfe paused, staring at the firepower.

"Wow," he muttered. Then he pointed at them. "These aren't—"

"No, they've been programmed to be non-lethal," Kestrel said, still considering. Then she raised her voice. "K95 to ground level."

The topmost gun lowered down to her on a mechanical arm. She plucked the handgun off and turned it over.

"Hm," she said. "Pretty good shape. Somebody broke off the safety, though..." She turned to Wolfe. "Which one do you want?"

"Um..." He thought a moment. "Something longer than that."

"Something you set against your shoulder?"

"Yes."

"Okay, um..." she thought again. "C14 to ground level."

A long gun descended, stopping in front of him.

"Pull it off," she instructed. "That's a hunting rifle, long range. Very precise."

He clicked it loose, then hefted its long barrel and graceful, slender stock.

"Interesting..."

"Come over here," she said, turned and entered one of the empty stalls. She approached the counter and looked down at the screen there. She felt Wolfe come in behind her.

"How about stationary targets first?" she suggested, touching the screen and selecting that option.

"How do *you* know so much about guns?" Wolfe asked. She smirked.

"I used to sell them, remember? Before you blew them all up."

"Right," he muttered. "Sorry about that."

"It's okay," she admitted, still smiling. "I didn't like that job, anyway."

The target tunnel ahead of them darkened, and then at the far end about forty meters away, a single red circle with a center dot appeared. Kestrel raised her gun in her right hand, sighted and fired.

A green bolt, thin as a needle and tipped in neon yellow, broke from her gun with an efficient *tang*. It split the center dot. The target splattered and disappeared.

"I...I didn't even see that," Wolfe stammered.

The target reappeared. Kestrel took a short breath, aimed and fired. The target splattered again.

Again. And again.

Ten more times, she shattered the centers of the virtual targets—and the lights blinked a multi-colored **1000 POINTS!** at her before flashing: **PLAYER TWO**.

"That's you," she said, stepping aside to make room for Wolfe. But he just stood there, considering her. She met his eyes—then blushed.

"What?" she wondered. He looked at her sideways.

"Who taught you to shoot like that?"

"I did," she answered. "When I knew I'd have to be selling them, I wanted to be able to actually help people shop. I learned to shoot all the guns on the wall of the store. Which was actually..." she looked at the ones nearby. "More than there are here."

He paused for a moment, then turned to the corridor.

"All right, what do I have to do?"

"Just hit the target," she told him. "Like I did."

"Do I have to reload this thing?" he asked, lifting it up to look at it.

"No. Just pull the trigger."

"I can do that," he muttered, raised it and set it against his right shoulder—like it fit there. Like he had done this a thousand times. A million.

The target appeared.

He shot it.

Right in the center. Even better than Kestrel's aim.

Thirteen times, he shot the middle out of the target—and his gun kicked, uttering a snapping growl each time it fired.

1000 POINTS! the system declared. **ROUND TWO!**

"Where did *you* learn so much about guns?" she asked, studying him.

"Here and there," he answered, his attention on his lowered rifle. "From my father first."

He didn't offer any more, so reluctantly, Kestrel stepped up again, readying her gun.

"Moving targets, now," she said under her breath. "These are a little harder..."

A shape coalesced at the end of the tunnel. Glowing. Man-shaped. Wearing armor, holding a handgun. And he bared his teeth and ran right at her. She took a breath, aimed—

"No."

Wolfe's hand suddenly landed on her arm. She jerked, then twisted to face him. The hologram man roared and charged right up to them, then dissolved.

"What?" Kestrel cried. "What's—"

"No targets that look like people," Wolfe said, keeping his hand on her arm even as another hologram man charged up and dissolved. She just stared straight up into Wolfe's serious gray gaze.

"Why not?" Kestrel wondered, her voice quiet. He considered her face a moment.

"Have you ever really done that, Brown Eyes?" he asked, low and fervent. "Looked down the barrel of a gun and shot a man?"

She shook her head once, seeing nothing but him.

"No."

His hand relaxed on her arm.

"Good," he whispered. "Don't start."

Kestrel swallowed, watching as he turned away, his brow furrowing.

"How...How about..." she fumbled, turning back to the controls. "Zigg-bots?"

" *What* are Zigg-bots?" Wolfe demanded, incredulous.

"Half alien, half robot green flying...things," Kestrel supplied. "They're not real."

The hardness faded from his features. He glanced down, on the verge of smiling, then nodded.

"Okay," he allowed. "Guess I can shoot up some Zigg-bots."

"This whole setup makes me nervous," Wolfe growled, climbing into the dingy copilot's next to Kestrel.

"Shut the hatch, there—the game won't start till you do," Kestrel said, slamming her own side door closed and settling into the cockpit.

"This thing has restraints..." Wolfe realized, pushing them out of the way so he could sit back in the snug black seat.

"You don't need those," Kestrel waved him off, glancing over the weathered control board's hundreds of blinking lights and buttons. "But you should know—I'm very bad at this."

"Wonderful," Wolfe said under his breath, then reached out and slammed his door shut.

The cockpit lights dimmed, the front screen darkened, and the blue words at the beginning of the game flashed to life in front of them.

ORTHEUS
THE ULTIMATE GAME OF SKILL AND STRATEGY

Kestrel grabbed the levers, which had been wrapped around with black electrical tape, and felt for the buttons.

"Your job will be to shoot. There's your guns," Kestrel told him, pointing.

"These?" he said in disbelief, wrapping his hands around two joysticks on a moveable platform.

"You can pull them closer to you—yeah, like that," Kestrel nodded. "The right one is the right gun, the left one is your left gun."

"Look, if we're going to do this, you'd better use the right terms," Wolfe declared. "Starboard and—"

"Port, all right fine," Kestrel finished. "Didn't know you flew."

"I don't," Wolfe said, wincing as he tweaked the joysticks back and forth. "I've only been on an airplane twice in my life. As a passenger."

Kestrel's eyebrows went up.

"Really?"

"*Begin!*" the computer ordered.

The music started—frantic and intense. Kestrel's head whipped around to face front. The words dissolved into a simulated view of glittering space—it looked *absolutely* real—and off to Wolfe's side of the screen, the soft curve of a blue planet glowed.

"What are we doing?" Wolfe demanded.

"We have to safely land on the planet to get our orders for the next mission level," Kestrel said, swinging the ship around so the planet filled the screen.

"What's the catch?"

"There's an enemy blockade in the way."

"And we're all by ourselves, here?"

"Yep."

"Do we have any special advantage?"

"No," Kestrel shook her head. "We're *supposed* to get a secret weapon—some sort of time-travel portal—but that's not until level three."

"What's that out there?" Wolfe pointed.

"Oh, hold on!" Kestrel cried. She hit the accelerator. The shapes in the viewscreen got drastically larger—then formed into claw-like fighters that screamed toward them, firing yellow bolts.

"Shoot, shoot!" Kestrel ordered.

"How?" Wolfe demanded.

"Pull the triggers!" Kestrel said, then yanked on her controls to send their little ship into a sharp bank. The cockpit itself didn't flip upside down, but the screen did, making Kestrel *feel* as if they were doing loops. She straightened it out, then glanced at her readings.

"Where did they go?" she wondered.

"I'd like to know how I'm supposed to get a clear shot off when you tailspin us like that," Wolfe muttered, pushing himself off the wall and thudding back into his seat.

"You'll get a chance, here come some more," Kestrel said, accelerating again as three more fighters emerged.

"Hold it steady this time," Wolfe said.

"I *am*—"

The fighters bore down on them, then flew by and strafed them—but not before Wolfe got off three solid shots. One nicked an enemy wing.

"Almost," Kestrel said tightly as the cockpit shook, then stabilized. She looked at her readouts. "All right, we just have to make it through three more waves without sustaining any more damage—"

Ping, ping, ping!

Kestrel flinched as the viewscreen flashed and the ship jiggled.

"Like that?" Wolfe said wryly.

"Where did that come from?" Kestrel gasped, looking around. Then she found her status screen. "Uh, oh."

"What?" He glanced at her.

"We lost our starboard engine."

Just as she said that, the view began to list to the right. The planet loomed up in front of them, filling the whole screen. Kestrel twisted the controls to the left, grimacing. The listing slowed, but did not stop. The red speedometer numbers climbed.

"Um..." Kestrel managed. "We're...I think we're gonna die."

"That's probably a good assessment," Wolfe nodded, sitting back and folding his arms. They blazed forward, entering the planet's atmosphere. The whole screen turned white.

The controls went limp in her hands.

The screen turned black.

You were incinerated upon entry, the computer blinked.

"Oh, *no* kidding," Wolfe snorted. "Good thing we have a computer around to tell us these things."

Kestrel sat back, a wave of melancholy overcoming her.

"I've never been very good at this game," she murmured, rubbing her thumb on the stick. "Marcus always beats me."

Silence fell, and she could feel Wolfe looking at her.

"Well," he finally said, drawing a breath and taking hold of the door latch. "Now that you've made me sick, I think I need a change of scenery. And a drink."

Kestrel looked at him sideways.

"What kind of drink?"

He shrugged and pushed the door open.

"Anything but that syrupy coffee."

"I don't know what's on this level," Kestrel warned him as the lift plunged. "Usually the bottom level is reserved for night life after crossing the Liquor Line—"

"I keep hearing about this Liquor Line," Wolfe said as the lift slowed and the doors whooshed open. He stepped out. "What is it, exactly?"

"It...You don't know?" Kestrel frowned at him, keeping pace next to him.

"Never paid attention."

"Alcohol of any kind is illegal inside the Liquor Line," she explained. "Once you get past that, it *is* legal, but you can't get in fights or break things or drive anything."

"Aha."

"If you want to smoke or do other...questionable things," Kestrel made a face. "You have to get further out into space, past the Vice Line. It's so far away from any real government that you can get away with pretty much whatever you want."

"The wild west," Wolfe mused, heading down the quiet hallway, hands in his pockets.

"The what?" Kestrel wondered, but he didn't supply anything more. Kestrel was forced to push that aside and cast around as she walked.

The floors and walls on this level were obsidian black—mirror-like, with deep sparkles. The ceiling shone like silver, random pinprick lights offering more than enough illumination to see clearly. When they walked, their footsteps caused low, reverberating musical notes, like the plucking of piano strings.

On both sides of the hallway, doorways stood locked and barred— doorways to dark dance clubs and lifeless cocktail lounges. No music played. And nobody else walked the corridors. Kestrel shivered.

"It's eerie down here," she decided.

"It's quiet," Wolfe sighed, running a hand through his hair and lifting his head. "I can actually hear myself think for once. Things aren't constantly..."

He trailed off and stopped, brow furrowing. Kestrel stopped too.

"What?" she asked.

"Sh," he held up a finger. "Hear that?"

Kestrel paused, listening. For a long moment, nothing. She opened her mouth to say no...

A voice. Then, a low tone—*not* a voice.

Then, laughing.

"C'mon," Wolfe urged, and started forward. Kestrel followed. They rounded a corner, then slowed in front of a wide door.

A door with a frame made of *wood*.

No laser gate barred the entrance, but not many lights were on inside. However, Kestrel *could* see the interior: polished cherry wood, a low ceiling. Tall-backed booths, a bar in the back, bordered by sparkling glasses and bottles. A wooden floor, scuffed and pockmarked.

The voices came from inside there. As did the low, jingling tones.

Wolfe stepped inside.

"I don't think they're open..." Kestrel cautioned, but he didn't hear her. Biting her lip, she ventured in after, hoping no alarms were about to go off...

They maneuvered through the maze of booths and tables and finally came out in front of a well-lit, short, small stage next to the bar. And on that stage sat three casually-dressed young men. One black-bearded man sat perched on a stool, his arms wrapped around a long-necked, broad-chested wooden stringed instrument that looked taller than he. A blonde man sat on a box, a little stringed instrument resting on his lap. And the last, a red-head, sat on the edge of the stage, holding a medium-sized stringed instrument. They were all in the midst of laughing heartily.

Then they caught sight of Wolfe and Kestrel. They stopped and turned. The red-head's bright eyes widened.

"Hello," he said, in an accent—it sounded Scottish. "Er, we're not open yet..." He glanced at his fellows. "Don't cross the Liquor Line for another few days. We were just practicing."

"Can we help you?" the bearded man asked, standing up off his stool— he had an accent too, but a different one. Australian?

"We were just exploring and I heard your guitar," Wolfe gestured to the instrument the red-head held. "It's a nice one."

"You heard that?" the man seemed surprised. "I was just diddling around..."

Wolfe grinned.

"It's been a while since I've heard a *real* acoustic guitar," he said. "You don't forget that sound."

"Aye, you don't," the young blonde man agreed.

"My name's Jack," Wolfe stepped in and held out his hand.

"Jim," the red-head answered, shaking Wolfe's hand and smiling.

"This is...This is April," Wolfe turned and indicated Kestrel.

"Nice to meet you, ma'am," the black-bearded man nodded to her.

"This is George," Jim pointed to the bearded man. "And this is Kie."

"Pleasure," Wolfe said.

"So," Jim's brow furrowed at him. "You play?"

"I did," Wolfe nodded, putting his hands in his pockets. "But I wound up losing my *own* guitar in a fire, actually."

All the men grimaced.

"That's terrible," Kie moaned.

"Yes, it is," Jim agreed. "Would you like to...?" He half held out his guitar to Wolfe. Kestrel watched him.

"You sure?" Wolfe asked. Jim raised his eyebrows solemnly.

"Least I can do for somebody who lost his instrument that way."

Wolfe smiled again, and grasped the neck of the guitar.

"Thank you," he inclined his head. "I'll be careful with her."

Wolfe sat down on the edge of the stage next to Jim, running his eyes and his fingers over the instrument. He took hold of the neck of it with his left hand, then let his right hand hover over the strings.

A reflexive, broken smile crossed his face.

"Long time..." he murmured. He set his fingers on the strings, breathing slowly. They all watched him. Kestrel didn't move.

He began to play.

Soft, individual notes—rich and deep and flowing together like a stream over smooth rocks. His left hand fingers pressed down and released the strings with firm, gentle purpose as he bent his head, listening as the tones reverberated through the wooden chest of the guitar.

Kestrel's breath stole from her body. She'd heard guitars before—guitars made of metal and carbon and plastic and even glass—but never wood.

And never alone, without being plugged into an amplification system and accompanied by pounding drums and synthesizers...

She'd never heard anything so beautiful. So honest.

It cut straight into her heart.

Jim, George and Kie gazed at Wolfe, utterly still, as if listening with all their beings. Wolfe played more carefully, more deliberately, drawing the soul out of the instrument.

And then he started to sing.

A deep voice. Untrained, smooth and simple. And as the words left his lips, Kestrel felt a lump rising in her throat.

"Oh, Shenandoah,
I long to see you,
Away, you rolling river.
Oh, Shenandoah,
I long to see you,
Away, I'm bound away,
'cross the wide Missouri."

Jim glanced at George in startled recognition. Then they began to hum along—harmonizing, adding two more layers to the profound melody.

"Oh, Shenandoah,
I love your daughter
Away, you rolling river
For her I'd cross
Your roaming waters
Away, I'm bound away
'cross the wide Missouri."

Wolfe stopped singing, and played the chorus one last time as a strange, thrilling pain danced through Kestrel's chest. She pressed her fingers to her mouth as the notes wandered through the darkened pub, lingering like the summer wind, slowing down...

Fading. And ceasing as he strummed one last chord, and lifted his hand from the strings.

For just a moment, silence fell. Then, Jim beamed and clapped his hands. The other two instantly joined, and Kestrel felt herself smiling.

"Oh, well done!" Jim commended. "That was gorgeous, mate!"

"Thank you," Wolfe said, letting his hand stray across the strings again in a quick *thrum*. "It's a really nice instrument."

"Almost a hundred years old," Jim declared proudly. Wolfe raised his eyebrows at him.

"Really?"

"Yeh, belonged to my great-grandfather," Jim said.

"You've taken good care of it," Wolfe nodded, looking at it again. He took a breath, and braced himself. "Well, we'd better—"

"Do you know any duets?" Kie cut in. "Any group tunes?"

Wolfe hesitated.

"I...Well, I don't know if you guys would call 'em by the same names..."

"Well, play a lick," George suggested.

"Okay, um..." Wolfe cleared his throat and thought a moment. Interested, Kestrel stepped closer, folding her arms and leaning sideways against the back of a booth.

Wolfe set his fingers on the strings, then plucked eight notes—the first three were the same note, then the others ducked down and swung back up again. He stopped and looked to them. Then, Jim got up.

"I'm going to need my banjo for this one." He hurried off the stage to open a different case.

"You know it?" Wolfe asked, surprised.

"We call it *Gold Rush,*" Kie said. Wolfe smiled wryly.

"When I learned it, it was called *Cripple Creek,* but as long as the notes don't wander too far apart, I think we'll be all right."

"We should be," Jim nodded eagerly, sitting down with a very long-necked instrument—the place where he strummed the strings looked like a small drum. Wolfe shifted toward the group, watching Jim.

"Ready?" Jim looked at the other men. They sat poised.

"A one and-a-two-and-a-three—" he said—

And off they went. George kept steady, pulsing time on his tall, big-chested instrument, and Kie, Jim and Wolfe's fingers simply flew over their strings, their left hands effortlessly sliding up and down to change chords.

Kestrel found herself grinning like an idiot, completely unable to keep her eyes off them. The rollicking, multi-layered song swung and reeled through the pub, lightning fast, happy and reckless—and none of them missed a beat.

They raced along, exchanging challenging grins as the pace picked up to a blinding speed, built and got louder—

Then, the song turned, spun around on itself, tied up in a nice little tag and finished with a flourish, each man striking the strings and then lifting his hand in finale.

Kestrel burst into applause. Kie laughed, George and Jim inclined their heads to her. Wolfe hid a quiet smile.

"That was amazing!" Kestrel cried, stepping closer to them. "That was the most amazing thing I've ever seen. Or heard."

"Thank you, lass," George said warmly. "Do you play anything?"

"Oh—no," Kestrel said regretfully. "I can sing, but I never learned how to play anything like that."

"What, and he won't teach you?" Jim asked, sending Wolfe a berating look. Wolfe chuckled.

"I would if she asked," he said, glanced up, and met her eyes for a moment. She stood still. His smile gentled. Then, Wolfe stood up, and held the guitar out to Jim.

"I'm honored you let me play this," he said as Jim set his banjo down and got to his feet.

"It was an honor to hear you!" Jim said as he took back his instrument, and the other men agreed.

"Glad to have met you," Wolfe stuck his hand out again. Jim grasped it, his brow furrowing.

"This isn't goodbye then, is it? Are you getting off at a stop, soon?" Wolfe hesitated.

"Well, no, we're going all the way to the Triple Star System..."

"Then come back tomorrow evening, mate, if you're not busy!" Jim invited. "In fact, any evening! Play some with us! And bring your pretty girl!" He winked at Kestrel. She blushed. Wolfe laughed.

"Thank you," he gripped Jim's hand and shook it. "Thank you, we'll try to come."

"Goodnight!" Kie called.

"Goodnight," Wolfe waved to all of them.

"Goodnight, April," George bid her. "Come back to see us!"

"I will!" Kestrel promised, and together she and Wolfe left the pub.

They walked for a while in silence, the tunes still ringing through

Kestrel's memory. Finally, she lifted her head and looked at him.

"That first song," she said, her voice quiet. "It was beautiful."

He shrugged, smiling.

"I'm a little rusty."

"Didn't sound like it," Kestrel said. "I could listen to that all night."

His smile broadened, though his head stayed down.

"Thank you."

"I've never heard the song, though," she remarked. "Where did you learn it?"

He sighed, lifted his head and glanced at the ceiling in thought. He put his hands in his pockets.

"Hm. I don't even remember. I must've been pretty young—thirteen or fourteen."

"What's it about?" Kestrel wondered.

His eyes grew distant.

"It's about..." he said slowly. "About leaving home. About leaving a familiar place...familiar people. And never seeing them again."

Kestrel swallowed. And she eased just a little closer to him as she walked. His arm bumped her shoulder. They didn't say anything for the rest of the short jaunt back to their level—but he didn't move to distance them.

NINE

DAY SIX

The next day took a different turn. Kestrel actually slept well in her bed—woke up at nine o'clock, a vast improvement from five or six in the morning. She and Wolfe got ready and trundled down to the second level to eat at a pancake place for breakfast. There, they happened to overhear some other passengers discussing ship tours, so they headed down to the concierge to inquire, then booked an afternoon tour of the Map Room.

It was spectacular. Like nothing Kestrel had ever seen. With a group of twenty other people, they entered a pitch-black dome that soon illuminated, with a flick of the tour-guide's finger, to form a three-dimensional map of this quadrant of the galaxy. Marveling, she and Wolfe literally wandered among the stars, listening as the guide talked about the different planets—most of them inhospitable—and the great fleet of space stations that moved with the speed of tectonic plates between the celestial bodies. They could touch the space stations, pinpoints of floating light, and their names, populations, trades and sizes would pop up above them, along with rotating portraits of their governors.

Then the guide pointed out the *Exception*'s route, activating a blue laser line that shot out from Earth, cut across a good portion of the room, and ended at the other side. She showed them where they would stop tonight: the Argoth Station, and then the Darrow Station, where they would be stopping several nights down the way. Wolfe passed by those stations without a glance and headed straight for the terminus of the line. His eyes, reflecting the light of the laser, fixed on the Gain Station.

"It orbits a planet," he noted.

"Yes," Kestrel said. "Alpha Centauri Bb—actually, people just call it Alpha. And *it* orbits the star Alpha Centauri."

"Can you live on it? The planet?" Wolfe wanted to know.

"It used to get hotter than a thousand degrees," Kestrel said. "But now there's a planetary heat shield, and a lot of scientists who work on the Gain Station have homes there. I heard they're making a jungle, and they're working on an ocean."

"Hm," was all Wolfe said.

They continued with the tour, Wolfe growing steadily quieter, brooding. The guide led them back out into the bright swimming pool room, thanked them and dismissed them. The crowd dispersed, and Kestrel's hearing filled with the racket of all the hundreds of kids splashing in the swimming pool, under the light of the orange-and-red window far above.

"Want to look through the vendors?" Kestrel suggested. Wolfe blinked, coming out of some sort of reverie, and nodded.

Kestrel started forward, maneuvering around the fake palm trees and rows of deck chairs by the pool, toward the first little red vending tent. She slowed down in front of it and folded her arms, casually eyeing the silver jewelry laid out on black velvet. She felt Wolfe sigh behind her, but didn't turn. Not until she heard a plaintive keening sound coming from down around their knees.

Kestrel spun—and her eyes went wide. Standing in the middle of the walkway next to them was a tiny boy. He had light hair, wet and plastered to his head, and he wore tight black swim trunks with pictures of sharks on them. He held both arms up, bent at the elbows, and his face contorted with an impending scream.

"A baby!" Kestrel cried. "What—Where are his parents?"

Just then, the child burst out bawling, tears spilling down his cheeks. But nobody swooped in to rescue him—nobody came darting across the plaza.

Wolfe moved.

"Hey, hey there, little man," he soothed in his deep voice, stepping to him, bending down and scooping him up. Kestrel stared. Wolfe set the baby easily against his side, wrapping his right arm around him and smoothing his wet hair away from his forehead. "Where's your Ma and Pa, hm? Easy, easy. Yeah, I'd be screamin' too."

"Guh," the little boy choked, rubbing at his eyes, then he opened them—they were bright green and watery, and he pouted hard.

"You bet," Wolfe nodded, as if he understood him. "Here, let's go see if we can find your folks." And he strode off in the direction of the reception desk. Kestrel instantly caught up with him.

"He can't be more than a year and a half old," she whispered urgently. "What are his parents thinking of, leaving him alone like that? He could have drowned, or been kidnapped!"

Wolfe didn't answer, but his look darkened and she knew he'd been thinking the same thing.

"Excuse me," Wolfe said to the tall receptionist. He turned his head and hefted the child lightly. The baby calmed down to a whimper. "We seem to have found someone's kid."

The man's eyes went wide.

"Oh, wow. Thank you, sir—let me just make a quick call." He picked up his communicator and spoke rapidly into it, occasionally studying the child. Kestrel stepped closer, reaching up to stroke the back of the baby's head.

"It's okay, sweetie," she cooed, tilting her head and smiling so he could see her. "We'll find your mom soon. Don't worry."

"You want to hold him?" Wolfe asked. She met his eyes. Wolfe was looking at her with some interest.

"Isn't he all wet?" she wondered.

"Yeah."

She shrugged, her smile broadening.

"Sure."

He gently leaned toward her and handed the little boy over. Kestrel rested him on her left hip, snuggling him closer, wrapping both arms around him. The boy watched her, and mumbled something to her that didn't contain any words, but Kestrel nodded fervently.

"Oh, I know it," she said. "This is the pits."

The boy sniffed, more tears leaking out, and he let his forehead head *thunk* forward onto her shoulder. Kestrel shot a stricken, sympathetic look at Wolfe. He lowered his head and grinned.

A cry rang out through the lobby. Wolfe straightened and turned around. Kestrel caught sight of a man and a woman racing toward them, dodging between the tables and chairs, the woman in the lead. She had strawberry-blonde hair that flew out behind her—the man had dark hair and wide green eyes.

"My baby!" the woman yelped—in Romanian. Kestrel hurriedly held him out to her. She snatched him up and pressed him to her with all her might. The man, her husband, clutched them both, breathing hard. After a panicked moment, the woman found Kestrel and tearfully spoke to her, again in Romanian.

"Thank you so much! We had no idea what happened—he was with us one moment and gone the next."

"Oh, it was no trouble," Kestrel answered in the same language. "He was a little frightened, but I think he's all right!"

"Thank you, thank you," the husband said as well, taking Kestrel by the hand. "We are indebted to you."

"No, no, it's fine," Kestrel assured him. "We're just glad he's safe."

The couple thanked them dozens of times more, then hurried away, their son in their arms.

"Bye, little man," Wolfe said quietly, waving to him. And the child, leaning over his mother's shoulder, lifted his hand and waved his fingers. Wolfe chuckled, and stuffed his hands in his pockets.

"You're right," Kestrel sighed, glancing down at herself. "He *was* all wet."

Wolfe chuckled louder, then started to head back toward the lifts.

"You hungry?" he asked.

"I could eat," Kestrel answered. Together, they boarded the lift, and waited for it to rise to the commerce floor.

"What language were they speaking?" Wolfe wanted to know.

"Romanian."

"You speak Romanian?"

Kestrel nodded.

"I speak quite a few languages." The doors opened. They stepped out.

"Where did you learn?" he pressed.

"I had a language and literature emphasis all the way through secondary school," she said as they walked. "Then I went to the Missouri University for Linguistics and Literature to be a manuscript technician at a museum."

"What's a manuscript technician?" Wolfe asked as they detoured around a large group of babbling teenagers.

"They preserve and translate old documents," Kestrel explained, matching step with him again. "I think it's fascinating, all those ancient stories."

"So you read a lot," he concluded. She grinned.

"I suppose so."

"And what's your favorite ancient story, Brown Eyes?"

"Hm..." she thought a moment. "Probably *Rip Van Winkle* by Washington Irving."

Wolfe barked out a sudden laugh. She turned to him, startled.

"What?"

"Nothing," he said, rubbing his forehead. "It's been a long time since

I've read that one."

Kestrel thought for a moment, then risked a question of her own. "Do *you* know any other languages?"

He straightened as he walked, then spoke in a low, purposeful tone. *"Accipere quam facere praestat injuriam."*

"Latin!" Kestrel realized. *"'Better to suffer an injustice than to do an injustice.'"*

He nodded.

"Is that why your tattoos are in Latin?" she ventured. "'Justice' and 'Vengeance'?"

His jaw tensed for an instant, and he looked the other way. He cleared his throat.

"A while back," he began, keeping his voice down. "I did a stint as a cage fighter. Only took me a couple times of getting my hand broke and my face spat on for me to learn that if I didn't have at least two tattoos..." he shook his head. "None of the other guys would respect me as one of them."

Kestrel let that sink in. Then, she turned to him.

"Why 'justice' and 'vengeance'?"

"They're the same thing, Brown Eyes," he said frankly. "Just coming from different angles."

"Hm. I suppose..." she murmured. She thought a moment. "I don't really have much experience with either."

"Good," he declared, and they kept walking.

They found a place to eat an early dinner. Wolfe didn't seem inclined to talk much, though Kestrel watched his pale face the whole time. They finished, and she suggested going to the pub. He brightened up at that, and they started walking that direction. But halfway there he had to stop, press his hand against the wall and catch his breath.

"Sorry, Brown Eyes," he said, shaking his head. "I'd better go back to the room."

"Are you all right?" she asked, stepping nearer.

"Yes," he assured her, nodding firmly. "I just don't think space travel is agreeing with me. I need to lie down for a little bit."

"Okay, let's go," Kestrel said, waiting for him to start back to the lift.

"Why don't you go on to the pub?" Wolfe urged. "Don't let me spoil your evening. That bass player was looking forward to seeing you."

Kestrel blinked.

"George?"

"Right, that was his name," Wolfe tried to smile. "Don't want to disappoint him."

Kestrel looked at him a moment, trying to decide if he was serious.

"No, thanks," Kestrel decided. "We'll both go some other time."

"Fair enough," he murmured, looking whiter. And they headed back to the room.

As soon as they arrived, Wolfe took off his jacket and eased down on his bed, closing his eyes. Kestrel paused for a moment, squeezing her fingers together, then decided to just go in, take a long shower and go to bed early.

Kestrel opened her eyes. The room was dark. She took a breath and lifted her head.

1:07

Something inside her turned over. She rubbed her face...

And heard it. The sound that had woken her up.

Coughing.

Hard, rattling, violent coughing.

Punctuated by short, desperate gasping.

She threw her covers off herself and darted to the door in her pajama pants and shirt, never minding about her robe, her long braid lashing her back. The door hissed open—

She skidded to a halt on the edge of the step. The standing lamp was on to a quarter power, but Wolfe wasn't in the bed. She opened her eyes wide, trying to see through the darkness...

A light. A sliver of light at the bottom of the bathroom door.

More coughing barked through that door—ragged, frantic, full-bodied. Kestrel hopped down, stumbled through the dark room, felt her way behind the chairs and slowed to a halt right outside the door. She put her fingers to her lips.

He stood just on the other side. She could feel him. His watery gasps shivered through her, his coughs echoed like slaps.

He suddenly choked.

Kestrel's heart jolted. Her hand flew up to beat on the door—

"*Gah*," he grunted, swallowing audibly. She heard him shuffle, perhaps turn around...

Hissing broke out from the shower.

Kestrel frowned.

Wolfe began taking deep, purposeful breaths in between his spasms of coughing. And she felt heat radiating through the door.

His coughing eased. The heat increased.

And she realized what he was doing.

He had turned on the hot water, letting the steam fill the little bathroom and relax his muscles.

Within a few minutes, his fit had subsided. She heard him clear his throat once in a while, but that was all. The knots in Kestrel's stomach slowly untied themselves.

Gradually, she pulled herself back away from the door and slipped back to her room.

She bit the inside of her cheek and got in bed, pulling the covers up to her shoulders. She turned onto her left side, so she could see the glow of his lamp through her door. She listened as the bathroom water ran and ran. She listened as it eventually turned off, and the door opened. She listened as he sat on the edge of his bed and turned off the lamp. And it was only after she heard him settle down into his bedding and lay quietly that she could relax and drift off.

TEN

DAY SEVEN

Kestrel, dressed and ready, stood in front of the coffee maker in the kitchenette, gazing back over her shoulder at Wolfe.

He lay on his back in his bed, the covers thrown half over him, one hand resting on his chest—asleep. She watched the steady rise and fall as he breathed.

She turned back to the coffee maker and poked the picture of plain black coffee. The machine buzzed to life, and within moments, hot liquid poured into a short ceramic cup.

Wolfe stirred, groaned. She faced him. He rubbed his face, then lowered his hand.

"What's that smell?"

"Coffee," Kestrel supplied. He blinked, sucked in a breath, and halfway sat up. His night shirt hung unbuttoned—he closed one eye, swung his feet around and set them on the floor.

"Smells good," he commented roughly, buttoning his shirt. Then he stood up, tugged out his suitcase from beneath the bed and opened it. "Sorry, let me go make myself decent." He pulled out a set of clothes and strode past her into the bathroom. The door shut. Kestrel moved the cup of coffee off to the side, then selected a fruity hot tea for herself. It instantly started to brew.

She stood there, leaning back against the counter, sipping her tea until she finished it. She faced the maker again, bit her lip, and was trying to decide what she wanted next when the door opened.

"What's this contraption?" Wolfe asked, coming to stand close next to her. He was dressed in a black shirt, jeans and boots; clean-shaven, his hair mostly combed. And he didn't smell like smoke anymore. He smelled earthy—with the barest hint of a sharp, masculine cologne. Kestrel's breathing unsteadied for a moment, but she made herself stand still.

"Oh, *now* you're putting me on," Kestrel chuckled in disbelief, picking up his coffee and handing it to him. "You know what it is."

"Thanks," he said.

"Do you think I should have a hot chocolate or a mocha?" she asked.

"Hot chocolate," he said, sipping his coffee. "At least it's being honest with itself."

Kestrel snickered, then pushed the button. The chocolate poured into the small cup and foamed, leaving whipped cream on the top, and she picked it up and took a careful sip.

"Ooh, that's hot," she murmured, touching her lip.

"Got to watch out for that," Wolfe grinned, taking another sip and then crossing to the sitting room chairs. He eased down into one, settling back. Kestrel watched him.

"How do you feel?" she called.

"Fine," he answered. "Why?"

Cradling her drink in both hands, Kestrel ventured toward him and sat in a chair to his right. She hesitated.

"I heard you coughing last night."

He gave her a sideways glance, then shrugged.

"My cold is hanging on longer than I thought. Probably because of those cigarettes," Wolfe assumed, taking a long drink and then setting the coffee down on the entertainment console. "Picked smoking up a while ago—just a bad luxury I allowed myself once in a while. I think I'll get better now that I've stopped."

Kestrel nodded, unsure.

"So," he sat forward and put his elbows on his knees. "What's there to do today?"

Kestrel looked at him. His gray eyes were brighter, probably from the sleep he'd gotten, but his shoulders still seemed heavy, his smile tired.

"What if we went to see a 4-D?" she suggested.

"A what?" he asked, taking another swig of coffee. She stared at him.

"You *cannot* tell me that you've never been to a movie."

He chuckled darkly.

"My life till now hasn't exactly allowed me a whole lot of leisure time."

"Well, we have to fix this," Kestrel determined. "I saw an ad for a theatre on level six—we can go get something for brunch and see what's playing."

"Sounds good," he nodded. "Lead the way."

P

"*The Almost King,*" Kestrel said, watching the names flicker by above the box office. "That looks good."

"What is it?" Wolfe wondered, looking at the same thing.

"I heard about it—it's about some ancient hero a really, *really* long time ago. He does some great things but when his people offer to make him king, he turns it down."

"Hm," Wolfe grunted. Kestrel wrinkled her nose as she scanned the other titles.

"The others aren't any good," she shook her head. "Nothing interesting."

"You know more about this than I do," Wolfe confessed.

"All right, let's give it a try," Kestrel said, striding toward the doors. They opened into an extremely long hallway riddled and strung with colorful flashing lights. Movie music themes from various famous stories greeted them as they walked in. Dozens of doors waited on either side of the hall, each one with a movie name blinking above it.

THE ALMOST KING

Kestrel stopped in front of that door and faced the computer console.

"*How many are in your party?*"

"Two," she answered.

"*Please insert your card.*"

Kestrel did, then put it back in her pocket.

"*Enjoy the show.*"

The door opened, and they stepped into a large, tall, square room. The walls, floors and ceiling glowed soft blue. As they approached the center, two slots opened in the floor, and two chairs on short poles rose up.

"*Please be seated,*" a pleasant computer instructed. "*Fasten your lap restraints, and keep your feet on the foot rests at all times.*"

Kestrel turned around and sat down on the chair on the right. Wolfe sat next to her, on *her* right. They both fastened their lap belts, and then Kestrel lifted her heels and hooked them easily on the bar that stuck out of the sides of the pole that elevated her chair. She looked over at Wolfe, who sat uneasily in the short-backed chair.

"Ready?" she asked.

"I'm not sure what to be ready for," he admitted.

"It's just a movie," Kestrel shrugged, smiling.

"Ladies and gentlemen," the computer said. *"The lights will be dimming during your show. However, the exit sign will be lit all during the performance. Please locate it now."*

Kestrel glanced over to the left and found it, then nodded.

"Thank you, and enjoy the show."

The ceiling, walls and floor faded to dark. For a moment, all was silent. Then, a low, stealthy musical score rose up as light arose.

They sat in a gray field beside a dirt road, which was bordered by a tangled black forest. The sky hung dark and overcast, only moonlight peering through the cuts in the clouds.

Wolfe sucked in his breath, startled. Kestrel smiled to herself, looking all around as well. Mist rose up and wove along the ground just below their feet, and the scent of damp forest, and frost, filled her lungs.

The soundtrack grew restless. Far ahead of them, in the depths of the shadows, something pattered.

A patter—that became a rumble.

And suddenly, out of the darkness and into the white moonlight, burst a single horse and rider.

Wolfe jerked.

The horse's hooves flashed and thundered across the earth. The rider hunched over its neck, holding on for dear life, his coat bannering out behind him, his tricorn hat pushed down low on his brow. Gold writing faded to life beneath him, then disappeared:

April 19th, 1775

Then, all at once, Kestrel and Wolfe seemed to be flying alongside the rider. They swooped closer to his flank, the forest behind him blurring with the speed. His breath and the jet-engine breaths of the horse pounded in Kestrel's ears as the wind rushed against her face and through her hair. They turned slightly, and Kestrel glimpsed buildings up ahead. Crude, wooden ones. The rider pulled off the main road and darted into the yard. Kestrel and Wolfe seemed to follow right with him, pausing beside a barn.

Lamps lit inside the little house. The door opened—a man in a long nightgown stepped out on the porch, holding a lantern.

"Mr. Revere!" he called. "What news?"

"The British are coming!" the rider gasped. "Ready the militia! I go to spread word further!"

"Godspeed!" the man at the house urged him, and Revere wheeled his horse around, gave it a lash, and away he shot. But Kestrel and Wolfe did not follow him.

Instead, their surroundings melted away, then clarified to become the cramped interior of the glowing house, now boiling with activity. It smelled like coal fire, dust and straw. The scruffy man set the lantern down, hurried around a wooden table and shook his tall sons, who slept in cots along the walls. They got up, asking him dozens of questions and throwing off their patchwork quilts. Then, they all pulled on their trousers and coats and shoes and hats, dug out their long, gleaming musket guns from beneath their beds, loaded up their ammunition and charged out into the night.

Kestrel and Wolfe's surroundings then transformed into a frenzied tapestry of a dozen different homes, all of which were awakening, donning their clothes and gathering their weapons. Mothers wept, wives gripped their husbands tight, and men dashed out the doors and toward the moonlit roads. Then, all of the tapestry coalesced into one scene—a scene into which Kestrel and Wolfe immediately plunged. They moved amongst the walking ranks of men as they hurried through the woods, and the sky lightened with the dawn. Ahead of them, an open space waited. A meadow. Kestrel could see the tall grass. The men, all around them, muttered encouragement to each other. Their weapons clinked against their belt buckles, their clothes rustled, their boots snapped on twigs and underbrush. Branches passed overhead, whispering with their passage.

They drew to a halt on the edge of the meadow. Kestrel looked around her—they stood in the second line of troops. One tall, young, gangly soldier poised on Wolfe's right. An old, grizzled warrior hunched to Kestrel's left. In front of them, the men held their muskets across their chests, quieting.

Listening.

But one of them was breathing hard, right near Kestrel. She glanced around. All the rustic soldiers stood still. She blinked, and looked at Wolfe.

He swallowed, staring past the shoulders of the front line, his jaw clenched. Kestrel opened her mouth...

"Ssst," the captain lifted his hand, then pointed. Kestrel's head whipped around.

Across the field, a bridle rattled.

Their line of men stiffened.

And out of the murky fog of the dawn melted nine-hundred red-coated, black-hatted British soldiers. And a good many of them rode on horseback.

"Hold your ground, men," the captain muttered.

Wolfe's breathing labored, tightened—sped up. Kestrel sat up and glanced at him again, wondering what was wrong...

Both lines began to shift, restless, nervous. Challenging.

"Steady," the captain held up a warning hand. "Hold your fire until—"

BOOM!

Smoke exploded through the air—a flash, an impact, a thundering snap.

Wolfe lashed out and snatched Kestrel's arm. She jerked.

"What—" she yelped.

The shot echoed through the forest. The lines rattled.

"Ready!" the British captain shouted, raising an arm. The British lifted their rifles and aimed straight at them. The Minutemen aimed back.

"Oh, God—" Wolfe moaned—

"Fire!"

Shots burst out from both sides. Explosions peppered Kestrel's hearing. The air swam with gunsmoke. A soldier next to Kestrel screamed, threw up his arms and fell to the ground—

Wolfe moved.

He threw himself out of his chair—his feet hit the floor—

The scene disappeared instantly.

The floor, walls and ceiling blinked to bright blue.

Kestrel stared up at Wolfe, who stood right in front of her, *over* her, his hands reaching past her shoulders to brace on the back of her chair, his eyes screwed shut. Bent over her, leaning in very close.

"Hey," she whispered, shaken. He opened his eyes. For a moment, they didn't focus. Didn't see anything. Then he blinked again, three more times...

He met her gaze.

He drew in a deep breath, withdrew and stood up, passing a hand across his face.

"People do this for entertainment?" he grated, facing the far wall. "Stand right in the middle of a battle without any weapons?"

"It isn't real," Kestrel murmured.

He looked at her.

And what she saw reflected in those bright, weary gray eyes silenced her. He let out a sigh that shuddered.

Her heart twisted and clenched.

"I'm...I'm sorry," she breathed, her throat catching—though she was at a loss as to why she was apologizing.

He softened.

"Not your fault," he said, sniffing and shaking his head. "Not your fault at all."

"You want to go?" she asked. He hung his head, then nodded twice.

"Yeah, I think we'd better."

Kestrel ate dinner alone. Wolfe had discovered that meals could be brought to the room, so he ate there. Kestrel, however, couldn't sit still any longer. She had to move, had to walk—had to clear her head. So she made three laps of the entire level before she settled down and found a small sandwich shop.

She sat in a booth and finished off her food slowly, then sat back and sipped her drink, watching the foot traffic out the window, fighting to keep the tension in her chest at bay.

"Pardon me."

Her head came up.

Standing beside her booth was a young man.

The same tall, good-looking, gold-haired, blue-eyed man she had seen at the beginning of the voyage. He still had his long camel coat, now draped over his left arm. Now he wore brown and cream-colored classy travel clothes. He smiled down at her, friendly and easy.

"Yes?" she asked, startled. He canted his head, his brow furrowing at her without his expression losing its amiability in the least.

"I'm sorry, but I couldn't help but notice how rapidly you walked through the level just a while ago. Several times, I believe."

He had an English accent—an educated, precise and delicate version, accompanied by a musical tenor voice.

"Ha, yes," Kestrel nodded, managing to answer his smile. "I um...I was tired of sitting in my cabin. Had to get some exercise."

"That's exactly what I was afraid of," he said, with interested seriousness. "I'm William Anthony, the ship's chief surgeon." He held out his hand to her. She took it. His hand was soft, but strong.

"I'm—uh," Kestrel started, mentally staggering before she realized what to say. "I'm April Johnson."

"A pleasure to meet you," he smiled again, inclining his head to her. "And in addition to that pleasure, I wanted to inform you of the existence of an entire level on this ship devoted to physical exercise of all kinds."

"Is there really?" Kestrel sat up, truly listening now.

"Oh, yes, it's been my personal project," he nodded, sliding into the booth seat across from her and laying his coat down. "A two week voyage is *far* too long to simply laze about, watching 4-D's and eating and shooting at things in arcades. People enjoy it the first week, but as the second week begins, passengers become dissatisfied. For a long while this was an apparent mystery to the management—until I came up with the simple answer: people need to *exercise*. A routine of exercise will make everyone happier, and more able to enjoy the other amusements."

"Makes sense to me," Kestrel acknowledged, enjoying the sound of his voice and his eloquent expression more than anything.

"I thought it would, after seeing your pace," he grinned. Kestrel laughed.

"Anyway, I shan't trouble you any further," he said, sliding out of the booth and picking up his coat. "But it's on level five, if you're interested in such a thing—and if you should have any questions, your cabin's communications service can easily ring me or my staff."

"And—what was your name again?" Kestrel asked.

"Doctor William Anthony," he said smartly, his sky-blue eyes lingering on her face. "Hope to see you soon, April."

"Thank you," she answered. And just like that, he was gone.

ELEVEN
DAY EIGHT

"Jack!"

The call rang through the giant hanger bay. Kestrel pulled her attention down from the underbelly of a sleek, copper-colored, two man transport to look across the vast metal floor. Red-headed Jim, grinning, strode out across it toward them, lit by the harsh lights far overhead. Kestrel sensed the rest of the small tour group move on to a larger, classic vessel, but Wolfe stepped up next to Kestrel and held out his hand before Jim had even gotten to them.

"Good morning, mate!" Jim greeted Wolfe, shaking his hand. He smiled at Kestrel. "Good morning, ma'am! Nice to see you again."

"Hello, Jim," Kestrel said brightly, finding herself happy to see him. Jim stepped back, glancing around.

"Taking the hanger bay tour, eh?" he commented. "How do you like this F37? Pretty handsome!"

"Yes, it is," Wolfe nodded, turning to assess the smooth, two-winged vehicle in whose shadow they stood.

"Ever flown one?" Jim asked.

"Nope," Wolfe said crisply. "Not quite brave enough."

"Don't believe that, not for a minute," Jim declared. "Say, what are you two doing this evening?"

Wolfe turned back around. Kestrel perked up, listening.

"Why?" Wolfe asked.

"They're opening the pub up at seven o'clock for snacks and non-alcoholic beverages," Jim explained. "Just to get the word out that it's down there before we cross the Liquor Line tomorrow, haha!"

"Good thinking," Wolfe smiled.

"You two ought to come!" Jim invited. "We've got more instruments—a cello, a piano, another guitar...You can even play with us a bit if you'd like, Jack. I know people would love to hear the way you play that guitar!"

Wolfe took a breath, the skin around his eyes tightening.

"I appreciate your asking me to do that, Jim, but I—"

"That sounds fun," Kestrel cut in. "I'll come."

"Glad to hear it!" Jim crowed, then raised his eyebrows at Wolfe. "You aren't going to let her come all by herself, are you? Pretty lady like her— someone's likely to steal her away from you!" He looked at her sideways and winked at her again. Kestrel halfway glanced at Wolfe, but his expression stayed neutral. Jim laughed and slapped Wolfe's arm.

"I'll see you tonight, lad," he said, walking off and pointing at Wolfe as he left. Wolfe watched him go, but didn't say anything about it. Then he straightened, frowning, and searched the reaches of the hanger bay.

"Looks like they've left us behind," he mused, and started off to catch up with the group, leaving Kestrel to mull things over on her own.

Kestrel assessed her reflection in the mirror of her bathroom. She and Wolfe had ordered room service for supper, and though they had talked while they ate around the entertainment console, the discussion had centered around the map room, and the three-hundred vehicles stored in the hanger bay, and how much each of them cost. Not a word about the pub.

Then, Wolfe had sat down to a game of solitary checkers, leaving Kestrel to amuse herself. For a while, she had vacillated by the foot of her bed, studying the clock, which had read 6:00. Then, she had set her jaw, spun, headed into the bathroom and shut the door.

She had showered, washed her hair thoroughly, then got out and dried. Then, while wrapped in a towel, she had used the hand-held, courtesy drying device that caused her chestnut hair to curl gently, showing off its layers, instead of ironing it straight as she usually did. And, after considering a moment, she had left it down, so it tumbled around her shoulders and down her back. After that, she had dug through her bag and found a long pair of pants that flowed rather than clung, and her light blue shirt with a v-neck instead of a high collar. She had dressed, then put on some makeup, using more color than usual around her eyes, and on her lips. As a last touch, she had slipped on the more delicate flats that had come with her bag, leaving her boots by her bed. Now, she smiled at herself, pleased with what she saw. Her dark eyes appeared bright now—she looked pretty. She even *felt* pretty, which was a rarity these days.

She drew herself up, still smiling, and strode toward the bedroom door, making certain she had her cards in her pocket. The door swished open, and she hopped down the step and started toward the front door.

"What—"

She halted, turning.

Wolfe had sat up on the edge of his bed, a checker piece held up in his left hand. He stared at her. His gray glance flicked up and down her form.

"What are you..." He stopped, and cleared his throat. "Where are you going?"

"To the pub, like I said," Kestrel answered. "I'm not even close to being tired yet—and I'd like to hear some more music." She paused. "Want to come along?"

"Well, I'm..." he started, absently fingering the checkers piece, but never pulling his eyes from her face. Then, he glanced at the board and cleared his throat again. "Sure. Why not?" He put the checkers piece down and got to his feet. He tugged on his leather jacket, then nodded, gesturing to the door. "After you."

"Thank you," she smiled. She stepped through, feeling him draw up beside her, and they headed to the lift in stride.

They had barely crossed the threshold of the tavern before a beaming Kie hurried up to them and motioned them in further.

"Jim will be glad to see you!" he declared. "He's saved a table for the two of you near the stage, so if you feel like joining in, Jack, you'd be welcome."

"Thank you," Wolfe said, surprised. "Thank you very much."

"Follow me," Kie bid them, and they trailed through the half-full pub toward the front. Low chatter filled the room as waiters wove between the crowded tables and booths, hoisting trays filled with fizzy drinks over their heads.

"No androids," Kestrel remarked to Wolfe.

"Must've figured out people enjoy being waited on by actual humans," Wolfe answered, striding around the last booth and coming out by the stage.

"Here's Jack!" Kie announced. The other men, much more dressed up than before, got to their feet and greeted him warmly, shaking his hand and slapping his shoulders. Wolfe appeared startled at first, but each friendly greeting made his frame relax a bit. The men also said hello to Kestrel, brightly calling her "April," expressing their gladness that she'd come along. Kestrel caught sight of the piano Jim had mentioned, snugged up next to the stage, with a cello sitting on a stand near it.

"Have a seat and relax," Jim suggested, pointing to a booth for two very close to them. "Have a drink—on the house. We were about to play an original composition of ours, then one or two others. When we get to the folk songs, we'll pull you up! Don't think we won't!"

"All right," Wolfe laughed, waving and backing toward the booth, then sliding into it. Kestrel followed him, sitting down across from him. The band assembled, getting their instruments in place, then sat down and began to play a fast, complicated tune at a reckless pace. The patronage listened to them with delight, sometimes clapping along.

"So why didn't you ever learn an instrument, Brown Eyes?"

Kestrel blinked, then turned to Wolfe. His hands clasped together on the table, and he watched her a moment before attending to the musicians. "Seems like you like music."

Kestrel smiled ruefully, looking where he did.

"I started playing synth-violin when I was little," she said. "But I never liked performing in front of people. My hands got sweaty."

He chuckled.

"So you gave up?"

She shrugged.

"I learned to sing. I like that." She laughed to herself. "And I can sing better than I could ever play the violin."

They fell silent. Kestrel watched the band for a while, then turned back to Wolfe. He was already looking at her.

Instantly, he glanced away. Kestrel's breathing quickened. She canted her head.

"Can I ask you a question?"

He chuckled, and his eyebrow twitched.

"Why not?"

"Why do you call me 'Brown Eyes'?" she wondered.

He raised his eyebrows, then shrugged.

"Keeps me from saying your real name," he answered, keeping his voice down. "That wouldn't be a smart thing to do around here, would it?"

"Probably not," Kestrel acknowledged, still intent on his face.

"*And*...that's the first thing I saw when I stepped out," he went on, even lower. "A pair of big, brown eyes." He looked at her again. Kestrel squeezed her hands together under the table.

He smiled quietly. It changed the whole aspect of his face. Lit his eyes, as if with candlelight; gentled the stern edges of his face, eased his scars, and softened his mouth. And in a sudden, silent rush, Kestrel realized something she hadn't thought about since she first saw him: he was handsome.

And then, words fell out of her mouth without permission.

"Where did you come from, Jack?"

He smiled again, lowering his head, then leaned back and glanced at the ceiling.

"A place very different from this one," he declared. "A quieter one. Less flashiness, less busy-ness." He waved his hand dismissively. He sighed, casting around the pub again, but seeming distant. "A lot of things were simpler. Prettier. More honest."

Kestrel's eyebrows drew together as she considered him, trying to fathom what he meant. Her mouth opened as another question formed...

The piano bench scraped. Kestrel looked over her shoulder as Kie sat down at the black instrument, set his hands on the keys and attended to George, who held his cello and bow at the ready. They nodded to each other, and Kie began.

It was a soft, swaying melody—very simple at first. Lovely. Like a walk through a forest in the fall. And then the cello began to hum, lilting between the harp-like notes of the piano. Kestrel listened for a little, but then her questions pressed against her breastbone again. She turned back to Wolfe.

"I was going to ask you—" she began.

"Do you dance?" he wondered, meeting her eyes frankly. Her eyebrows shot up, and her face turned hot.

"I...*no*," she shook her head. "No. I'm not...Not that kind of girl."

He stared at her a second, then laughed.

"*What?* What do you mean?"

"I don't..." she stammered. "I mean, dancing isn't..." She trailed off, not understanding why *he* didn't understand. Apparently very amused, Wolfe shook his head.

"I don't know what kind of dancing *you're* talking about," he said, grinning.

"What were you thinking of, then?" she frowned.

"C'mere," he said, sliding out of the booth and standing up. He beckoned to her with his fingers. She gulped.

"What are you..."

"C'mon, it doesn't *hurt*," he rolled his eyes. "Everybody ought to know this."

Kestrel shakily got to her feet, feeling off balance. He faced her.

"Do you know anything about waltzing?" he asked.

"I...Um, no," she confessed, knowing she was still blushing terribly. "What's—"

"Relax," he grinned. "I told you, it doesn't hurt. I'll teach you."

"Oh...kay," Kestrel managed.

"Come here and stand on my feet," he instructed. Kestrel's eyes flashed.

"Why—"

"Here," he said, took hold of her upper arms and pulled her to him.

Kestrel stumbled, then placed both her feet on top of his boots.

And all at once she was standing *very* close to him. *Right* up against him. Her head came up—she looked directly into his face. She couldn't breathe.

"Put your left hand on my shoulder," he instructed, apparently unaffected, as he guided her hand up to where it should be. Her hand rested on the smooth leather of his jacket and held on.

"Now, let me have the other hand," he said, grasping her right hand in his left, and holding it out to their sides. "And I put my arm around you like this." His right hand slid around her back and pressed against the center of it, just above the small of her back, making her stand up so straight...

He adjusted his grip on her right hand—she could feel a callous near his forefinger knuckle, but the rest of his skin was soft, his grip strong.

"Now," he said, glancing critically over their posture. "Your steps mirror mine. That's why you're standing on my feet right now. In a minute, when you get it, you'll stand on your own and dance. The trick is to follow my lead." He looked down into her face. She tilted her head back, gazing into his eyes. Eyes like the prairie sky before a storm...

She nodded.

He smiled.

"Okay, here we go."

He leaned slightly to one side, and stepped with the music. Her feet, on his, naturally followed. She had to hold on to him to stop herself from toppling backward—but then his arm tightened around her, keeping her where she was.

The next moment, she recognized the rhythm of the dance: *one*-two-three, *one*-two-three, *one*-two-three...

She started breathing again as her brain clicked in. She watched his features intently, listening to him with her whole body. He was all warm—his hand warmed her cold fingers. He still seemed amused by her. He watched her face in return. He flashed his eyebrows.

"You ready?"

"No—"

"Yes you are," he said, and pulled his feet out from under hers. Kestrel almost stumbled—

He swept her into a spin, pulling her tighter to him, making everything around her head and *in* her head swirl and blur—

And she was dancing. She gasped, her heart racing as her feet managed to keep up with his. The music built and swelled as they moved together, her body bent slightly back to fit against his, even as he smoothly guided her across the space in front of the stage.

He didn't take big steps—he kept everything simple, turning her gradually, still halfway smiling as he observed her. Kestrel curled her fingers around a crease in his jacket as they swayed. He lifted his head and looked around the pub, taking a breath.

"Looks like we have an audience." He smiled down at her again. "Or they just like the pretty picture."

"What?" Kestrel wondered.

"That's my job," he said. "To make you look good, kind of like a picture frame makes a painting look good. *You're* what everybody's supposed to be paying attention to."

Startled, Kestrel didn't know what to say to that. His eyes sparkled, and he dipped his head towards hers for an instant.

"That's a compliment, Brown Eyes."

She almost laughed, turning her face away.

"Well, I..." She drew herself up, trying not to trip, and met his eyes again. "Thank you."

They fell quiet, both of them smiling. Then, he drew another bracing breath.

"Okay, we're going to try a twirl."

"Um..." Kestrel winced. He laughed at her.

"Don't worry about it," and he pulled back from her, letting go of her with one hand but directing her with the other hand into a quick turn underneath his arm. Then, before she knew what was happening, she was back in his arms. She grabbed hold of his jacket and let out a surprised giggle, which made him chuckle in return.

"Very good, very good," he praised. "Only stepped on my foot once."

"Oh, I'm sorry!" Kestrel cried, withdrawing from him and missing a step. He immediately pulled her back to him, adjusting his grip on her and shaking his head.

"That's what these boots are for."

"Really," Kestrel said flatly. "To protect you from girls stepping on you."

"Of course."

Kestrel laughed again, much louder—but she didn't care, and Wolfe only gazed out over her head and grinned, then met her gaze. His expression became curious.

"You sure you've never done this before?"

She shook her head firmly.

"Never. Not once in my life."

"Well, you're very good," he admitted. "Must have a heck of a teacher."

Kestrel snorted, feeling a little giddy. He laughed at her again—a deep, rich sound that had lost all its rustiness. Then, too soon, the music ended.

Everybody clapped and cheered. Kestrel blushed, and hid her face. But before the noise had even started to die down, Jim called to them.

"Jack! April! Come here!" he motioned to them, and they hurried up to the stage.

"Did you say you were a singer of songs, lass?" Jim asked intently.

"I sing a little," she answered.

"How are you with ancient hymns?" George wondered.

"I know a few," Kestrel said. "Which one were you thinking of?"

"*Everlasting Arms,*" Kie told her. "Can you play it, Jack?"

Suddenly serious, Wolfe answered.

"Yes."

Kie held out a guitar to him. Wolfe took it, his whole bearing subduing. He sat down on the edge of the stage again, then attended to Jim.

"Come sit here," Jim invited Kestrel, patting a stool. "Give us a song."

Kestrel's heart started to pound, and she swallowed. But she liked the song and the men playing. She smiled, then sat down, hoping she wouldn't fall off. The crowd quieted. The piano started—and the guitar, cello and mandolin joined. Jim nodded to her. She took a deep breath, praying she remembered the right words.

> "*What a fellowship*
> *What a joy divine*
> *Leaning on the Everlasting Arms*
> *What a blessedness—*
> *What a peace is mine,*
> *Leaning on the Everlasting arms.*"

Her chest relaxed as the words flowed much more easily than she thought they would. Her voice rang easily, lightly through the pub, following the lovely old melody as if she'd sung it hundreds of times. And, out of the corner of her eye, she saw Wolfe. He played steadily, softly. But he looked only at her. She smiled at him, her heart swelling, her voice rising with the chorus.

> *"Leaning, leaning*
> *Safe and secure from all alarms*
> *Leaning, leaning*
> *Leaning on the Everlasting Arms."*

She turned to look down at the other musicians. They glanced affectionately at her. George closed his eyes, swept away. And Wolfe met her gaze—soft. Bright. Warm.

> *"Oh how sweet to walk in this pilgrim way!*
> *Leaning on the Everlasting Arms*
> *Oh, how bright the path grows from day to day,*
> *Leaning on the everlasting Arms."*

The music crecendoed all around her. She closed her own eyes, listening even as she sang.

> *"Leaning, leaning*
> *Safe and secure from all alarms*
> *Leaning, Leaning*
> *Leaning on the Everlasting arms!"*

The last chord thrummed through her. She opened her eyes. All the patrons clapped, and Jim reached up and squeezed her wrist.

"That was lovely. Just lovely. Thank you," he beamed.

"Thank you," Kestrel managed—then her attention was pulled to Wolfe. And she realized he'd never taken his eyes off her the whole time. He still didn't. The noise of the pub and the musicians all around them faded to the background. Then, slowly, Wolfe inclined his head to her. And she smiled at him.

TWELVE

DAY NINE

A sound.

Out in the lounge area.

Kestrel shot into a sitting position, her heart pounding before her eyes had even opened. She blinked, frowning around at her dark room. She pressed a hand to her chest and listened.

Talking. Hurried murmuring.

She pushed her covers off, snatched up her robe and put it on, then walked quickly to her bedroom door. It swished open.

Wolfe lay on his bed in the half-light of the dimmed lamp, his covers skewed. He twitched. He turned his head one way, then the other. He held his breath for long seconds, then drew sharp ones. She watched him, her attention narrowing, perched on the edge of the step.

His whole body thrashed. His right hand flew to his chest. He let out a strangled grunt through his teeth. His free hand tore at the blankets—and he let out a cutting yelp.

Kestrel leaped off the stair, dashed across the floor and sat down on the edge of his bed.

"Wolfe," she called, grabbing his right wrist. "Wolfe, wake up."

He groaned, his throat spasming.

"Wolfe—can you hear me?" she leaned closer, shaking him. "Wolfe, wake—"

With a tearing gasp, he knocked her hands away. She jerked back—

He grabbed her by the throat.

She didn't have time to scream—he sat up and his hands squeezed. She snatched at them—

His eyes opened. Met hers.

His violent grip instantly loosened. His breath released in a desperate, shuddering rush as his gaze darted all across her features. She started breathing again too—but she broke out into terrible shivering.

"Brown Eyes?" he asked, hoarse.

"Yeah, it's...It's just me," she said, her lip trembling.

"*Oh...*" he gasped, his hands slipping down to rest on her shoulders. "I'm sorry." His brow twisted and his gray eyes searched hers. Urgently, he reached up and brushed a strand of hair out of her face. "Are you...Are you okay? Did I hurt you?"

His touch startled her—sent a thrill of electricity darting down her neck.

"I'm fine," she stammered, swiping a stray tear off her cheek. "I'm fine, I'm fine."

"I'm so sorry," he choked, screwing his eyes shut and shaking his head. He rubbed his hand up and down her arm. "You..." He suddenly stopped, unable to go on. His hands went still, then tightened gently. "I wouldn't hurt you, you know. You *know* that I..." He gulped and lowered to a rough whisper. "I'd never hurt you on purpose." He lifted his head and met her gaze. His expression panged. "You know that, right?"

Kestrel looked back at him for a long moment, then nodded.

"Yes," she breathed. "I know."

He let out another sigh, closing his eyes and wrapping his hands around her elbows. Kestrel swallowed unsteadily as his forehead brushed hers. She could feel his warmth—almost feverish.

"I was...I was having a nightmare," he muttered, swallowing twice.

"About what?" Kestrel wondered. He smirked—a shattered expression.

"Wouldn't make any sense if I told you. They never do, when you say 'em into the open air." He took a careful breath, but didn't release her. He rubbed his thumbs against her skin. "They're nice little side-effects of the post traumatic stress I like to carry around."

Kestrel's shivering started to abate.

"What...What causes post traumatic stress?"

He swallowed, almost smiled—but couldn't bear to.

"War," he whispered simply, risking a glance at her. Their faces were very close. His eyes shimmered.

Kestrel stopped quivering. Her chest settled.

"Oh," she breathed.

"Yeah," he said, barely making a sound.

For a long while, they sat in silence. Wolfe slid his hands down and gripped her fingers, holding them there on top of the tangled bedclothes. Now that Kestrel wasn't shaking, she could feel the slight tremor passing through *his* broad-shouldered frame.

"So…" she finally said. "I shouldn't wake you up."

"Well, I'm…I was not enjoying that dream," he confessed. Then he squeezed her hands harder. His voice lowered. "But I don't want to…To do anything I'll regret. And if you wake me up like that…I might."

"Okay," Kestrel nodded. She paused. "What if I throw a pillow at you?"

He laughed. A startling jolt that seemed to surprise him as much as it did her. He nodded, and wiped at his eyes before taking hold of her hands again.

"Yeah, that might work."

"Good," she returned the pressure on his fingers. "I'll get a pillow and sit right over there, then, so you can go back to sleep without worrying about it."

Sudden confusion crossed his face. He gave her a penetrating look.

"Wait, you…You mean it?" he asked. "You'd wake me up?"

"Yes," Kestrel nodded. "I couldn't sleep through that, anyway."

He openly gazed at her, eyes brilliant, his brow slowly furrowing. She rubbed the back of his knuckles with her thumb, then tilted her head and smiled at him.

Something broke.

Singing. Well—a drunken *attempt* at singing—out in the hall.

Wolfe pulled out of her grasp, growling, and got out of bed. He crossed the room, barefoot. She could now see that he was wearing loose pants and a fitted sleeveless white shirt. He punched the door release and the door opened. The exterior light framed his canine-like scowl as he braced both hands on either side of the door and leaned out. He turned to the right, catching sight of someone.

"Hey, shut up!" he ordered. "It's past midnight—some folks are trying to sleep."

"*You* shut up!" came the drawled retort. "You're makin' more noise than I am!"

"Yeah, sure," Wolfe muttered, glaring, then coming back in and closing the door. He glanced at Kestrel as he came back to his bed. "I thought you said drinking was illegal here."

"We must have crossed the Liquor Line," Kestrel realized.

He paused, considering.

"How far is the Liquor Line from the Gain Station?"

"About six days," Kestrel answered. He heaved a sigh, raking his hand through his hair.

"Halfway there," he murmured. He sat heavily down on his bed next to her and rested his elbows on his knees. Sighing, he interlocked his fingers and lowered his head. "Better get some sleep before that wino decides to start singing again."

"All right." She took a breath got to her feet. He watched her.

"I'll be right here, armed," she said, sitting down in a nearby chair and pulling one of the decorative pillows into her lap.

"You won't sleep well in that chair," Wolfe warned.

"Yes, I will," she insisted. "I did the other night, remember?"

He sat still as she settled, and when she looked up at him again, that soft, open, ghost-of-a-smile look had not faded.

"Go on," Kestrel urged.

"Okay," he whispered, smiling crookedly. He shook out his blankets and turned his pillow over. "Goodnight." And he lay down on his side, facing her.

"Goodnight," she answered.

And it was only after he dozed off that she was forced to fight back more tears, swallow them, and continue her vigil until exhaustion finally overcame her—but the clamor aboard ship built, and didn't die down until dawn.

"Not sure this is a good idea," Kestrel said as the elevator sank. Wolfe drew himself up and shook his head once.

"Don't worry. This place isn't half as rough as other places I've seen."

Kestrel didn't know how to argue with him—but her gut stayed tense. Their elevator was crowded tonight: three other couples kept them company, decked out and dressed to the sparkling nines, the women draped across the men as they chatted and giggled. Kestrel and Wolfe had backed into a corner early on to make room for them. Now the smell of perfume stifled her.

One of the women, in a short-cut, twinkling red dress, with long, curling blonde hair, looked over her shoulder at Wolfe. Though a black-clad man stood with his arm around her waist, her jewel-like eyes flicked up and down Wolfe's broad form, then she gave him a long, alluring gaze and a saucy smile. Out of the corner of her vision, Kestrel saw Wolfe glance the other way. Kestrel caught the blonde's eye and buried her with a flashing scowl. The blonde quickly turned back to her date.

The elevator doors opened. The sparkling people exited first, laughing. Kestrel and Wolfe trailed after—though Kestrel noticed he had dipped his head to hide a crooked smile.

"What?"

"Nothing," he answered, then straightened. Kestrel frowned at him, but his smile remained. And now, the loud music kept Kestrel from forcing him to elaborate.

The nightclub level boomed and glimmered and danced. Hundreds of people flowed like the currents of a black river up and down the wide corridor and in and out of all the clubs, their feet creating pulsing tones, their voices a throbbing chorus. Multi-colored laser lights flickered and swayed from unseen places, shooting wavering patterns across all the walls and bodies.

A hand slid down and took hold of Kestrel's. She jumped, her face heating up—

Wolfe squeezed her fingers, then pulled her forward through the crowd, weaving between the sharply-dressed young men and the wildly-colorful young women.

It took much longer than usual to reach the pub. And when they did, they could hardly see past the front door: dozens of people blocked the way, facing inward. Wolfe's grip on her tightened. They pressed forward, Kestrel just ducking her head and wincing as they practically crawled between all sorts of noisy, cologne-doused people. Her face brushed shoulders and hair as she passed—she squeezed down on Wolfe's hand.

Music rang out overhead. The next moment, they emerged right in front of the brightly-lit stage, where Jim and his band played a ripping tune to a clapping, smiling audience. The band glimpsed her and Wolfe, then happily nodded toward the one empty booth in the whole pub—the one the two of them had sat in the other night. The two slipped into it, Kestrel letting out her breath in a rush.

"There's a few people here tonight!" she remarked, having to shout over the ruckus. Wolfe smiled, nodding as he glanced around.

The next moment, a waitress wearing heavy eye-makeup and a short blue dress, her flaming red hair piled on top of her head, came up to them and put her hands on her hips.

"Good evening! What can I get for you?" And she winked at Wolfe. Kestrel's stomach turned over. But Wolfe lifted his head and grinned right back at the waitress.

"I'll have a beer."

"What kind, sir?" she asked. "We have over two hundred."

His eyebrows went up and he blew out his breath. Then, he closed one eye in thought.

"Is there *any* chance in the *world* you'd have a Yuengling lager?"

"Of course, sir!" she assured him brilliantly.

"Really?" Wolfe said in disbelief.

"Yes!" she said.

"You've just made my day," he sat back as he kept looking at her, obviously satisfied.

"Glad I could help," she beamed. "A pint?"

"Perfect," he nodded.

"And for you?" the waitress asked Kestrel.

"I'll just have a sweet iced tea," she answered, striving to keep her tone pleasant.

"Very good," the waitress said. "Be right back with those." And she left. Kestrel glared after her.

"A sweet tea," Wolfe commented.

"I don't drink," Kestrel snapped.

"Relax, Brown Eyes," he said, that twinkle of amusement in his eyes returning. "I was just going to say that you must favor the Missouri side of Kansas City."

"Why?" she wondered.

"Sweet tea—favorite drink of southerners," he explained. "That and lemonade."

Kestrel managed a smile.

"My grandma lived in Louisiana," she said. "When we'd visit when I was little, that's all we drank, all summer long. Unsweetened tea was just—wrong."

He chuckled, then nodded.

"Completely understand."

The waitress returned, set down Wolfe's foaming glass first, then Kestrel's tall, amber iced tea. Wolfe shot the waitress a mild look of disapproval as she departed.

"What?" Kestrel wondered. He shook his head once.

"She should've served you first," he said, then picked up his glass and took a sip. He swallowed, then nodded.

"Not bad. How's yours?"

Kestrel closed her fingers around the cold glass, took a gulp of her own, and grinned.

"*Almost* as good as Grandma's."

He returned her grin. And the tension in her gut faded—replaced by odd warmth.

"Jack! Jack, come here, lad!"

Kestrel turned to see Jim beckoning to him through a thunderous applause. He held out his guitar. Wolfe sighed, then glanced at her sideways.

"Don't drink all my beer."

She snorted as he got up. He maneuvered around two people and took the guitar from Jim, then sat down. Kestrel cradled her tea in her hands and turned in the booth so she could see better.

In just a couple moments, the ensemble struck up a tune just as wild as the one before it, Wolfe's fingers flying over the strings. Kestrel felt a slow smile spread over her face as she watched. Wolfe turned more toward the other musicians, as if challenging them. Kestrel took another sip of her tea, realizing that they had picked up the tempo...

A figure obscured her vision. She glanced up.

A dark-headed young man stood in front of her booth. He wore a blue suit, but the collar of his shirt hung open, and he'd clearly spilled something down the front of it. He smiled at her—his brown eyes looked glazed over. He stuffed his hands in his pockets with too much force, then canted his head at her.

"What's a pretty kid like you doing sitting here all by yourself? Herself," he corrected, his diction a little muddy. He shook himself, then tried another smile. "And drinking *tea* no less."

Kestrel looked narrowly at him.

"I like it."

"Sure, sure, for picnics," he waved it off. "But we just crossed the Liquor Line! Have a little fun, girl." He leered at her and leaned down. "Lemme buy you a drink."

"No thanks," she answered. "I don't drink."

"Don't believe you," he said flatly. "Next you'll be telling me that you don't dance." He grinned wolfishly. Kestrel's face flamed. She knew what kind of dancing *he* meant.

"I don't."

"A hot thing like you?" he cried, far too loudly. "I know you *would*, if you had a little motivation..." He lurched in toward her again, putting a hand on the table. She stared him down, fighting to ignore the stench of strong liquor on his breath.

"I'm not feeling it," she said.

"I think you *will*," he whispered, getting closer. Kestrel started to sweat.

"C'mon, baby," he purred. "Gimme a chance."

"Back up."

The deep voice growled from behind him. Like a bear in the depths of a cave.

The young man stayed as he was for a second, then arched an eyebrow. Then he snorted, and turned his head. Kestrel quickly glanced past him.

Wolfe stood right behind him, drawn up to his full six-foot-three height. He lifted his chin, never breaking eye-contact with the other man. The young man smirked.

"What? Is there a problem?"

"You're bothering her," Wolfe answered. "I'd like you to stop it."

"Why?" the young man stood up and faced him, crossing his arms. "You her husband?"

Kestrel swallowed.

"No," Wolfe answered.

"Boyfriend?"

"No."

"Just a concerned citizen then, huh?" the young man smirked. Wolfe's eyes narrowed.

"You could say that."

"Then what are you doing bothering *me*?" the young man demanded. "I haven't done anything. And you're clearly too stupid to realize who I am."

Wolfe gave him a blank look.

"Should I?"

The humor vanished from the young man's face.

"My father *owns* the *Exception*," he retorted. Wolfe looked plainly at him.

"And that gives you license to annoy people in bars?"

Kestrel realized that a lot of the people around them had stopped what they were doing to see what was going on. She squeezed her hands together under the table. Wolfe never moved.

"It's *my* ship," the young man bit out. Wolfe gave him a critical smile.

"It's your father's ship," Wolfe amended, then regarded him frankly. "And you're not much without him, apparently. If I were you, I'd start looking for a life of my own."

The young man's face turned scarlet.

He grabbed Wolfe's beer and threw it in his face.

It splashed all over—into Wolfe's eyes. Wolfe stepped back, hands flying up—

The young man kicked Wolfe in the chest.

Wolfe crashed to the floor. The onlookers yelped and leaped out of the way. Chaos erupted. Kestrel jumped to her feet, banging her knees on the table. The young man sneered.

Wolfe coughed hard into his hand, his whole frame shaking.

"Well you're *not* me," the young man taunted.

Wolfe lifted his head.

His beer-drenched face hardened like stone. His eyes blazed.

Slowly, he climbed to his feet. Everyone watched, wide-eyed, commenting feverishly to each other. Wolfe wiped his face with the back of his hand, took two steps forward on the slick floor, and set his feet. He raised his eyebrows and looked straight at the young man.

"No, I'm not."

The young man bared his teeth, pitched forward and swung at Wolfe.

Wolfe blocked it with his left arm. His right hand flashed—

Struck the young man's nose.

The young man's head whiplashed backward.

Then, his body went limp, and he toppled to the floor.

Everybody exclaimed—some cheered, some clapped, others just gasped and moaned. Kestrel scrambled out of the booth, stepped over the young man and hurried up to Wolfe.

"Are you okay?" she gasped, her whole frame quivering.

"I'm fine," he said hoarsely, as if there was something in his throat. He rubbed his right hand fingers together and frowned down at them. Kestrel looked too...

Blood coated his palm. She started.

"What—Did you cut yourself?" she demanded.

"Jack! Are you all right?" Jim asked, hurrying up to them, followed by the rest of the band.

"I'm fine," Jack insisted. But Kestrel watched his face turn the color of ash.

Then—

"Jack, your lip's bleeding," George noted. Wolfe swallowed hard, his eyelids flickering.

"Did you bite yourself when you fell?" Jim guessed.

Wolfe coughed again, covering his mouth with that same hand.

"I'm all right," he said when he lowered his arm, his voice watery. "Just got to get out of all these people."

He turned, and shouldered his way through the crowd. People let him pass, but instantly closed the gap behind him, straining to watch him as he went. Kestrel, heart thundering, clawed through them, shouting "excuse me!" whenever she thought of it.

She burst out of the pub, into the crowded corridor, searching, searching...

Her heartbeat stalled. Where did he go—?

There. Heading toward the lifts.

She broke into a run.

His strides faltered. He started coughing again.

Kestrel reached him—

He fell to his hands and knees, his whole body wracked with furious choking.

She threw herself down beside him...

As blood spilled from his mouth onto the glassy flooring.

"Oh, *God!*" Kestrel cried—a plea to heaven that tore straight through her. "*Jack!*" She grabbed at him, but he was fighting too hard to breathe. Blood ran down his chin even as his skin turned completely white. He thudded down onto his right shoulder, grimacing. He twitched once, hard—twitched again. His eyes flashed open for an instant and found hers—silvery and stunned. He gulped, coughed and strangled—scrambled for her hands.

Tears streamed down her face as her icy fingers found his. Gripped them hard.

"Somebody help me!" she screamed at the top of her lungs, frantically searching the crowd. Everyone had stopped and now stared, stricken.

"*Help me!*"

Wolfe heaved a breath, shuddered, then his head fell back onto the floor. He kicked out. Blood leaked from the sides of his mouth and trailed down his cheeks. His hands went limp.

"Jack!" Kestrel dropped his hands and pressed her fingers to his throat. "Somebody *help me!*"

"Back up, back up."

The hurried English tones came from right above her head. Kestrel whipped around—

And through her tears, she saw the angelic, golden-headed form of Dr. William Anthony kneel on the other side of Wolfe, his sky-blue gaze intent on Wolfe's face. Anthony wore a white lab coat with full pockets. He pressed a firm hand to Wolfe's jugular, his brow furrowing.

"Pulse is thready," he mused. His expression tightened. "Hm. Gone."

"Gone?" Kestrel twitched, her tears turning cold.

"Hang on," Anthony said, bent down and tore open Wolfe's shirt.

Kestrel flinched back, squeezing her hands into fists. Wolfe's great chest did not rise or fall. Fleetingly, her gaze noted a maze of old scars that riddled his skin. Anthony dug in his pocket and pulled out a small square device, then pressed it to Wolfe's right pectoral. He dug in his other pocket and pulled out another machine, which he unfolded into a breathing mask with tank. He clamped the mask over Wolfe's nose and mouth, then flipped a switch. Next, Anthony pushed the small red dot in the center of the device on Wolfe's chest.

Wolfe's torso jerked. Anthony felt his pulse. His intense expression deepened.

He pushed the button again.

Wolfe jerked again—

Coughed, and gasped. Kestrel clamped her hands over her mouth.

Pounding footsteps assaulted her hearing. Anthony's head came up.

"Good—I need a breathing tube here, right away. Get me a stretcher," he snapped his fingers. "Move, move!"

Three other doctors dove down all around Wolfe—they shuffled Kestrel out of the way before she knew what was happening. They all pulled things out of their pockets, moving so fast Kestrel could barely track. One of them lifted Wolfe's head, pulled off the mask, forced his mouth open and shoved a tube down his throat. Kestrel hurriedly looked away.

Within moments, another white-clad doctor appeared with a floating stretcher. Anthony got out of the way as the stretcher lowered beside Wolfe. The stretcher flattened to paper thin, and slid right beneath Wolfe without moving him. Then, it lifted smoothly into the air, and a shield closed over him. The next instant, it lifted higher than head level, and shot off down the corridor. Kestrel watched it go.

"Are you all right?"

She looked up. Dr. Anthony stood there, watching her, concern in his eyes.

"Is *he?*" she asked. He smiled gently at her and held out his hand.

"He will be," he said. She reached out and grasped his hand. His fingers thawed her icy ones. He pulled her to her feet, then tucked her arm around his.

"Come on," he said. "We'll go with him, shall we?"

"Sounds good," she managed shakily, wiping at her face with her right hand as they started forward.

"He's very lucky he had you with him," Anthony said. Kestrel snorted, fighting back more tears.

"Yeah. I was *so* helpful."

He pressed her hand.

"I'm quite serious," he said. "You were his voice. I never would have come if I hadn't heard you."

Kestrel looked up at him again. He gazed at her kindly. The stab of panic in her heart faded, and she found strength enough to nod—but not enough to let go of him.

THIRTEEN

DAY TEN

Kestrel paced back and forth in the small, white waiting room. The faceless, box-shaped android behind the desk made no movement, and only emitted a low beeping sound. Kestrel's boots tapped endlessly on the tiles. She wrapped her arms around her middle, battling back the cold, and glanced at the glowing blue clock for the millionth time.

Two in the morning. He'd been in there for five hours.

Footsteps.

Kestrel spun to face the hallway.

Dr. Anthony, dark circles under his eyes, sighed and ran a hand through his curls as he emerged.

"Please sit down," he gestured to a chair. Kestrel immediately did so. He pulled another chair over and sat down across from her, setting his datapad in his lap. He regarded her seriously, tiredly.

"You're his next of kin, are you not?" He glanced down at his pad. "He is Jack Johnson, and you are April Johnson." He met her eyes. "His wife, then?"

Kestrel just nodded. Dr. Anthony sighed.

"Well, I have some rather difficult news," he began. "He has stage four Viridi Carcinoma."

Kestrel lifted her head and gripped her fingers.

"Cancer?"

"Yes," Anthony answered. "It translates literally to 'Green Cancer.' It's very specific type of cancer, almost exclusively found in veterans of the Halogen Police Action ten years ago."

Kestrel's brow furrowed.

"The weapons used in that action have since been banned, due to the disastrous side-effects," Anthony explained. "They were hand-held weapons that emitted a green beam of energy that surrounded a building-sized target, then caused it to explode. Anyone standing within a hundred yards of the reaches of that explosion who inhaled the fumes would *inevitably* contract this cancer. No exceptions." Anthony's eyes grew sad. "For years, the symptoms can often be dismissed as a simple chest cold—then the disease suddenly attacks the lung tissue, growing tumors that cause severe bleeding. As you saw, if left untreated, it's a strange and painful way to die."

Kestrel swallowed. Anthony's eyebrows came together as he considered her.

"Your husband would have been very young to fight—no older than seventeen," he noted. "Has he ever spoken to you about that part of his life?"

"No," Kestrel said. Anthony sighed, rubbing his forehead.

"I can understand why—not many veterans enjoy discussing it." He glanced down at his datapad. "The scarring on most of his upper body, however, indicates some severe trauma incurred during combat." He flipped through several images Kestrel couldn't see.

"Shrapnel wounds in the central chest area, suture marks; a very long, deep scar on his right side, and..." he paused, then glanced up at Kestrel. "He has a scar on his upper left pectoral, near his shoulder joint—a scar unlike any I've ever seen. It almost looks like a blunt puncture, and whatever-it-was traveled all the way through him and came out the other side." Anthony searched her face. "I'm sure you've noticed it. Do you have any idea what caused it?"

Kestrel's already taut stomach tightened further.

"No," she said again. "He's never talked about any of his scars with me."

"Hm," Anthony murmured thoughtfully, his gaze unfocusing.

"So this...Viridi Carcinoma," Kestrel ventured. "You said there's a treatment?"

"Yes," Anthony nodded. "And as soon as we stabilized him, we started it. It's both an intravenous and oral treatment—a breathing treatment. The intravenous treatment is pumping him full of vitamins and other strengthening essentials—as well as nano-bots to repair the mutated DNA—while the breathing treatment kills the cancer in his lungs. Then, in a few hours when that's done, his body will purge the tumor tissue, and we'll start on a different breathing treatment that will rapidly heal the delicate tissue in his lungs."

"Purge?" Kestrel repeated.

"Yes, he'll—well, he'll cough it all out," Anthony explained. "Under strict supervision, with all of us handy to make certain nothing obstructs his airway. It's a well-practiced procedure, and as strong as he is otherwise, he should do very well."

Kestrel felt sick to her stomach. And cold.

Dr. Anthony quickly reached out and took her hand.

"Are you all right? Do you feel dizzy?"

"I'm okay," she whispered, a tear falling. "When can I see him?"

"Not until later tomorrow," he answered carefully. "Probably after noon."

"Do you have someplace I can sleep here, then?" she asked.

"Of course," he said. "We have guest rooms for just such a purpose. And I can have someone go to your cabin and bring you whatever you need."

"Thank you," Kestrel sighed.

"Right this way," he bid her, standing up. She got up and followed him down the hallway.

At the far end, she could see several other doctors, nurses and androids bustling through different corridors. Dr. Anthony didn't have to lead her far, though, before he stopped in front of a door that opened silently. Inside, lit by a single soft lamp, stood a white bed, a chair, a desk and a wardrobe. She also caught sight of another door that probably led to a washroom.

"Try to get some sleep," Dr. Anthony advised. "Someone will come to get you if anything develops with your husband."

"Thank you," Kestrel said again, and entered the room. She sank down onto the bed as the door shut, thankful that at least now she could spend the sleepless night someplace soft and comfortable. She lay down on her side, curled up, and stared into the lamp. She took a breath to pray...

Then squeezed her eyes shut and let her heart loose into the silence, waiting to hear the sound of the door opening.

DAY ELEVEN

Kestrel pulled her knees up to her chest and wrapped her arms around them. This chair was stiff, but she didn't move from it. She sat next to the bed in the softly-lit ivory-colored room, directly beside Wolfe's left shoulder. White sheets swathed his tall form—his face looked about the same color. A needle protruded from the inside of his right elbow, connected to tubes and hanging bags of different liquids. She blinked slowly, studying his motionless profile.

Long eyelashes. A strong brow, dark eyebrows slightly drawn together. Perfectly-straight nose; a solemn, sculpted mouth—lips chapped by the forceful entry and removal of tubes. A hint of a beard tracing the edges of his jaw. Careless strands of hair fell across his forehead, covering the scar. His pale throat showed the marks of fingers and instruments pressing hard there. Bruise-colored taints beneath his eyes. Together, a handsome, weary, weathered, young face.

Kestrel glanced at the clock at the other end of the room. One o'clock in the afternoon. She hadn't eaten all day, but they'd just given her permission to come in half an hour ago, and she was in no mood to leave him now. Besides, she didn't have any appetite.

"What are you doing here, Brown Eyes?"

Kestrel's head came around.

Wolfe's face tilted toward her. He had opened his brilliant eyes—pale gray, like a morning in chilly spring...

He smiled briefly at her. Gentle lines appeared around those eyes.

"Hi," she gasped, reaching out to touch his arm for an instant before pulling back. "How...How do you feel?"

"I have to say," he said, his voice broken and hoarse. "If I told you I've felt worse, I'd be lying."

Kestrel tried to swallow the pain her throat, but it just graduated to her chest. She scooted closer.

"You'll feel better soon," she said. "Promise."

"So..." he asked, his smile gone now. He watched her gravely. "What have I got?"

"It's a...A rare type of lung cancer," she answered, trying to smile. He blinked once, swallowed once.

"I'm dead, then."

"No!" Kestrel said quickly. He frowned.

"But—"

"No, they caught it," Kestrel told him, taking hold of his forearm now. "When you collapsed in the hallway, you stopped breathing, but Dr. Anthony came and got you started again. Then they stabilized you and ran you through all the treatments." She nodded firmly. "The cancer's gone. You'll get better from here."

Wolfe stared at her.

"How did Dr. Anthony get there so fast?"

Kestrel paused. Something in his tone unbalanced her.

"I...I called for help."

He slowly lifted his eyebrows.

"*You* did."

"Yes..." she nodded, uncertain.

For a long moment, he gave her a piercing, stricken gaze, his eyes so vivid that they hurt her.

"Too bad," he finally whispered. "I wish you hadn't."

Kestrel's mouth opened, but her mind went blank. He let out a shuddering sigh, turned and searched the ceiling—and his brow twisted in sudden, weakened anguish. He gulped, and squeezed his eyes shut. A tear trailed down his temple.

Kestrel got up. She could hardly breathe—and what breaths she pulled in felt like she was sucking water. She closed her hands to fists, then turned and left the room.

Kestrel sat on the end of her bed in her cabin, slowly brushing out her hair. She had wandered listlessly through the ship after leaving him, then had finally headed back to the cabin. She had showered, put on clean clothes, then collapsed on her bed, completely exhausted. She'd slept for several hours, and woke up when her stomach began to bother her.

Now, she put down her brush and braided her hair, then got up and crossed to the door. She felt much better now—just very hungry—and she had to get out of this room. It was too empty. Silent. She'd go find something to eat, then decide whether or not she could bear going back to the hospital.

She stood still, leaning against the doorframe of his room. Watching his chest rise and fall as he slept. Listening to the silence.

Finally, Kestrel crept inside, striving not to make any noise, and sank down into her chair. She noticed that they'd taken the IVs out of his arm—now he just lay there in the dimmed light, shadows draping the corners of the room.

Footsteps near the door. Kestrel's head came up.

"Mrs. Johnson," Dr. Anthony leaned in, smiling at her. "I found this in his coat pocket." He held out Wolfe's book. "Thought you might like to read to him."

Kestrel got up, clearing her throat as she took it from him. Her fingers closed around soft, beaten leather.

"Thank you. Em...Read to him?"

"He's very, *very* tired," Anthony said, earnestly concerned. "But also very restless, due to the trauma he's been through. We've had to sedate his body, so he can relax—but it's quite possible his mind is still troubling him." Anthony nodded toward Wolfe. "Look at his face."

Kestrel turned, and gazed at Wolfe. His brow furrowed and his eyes occasionally moved beneath soft lids.

"I have been," she whispered. Anthony touched her shoulder.

"Let him hear your voice," he advised. "I have no doubt it will comfort him."

And he left. Kestrel held the book in both hands.

Hesitantly, she wandered back toward her chair, then sat down again. She stared at Wolfe, her chest tightening. She swallowed, and glanced down at the volume. Her fingers toyed with the front cover. She bit her lip, then opened it.

She stopped, her vision focusing sharply on the writing.

*Hand*writing.

She'd never seen handwriting outside of a museum. But these battered, stained pages bore neat, firm lines of flowing, ink-written words. Strident, leaning slightly to the right, smooth and beautiful. Slowly, Kestrel smiled, tracing the lines with her fingers as well as her eyes. She took a slow breath, and read them aloud.

> "'Let me not to the marriage of true minds
> Admit impediments. Love is not love
> Which alters when it alteration finds,
> Or bends with the remover to remove:
> O no! it is an ever-fixed mark
> That looks on tempests and is never shaken;
> It is the star to every wandering bark,
> Whose worth's unknown, although his height be taken.
> Love's not Time's fool, though rosy lips and cheeks
> Within his bending sickle's compass come:
> Love alters not with his brief hours and weeks,
> But bears it out even to the edge of doom.
>   If this be error and upon me proved,
>   I never writ, nor no man ever loved.
>   -William Shakespeare'"

Kestrel knew this poem—all literature students did. She read it to herself three more times before turning the page. She blinked. Another sonnet by that same author. Shifting in her chair, she read it aloud too.

"'No, Time, thou shalt not boast that I do change:
Thy pyramids built up with newer might
To me are nothing novel, nothing strange;
They are but dressings of a former sight.
Our dates are brief, and therefore we admire
What thou dost foist upon us that is old,
And rather make them born to our desire
Than think that we before have heard them told.
Thy registers and thee I both defy,
Not wondering at the present nor the past,
For thy records and what we see doth lie,
Made more or less by thy continual haste.
  This I do vow and this shall ever be;
  I will be true, despite thy scythe and thee.'"

Kestrel paused, sensing the undercurrent of a theme.
Something inside her stirred.
She looked up at Wolfe. His brow had not relaxed. His eyes moved again, without opening. Kestrel took a breath, and glanced at the next page. She began reading out loud before she had cast across the poem. But her voice faded as she went.

"'Her golden hair in ringlets fair,
Her eyes like diamonds shining
Her slender waist, her heavenly face,
That leaves my heart still pining

Ye gods above oh hear my prayer
To my beauteous fair to find me
And send me safely back again,
To the girl I left behind me.'"

The lines drooped downward as they traveled—a melancholy hand had written them. And the flourishes meandered, half-hearted, if they existed at all. It was suddenly hard for Kestrel to go on.

"'The bee shall honey taste no more,
The dove become a ranger
The falling waters cease to roar,
Ere I shall seek to change her

The vows we made to heav'n above
Shall ever cheer and bind me
In constancy to her I love,
The girl I left behind me.'"

Kestrel halted. Her whole being suddenly felt hollow.

She swallowed hard, unable to look anywhere near him. She silently re-read the poem, her lip trembling. Then, quickly, she turned the page. She took a bracing breath, abruptly relieved at what she saw, then spoke more confidently.

"'Job, chapter three. 'Let the day perish wherein I was born, and the night in which it was said, There is a man child conceived. Let that day be darkness; let not God regard it from above, neither let the light shine upon it. Let darkness and the shadow of death be upon it; let the blackness of the day terrify it.'"

Kestrel stilled—and a horrible chill swept through her. Her breathing quickened. She kept on reading aloud, rapidly, barely above a whisper.

"'Let the stars of the twilight thereof be dark; let it look for light, but have none; neither let it see the dawning of the day: Because it shut not up the doors of my mother's womb, nor hid sorrow from mine eyes.'"

Kestrel's vision clouded. She put her fingertips to her mouth even as her lips kept breathing the words.

"'For now should I have laid still and been quiet, I should have slept...'" She swallowed hard. Her throat spasmed. "'Wherefore is light given to him that is in misery, and life unto the bitter in soul; Which long for death, but it cometh not; and dig for it more than for hid treasures; Which rejoice exceedingly, and are glad, when they can find the grave? Why is light given to a man whose way is hid, and whom God hath hedged in?'" She lifted her eyes to

149

Wolfe's face, lowered her hand and gasped out the last line as her tears tumbled. "'For the thing which I greatly feared is come upon me.'"

Kestrel shut the book, her face unwillingly twisting as she wiped away hot tears and fought for breath. Her whole frame hurt, centering somewhere behind her heart.

She bent and set the book on the floor, then scooted her chair so close to the bed that her knees slid underneath it. Then, she reached out and picked up his left hand with both of hers. She ran her fingers across his knuckles, traced the old scars, and felt a lump in a bone that had broken and healed improperly. She squeezed, forcing warmth into his cold skin, unconscious of her trailing tears. His forehead still furrowed. She smiled at him.

"What have I to dread? What have I to fear," she whispered.

"Leaning on the Everlasting Arms?

I have blessed peace with my Lord so near,

Leaning on the Everlasting Arms." She canted her head, and sang softly, just loud enough for him to hear.

"Leaning, leaning
Safe and secure from all alarms
Leaning, leaning...
Leaning on the Everlasting Arms."

Wolfe drew in a deep breath. Kestrel stopped, watching him.

He sighed—a deep, full-bodied sigh, unburdened and even.

And he curled his fingers around hers.

Kestrel's heart leaped, and she returned the pressure. She blinked and cleared her eyes, called up another verse and recited it as best she could.

And through the rest of the night, she whispered old hymns to him, until all of the aching tension in his face melted away, and he slept.

FOURTEEN

DAY TWELVE

Kestrel drifted up out of a deep sleep at the sound of low male voices murmuring back and forth. She took a sleepy breath—then felt a stiff pang in her neck. Her forehead tensed as she tried to wake up...

"...and I think she's only left this room once since we allowed her in."

"Yeah. She's a good girl."

Kestrel knew those voices. Dr. Anthony. And Wolfe. She opened her eyes and lifted her head.

"She must have heard us talking about her." Dr. Anthony, standing on the other side of Wolfe's bed, grinned. Kestrel closed one eye and rubbed her shoulder.

"I fell asleep in the chair..." she mumbled. Out of the corner of her vision, she saw Wolfe turn his head toward her.

"I wanted to wake you up so you wouldn't get a crick in your neck," he said, still hoarse. "But when I tried to move, all my gut muscles threatened to kill me. So I didn't."

"Well...I might forgive you this one time," Kestrel managed a smile at him. He returned it—gently.

He looked better. He had a little color in his face, his eyes had warmed, and his smile had gained strength. Kestrel's gaze lingered.

"Good morning," she said.

"Good morning," he answered. He took a breath and raised his eyebrows. "Even though *I've* been awake since five. Who gave you permission to stop singing?"

Kestrel chuckled, rubbing her neck again.

"She sings?" Dr. Anthony asked. Wolfe glanced at him, beaming.

"Yep—a little song bird," he told him. "Prettiest voice you'd ever want to hear."

"Lucky man," Anthony decided, striding around the bed. Kestrel sneaked a glance at Wolfe—just as something almost like sadness crossed his eyes.

"Call if you need anything. We'll be sending food in shortly—see if you can keep it down," Anthony said brightly, then left the room. Kestrel shifted in her seat, watching him go.

"You look tired."

She looked at Wolfe, who had spoken. He regarded her with quiet earnestness, his eyebrows drawn together. She sighed.

"I am."

"You don't have to hang around guarding my broken-down bones," he chastised. "You should go back —"

"I don't like it in the cabin," Kestrel cut in. "It's too quiet without you."

He stopped, as if in mid-thought, studying her. He swallowed, then took a careful breath.

"Look, Brown Eyes..." he began, his voice low. Kestrel's breath caught.

Sharp knocks on the doorframe. Wolfe started, blinking. Kestrel jumped and turned toward the door.

"Jim!" she cried.

"My friends!" the brown-clad musician called, his expression a mix of pleasure and pain. He came in, his guitar case slung over his back. "Oh, Jack, we all heard," he said, coming up to stand by Kestrel. "How are you feeling, mate?"

"Much better, thank you Jim," Wolfe mustered a smile for him. "Where's the others?"

"That Brit doctor wouldn't let us all in," Jim huffed. "Said we couldn't crowd you. So I got sent as a spokesman."

"I'm glad you came," Wolfe told him.

"How's the little wife holding up?" Jim asked, affectionately patting Kestrel's shoulder.

"Oh!" she said in surprise. "I'm...I'm doing okay."

She felt Wolfe looking at her again—softly. Sadly. The strange ache in her chest came back. She forced herself not to show it, instead returning Jim's friendly gaze. Jim turned to Wolfe again, the pain in his features overcoming the pleasure.

"I hate to have to say this, mate, but we're bound to leave you."

Wolfe's brow furrowed.

"Why?"

"We're disembarking, almost this moment, to the Darrow Station,"

Jim explained apologetically. "We've been commissioned to perform there every night this month. It's why we boarded this ship in the first place."

"Sorry to see you go," Wolfe said, lifting his left hand. "But I'm glad we met."

"Aye," Jim beamed, gripping Wolfe's hand. "And it's a small galaxy— I'm sure we'll all meet again."

Wolfe's eyebrows twitched together, but he nodded firmly.

"I'm sure we will."

"Take care of this gem," Jim advised, dropping Wolfe's hand and planting a kiss on the top of Kestrel's head. "She's a keeper."

Kestrel blushed, lowering her face.

"Goodbye, Jim," Wolfe said.

"Goodbye," Jim said, backing toward the door and waving fondly. "Smooth sailing."

And he was gone.

Silence fell in his wake.

Then, Kestrel felt Wolfe bracing himself again to tell her something...

"Good morning!"

A white-clad nurse strode in, followed by a multi-armed android bearing two food trays. Two rolling stands immediately discharged from the android's belly—one rolled out in front of Kestrel, popped up and formed a little table. The other zipped to Wolfe's other side, extended and leaned across him, then unfolded in the same manner, though without touching him. The nurse then set trays down in front of the two of them, then cheerfully advised them to "Eat up!" before she and the android left.

Kestrel glanced down at the food. It looked mostly like different colors of slop. The gears in Wolfe's bed groaned as it moved him into an easy sitting position, and he considered the food.

"What is this?" he asked. Kestrel shrugged, picking up a utensil.

"Vitamins, minerals, protein..." She poked at it. "Stuff that's supposed to be good for you."

"Why does it look like *this?*" Wolfe wondered.

"Mom always said," Kestrel told him. "That if a patient starts complaining about the food, he's healthy enough to leave the hospital."

"So, the more crowded the hospital, the worse they make the food," he concluded. Kestrel snorted, chuckling.

"Maybe." She poked it again. "It's good motivation, anyway."

"Got that right," he muttered—but he ate. And despite the way it looked, it tasted pretty good, and Kestrel was able to finish it all.

Kestrel strode through the quiet halls, detouring around all the places where they served liquor. The clock in the cabin had read 9:30 when she'd left. It was probably closer to ten, now.

She'd spent most of the day with Wolfe, sometimes talking, sometimes watching live *Ortheus* tournaments on the entertainment screen—most of the time sitting in silence as he slept, overcome by exhaustion. Kestrel had finally left him around five to go eat at a restaurant, then take a shower and change clothes. Now, she headed back to the hospital, passing only one or two people on her way. She didn't relish the idea of sleeping in that hard chair again, but she knew she wouldn't sleep at *all* if she stayed in that hollow cabin.

Sighing, she passed through the hospital doors, noticing that the lights had powered down to a soft glow for the night. She trailed down the hallway, turned two corners, then drew near Wolfe's door. She passed through...

And halted.

He slept soundly, lit only by the small lamp near the top left corner of the bed. But right beside his bed, near his left arm, stood a white-swathed cot, complete with blanket and pillow.

"I knew you would be returning this evening," said a voice behind her. She turned to see Dr. Anthony. He smiled in greeting.

"I didn't want to find you in that wretched chair again," he continued. "But I know what it's like to be unable to sleep without your spouse there."

Kestrel ducked her head, then nodded.

"It's not quite as good as the same bed," Anthony said. "But close enough, I hope."

"Thanks," Kestrel managed. He inclined his head.

"Goodnight, Mrs. Johnson." He departed.

Kestrel stood there for a long time. Wolfe slept on. She gripped her fingers together. Then she scolded herself.

She'd been planning on sleeping here, anyway. In that awful chair or on the floor or wherever. Having a cot was just a blessing. Fighting back any remaining misgivings, she stepped closer, kicked off her shoes and climbed in on the left side of the cot. Mercifully, it didn't squeak. She pushed the covers back, gingerly slid underneath them, then snuggled down into her pillow, facing Wolfe. She lay still.

The sound of his breathing washed over her. Steady, soothing, like waves on the sea shore. Warmth covered her. She blinked sleepily, absently wondering when the last time had been that she'd actually slept *well*...

She didn't have time to remember accurately. She fell deeply asleep in a matter of moments.

Kestrel rose out of sleep. Something had changed. The atmosphere, the room...

Wolfe's breathing. It sounded different. Become irregular, or...

Unsteady. Distressed.

Kestrel woke up—but she didn't open her eyes. She listened, every muscle frozen.

He was crying.

She felt him, lying very near to her. On his side, facing her. She felt the air shudder with him. Through her lids, she could see the room was dark, maybe lit by a tiny floor light somewhere near the door. She sensed the warmth of him, the startling closeness of his body. She forced her eyes to stay shut.

"What are you doing to me, little bird?" he choked, his voice almost unrecognizable. "Why couldn't you have just let me be?"

And then his warm, shivering hand met the side of her face. Trembling fingers brushed her hair back.

"Stubborn..." he muttered, swallowing hard, his hand laying on her cheek. "...sweet-hearted girl."

He sniffed and quickly withdrew his hand. He cleared his throat, shifting feverishly beneath his blankets. He fell still. And Kestrel had to fight to keep from letting out a wordless cry.

Long minutes passed, and he didn't say anything more. Kestrel listened hard, counting his breaths, until she realized he must have fallen asleep again. She opened her eyes.

He lay there in front of her, on his side. She couldn't see more than his dark outline—but she *could* see that his right hand lay on her cot. Her throat contracted as she again fought back foolish impulses, and she made herself try to go back to sleep.

DAY FOURTEEN

Kestrel sat alone on the sun deck, listening as the fountain played in the far corner, watching the light flicker off the dancing water. But despite its soothing sounds, and the quiet of the abandoned deck, everything inside her churned.

She hadn't spoken to Wolfe today. She'd gotten up near six in the morning, before he'd awakened, and left for the cabin. She'd cleaned up, loosely braided her hair, washed some clothes, and gone to breakfast—and when she thought about returning to the hospital, her whole stomach flipped.

So she'd wandered, doing laps through the commerce corridors, then finally lighting in a corner table on the sun deck, staring off, her entire ribcage clenched.

"*Passengers disembarking at the Gain Station,*" a computer voice boomed. "*Please be advised: we will be making dock this afternoon at five-o'clock Kansas City time. Please have all of your belongings packed and be in the lobby no later than four-thirty. If you require assistance, please contact ship's crew and we will be happy to help. Thank you."*

Kestrel's gut rebelled again. She glanced at the clock. It was already two-thirty.

Stiffly, she stood up, her skin going cold, and traipsed the long way back to the hospital.

"Hello, Mrs. Johnson," a sweet brunette nurse greeted her as soon as she entered Wolfe's wing. "Your husband just left!"

Kestrel stopped.

"What?"

The nurse nodded.

"Dr. Anthony checked him over this morning and found that he's recovered beautifully," she said. "Your husband told Dr. Anthony that you had to disembark to the Gain Station, and Dr. Anthony said he was in good enough shape to do that, though he'll still have to take it easy. Last night's good sleep did the trick." She winked at Kestrel. "He signed out and said he was heading back to your cabin."

"Oh. All right," Kestrel answered the smile, albeit weakly. "Thank you very much."

"Have a good day!" the nurse bid her as Kestrel turned and left the hospital. She trailed back toward the lifts, boarded, waited, then emerged into the familiar hallway.

Kestrel stopped in front of the cabin door, staring at it. All of a sudden, it seemed like a wall instead—she felt that powerless to open it.

"*Attention passengers disembarking at the Gain Station...*" the computer said, repeating its message. Kestrel gritted her teeth, reached out with her card and waved it in front of the reader. The door hissed open. She stepped forward—

Wolfe stepped out toward her. They almost ran into each other.

They both jerked to a stop.

Her eyes flew to his—locked with his.

He wore jeans and a gray t-shirt and boots. He had cleaned up—and he looked directly at her, unflinching. Kestrel's cheeks flamed.

He stood still a moment, then cleared his throat.

"I was...just coming to find you." He sounded strange. Hesitant. She couldn't answer.

He glanced down and stepped aside, motioning her in. She avoided looking up at him as she passed, though her whole right side tingled as she did.

"They released you from the hospital?" she managed, scanning the room, looking anywhere but at him.

"Yeah, I..." Wolfe began. He cleared his throat again. "The doctor said I was fit enough to go."

She bit her lip and nodded—the only reply she could risk. She took a breath and drew herself up, then headed toward her room. She felt his attention follow her.

She left the door open, but didn't peer through it a single time as she dug out her suitcase and started piling her clothing into it. Her hands shook. Several times, she had to stop and steady herself before she could go on.

Finally, Kestrel paused, considering her open bag. She'd packed everything in her room, but she was still missing several articles of clothing.

She'd left them in the dry washer.

Kestrel stood there for a full five minutes, paralyzed. She closed her hands into fists, her brow knitting as she dared a glance to her left, out the door.

She could hear him moving around out there. Packing, just as she had been. She steeled herself, turned and stepped through the door.

He stood with his back to her, facing his bed, his bag open on top of it. Her feet, usually quiet, suddenly sounded loud on the carpet.

Wolfe went still. But he didn't turn. Kestrel swallowed, stepped down the single stair, then cautiously made her way to the dry washer. She reached it, stood in front of it. Out of the corner of her eye, she glimpsed Wolfe holding a folded white shirt in both hands, unmoving. She gripped the cold handle of the washer and pulled it open.

She leaned her shoulder against the door of it to keep it ajar, then reached in to draw out her soft garments. She attempted to fold them as she did, the scent of lavender wafting up.

She felt him turn his head. Felt him watch her. Like beams from the summer sun—like the undertones of low music.

Kestrel dropped a shirt on the floor. She adjusted her stance against the door to hold it in place, then bent to pick the shirt up.

"Here, I've got that," Wolfe murmured—and he stepped up and took hold of the door above her head.

"It's...It's okay, I've..." she tried, suddenly breathless. She swallowed, closing her fingers around the fallen shirt and squeezing her other laundry close to her chest. She started to stand up.

"Looks like I've got a shirt..." he muttered. "...in here too, let me—" He pushed the door back and leaned in around her to reach into the machine.

His broad chest brushed her shoulder. Her heart thundered.

He stopped—half bent over her. Millimeters away.

Both of them went completely still.

Slowly, Kestrel turned her head to the right. She managed a tight breath as her eyes trailed up toward his face.

He towered over her. So close—she could feel every one of his deep, tense breaths.

Terror overpowered her. She looked straight up into his eyes.

Brilliant, penetrating eyes.

His hand clenched the door of the washer, his knuckles going white. His brow knotted, his gaze flittering over her features. Startled. Captive.

Kestrel's breathing sped up as she wavered closer to him, memorizing every angle of his rugged face. His lips parted, to almost speak—and all at once, his mouth was all she could look at. And she stopped breathing when he bent down toward her, tilting his head...

His hair brushed her forehead. Her frame lifted as her wide eyes met his again—

The door buzzed.

Kestrel lost her balance, her vision blacking out for an instant as she turned toward it. Wolfe pulled away from her, letting the washer door slam shut. She pressed a cold hand to her hot face.

"Come in," she called. The door whooshed open. Dr. William Anthony stepped in, a pleasant smile only barely concealing an intense expression.

"I'm glad you're still here," he said. "Mrs. Johnson, may I have a word with you? Out in the hallway here? It won't take a moment."

"Sure," Kestrel said listlessly, her heart still hammering against her ribs. Rubbing her forehead, she stepped out after him, leaving Wolfe behind. The door shut behind them. Kestrel fought to focus on the doctor's face.

"Mrs. Johnson," Anthony began, just above a whisper. "Under normal circumstances, I would classify what I am about to tell you as 'none of my business.' But since you assured me earlier that he has never discussed this with you, I feel obligated to inform you of my suspicions, for no other reason than your protection."

Kestrel started.

"My protection?"

"Yes," he nodded. He paused, considering her. "Your husband's scars. You said you know nothing about them?"

"I don't," Kestrel admitted.

"I have just come from conducting some research," the doctor went on. "And it confirmed what I had first surmised." He stepped closer to her, and lowered his voice further. "At some point, your husband underwent surgery—massive, critical surgery—that was apparently very successful. However, the style of suture indicated by his scars has not been in use in *any* hospital in the known galaxy for more than two-hundred years."

Kestrel stared at him. Anthony nodded once more.

"Facts he has attempted to hide verbally are written upon him physically, Mrs. Johnson," he whispered. "And that is why I am led to believe that your husband is an illegally-practicing Time Traveler."

FIFTEEN

"A *Time Traveler?*" Kestrel repeated, her heart staggering before fluttering erratically.

"Yes," Anthony nodded. "That is the only explanation. No surgeon is even *taught* that technique anymore—it's considered abrasive and cosmetically ugly. Our stitches are invisible, and have been for more than a hundred years. *His*..." He gestured to the door, then shook his head. "As I said, it is the only explanation."

"What are you going to do?" Kestrel wondered, her blood turning to ice. Anthony sighed.

"I believe you are ignorant of his crimes. I can see it on your face. Which is why I want to do all I can to spare you."

Kestrel blinked.

"What?"

"I'm calling the ship's authorities to come and arrest him," Anthony told her. "They will hold him in the detention block and take him back to Earth to be tried. If you can keep him here until they come in a few minutes, you won't be arrested or implicated as an accomplice."

Kestrel couldn't do anything but stare at him. Anthony gave her a soft look.

"It's clear you don't know your husband, Mrs. Johnson. Please do the right thing now."

He reached out and touched her chin, giving her a long, steady look— then passed her and strode away down the corridor. And as he did, he lifted a communicator to his mouth and murmured into it.

Kestrel's entire body went cold. For an endless moment, she couldn't see anything in front of her. The ground seemed to be tilting underneath her feet—and there wasn't enough air. She reached out her left hand and fumbled for the door release...

It opened before she touched it. Her head came around.

Wolfe stood just inside, his hand on the inside button, his head bowed. Her hand suspended. He lifted a sideways look to her. And that pain and sorrow filled his frame again.

"Come here, Brown Eyes," he murmured, taking hold of her fingers and tugging. "I need to talk to you."

Numbly, she followed his lead—then snapped back to the moment. She gripped his fingers. He stopped, turning toward her.

"They're...They're coming to arrest you—" she gasped.

"I know," he nodded.

"But there's—"

"Nothing I can do," Wolfe said, dropping her hand. "That doctor's had me pegged since the second he saw me."

"*What?*" Kestrel cried. "Pegged for—"

"He told me what he just told you," Wolfe cut in. "He sent me back to the cabin to make sure I didn't cause a scene in the hospital—endanger other patients." Wolfe's voice quieted. "And he told me that if I cooperate, he'll leave you out of it."

"But you can't just—" Kestrel tried.

"He's put out a ship-wide warrant," Wolfe said. "They'll come after me in less than five minutes." His jaw tightened. "And there's something I have to tell you before they do."

Kestrel fell silent, bewildered. Wolfe gazed at her a moment, then turned and strode toward the opposite wall, setting his hands on his hips. He stopped, and lowered his head again. He ran a hand through his hair, then raised his head—but his whole body seemed to ache.

"I was born..." he began, his voice low. "June 15th, 1842, in St. Louis, Missouri. I didn't have any brothers or sisters—lots of cousins, though. I lived with my parents in a huge white house not far from the river. I went to school at Harvard University. Studied law." He stopped, his head reflexively coming around—and she saw sharp anguish written on his profile. He smoothed it, and went on. "While I was there, my parents...My parents died in a skirmish between the Northern and Southern armies. Both of them. In the same afternoon."

Kestrel wrapped her arms around herself, standing completely still, hardly daring to breathe. He went on.

"So I left school and joined the Second Massachusetts Cavalry . Got shot at Cedar Creek, in Shenandoah. Here." He faced her, and rubbed the upper left part of his chest. The place where Dr. Anthony had said he'd seen a puncture scar. "President Lincoln gave me a medal." He put his hand in his pocket, fumbled around, and pulled out two jingling pieces of metal dangling from ribbons. His jaw muscles clenching, he divided them and held one out to her. Kestrel took it. Its worn surface sat lightly in her palm, the ragged, faded ribbon draped over her fingers. A star, with a wreath around it. Her lip trembled.

"After the war, I lived in Boston for a while," he continued. "That's where I met Adelaide."

Kestrel's head came up. He was studying his other medal, rubbing his thumb across it.

"I thought she was the prettiest thing I'd ever seen. Hair like sunshine," he said. "She and I both hated city life, even though she'd been born there. We wanted some fresh air. Different scenery. So we got married and headed west. Bought a claim in Kansas. Built a homestead, started raising cattle." He fell silent. He stopped moving. "We'd lived there for about a year when they came."

Kestrel closed her fingers around the medal she held. He did the same to the one in his hand. He stared at the floor.

"Ada was inside the house, cooking supper. I'd just finished splitting some logs and had headed down to the creek to wash up when three…Three machines showed up out of nowhere. About eight feet tall, each of them. Shining metal. Two men stepped out of each one. They were dressed strangely—all in tight black suits, wearing helmets that covered their faces. They had weapons. I ran back to the house and got my Colt and my rifle and came out and confronted them. I told Ada to stay in the house. The men told me they didn't want a fight, but they'd shoot me if I didn't put my gun down. I told them they were on my land, and *they* ought to put down *their* guns. They refused. I shot at the ground by their feet. Everything escalated. They aimed at my house. I shot one of the men. Then they all shot at me. I shot three more of them dead before running out of ammunition in my rifle. Then, one of the men got off a shot at my house. A bright, green beam. Like lightning. It swallowed the…the whole house. I got up and ran to it."

Wolfe stopped. He rubbed his thumb back and forth, back and forth across that medal.

"She died," he whispered roughly—and Kestrel saw his eyes shining. He stood for a long moment, his throat locked, his thumb tapping the medal. Then he reached up with one hand and wiped his face. Pain ate up the inside of Kestrel's chest.

"The house blew apart and she died," Wolfe breathed. "And I fell into one of the open machines and the door shut."

"You..." Kestrel tried. "You *did* time travel."

He nodded, his head still low.

"Not on purpose, but yeah." He shifted his weight. "I went into a sort of...coma, I guess. And when I woke up, the machine was standing still. It opened, and I came out...into someplace else." He frowned down at the medal in his hand. "I don't have time to go into details, but...Everything had changed. I was in the 1960's. Wandered around for a while, fell in with a crowd. I was so...So sick. Angry. I wound up taking a man's place in the draft. I went to Vietnam. I fought. I'd already been a soldier in hell—this was different, but not new. And I was good. They saw that. I started taking the most dangerous assignments—ones that the other guys wouldn't take because they were scared they wouldn't come back. Sure enough, in the middle of a raid in the pitch black jungle, I got shot. Died. Heart stopped and everything. I thought I was...But they got me to a mobile hospital and resuscitated me on the table." He chuckled, and shook his head. "I coulda strangled that doctor."

Tears pricked Kestrel's eyes. She drew a little closer, her knees weak, and sank down on the armrest of one of the chairs. Wolfe stayed where he was, then held out the other medal to her.

"Got a purple heart for that one."

Kestrel took it listlessly, feeling it almost sear her hand as echoes of his screams rang through her mind. George Washington's features had been all but rubbed out.

"Also picked up smoking during that stint. Didn't really give it up till now," he added. "I, uh...They shipped me back to the states. After six total months had passed, the machine lit up again. I realized then that I had to get on it. I figured it was set to some sort of automatic recall—that it was heading back to its own time. Maybe in increments, but sure and steady. I knew it would eventually take me to the man who'd murdered my wife. So I got on. This time, it took me to the year 2050. I didn't have an ID or anything, so I was forced underground. Took a job as a cage fighter. I think I told you about that." For the first time in an age, he looked at Kestrel. Her heart skipped a beat. He went on, rubbing his left inside forearm.

"I got my tattoos then: Vengeance and Justice. That's what I was after. I knew if I found the man who had done this to Ada, I could make him undo it. But I was getting myself bloodied every night, and not learning anything. If I ever said anything to anybody about time travel, they looked at me like I was crazy. Except Robert Conrad." He almost smiled. "He found me down there—literally picked me up off the mat where I was bleeding all over. Told me that a gentleman like me didn't belong in that pit. He hired me as a personal bodyguard. Fed me, clothed me, gave me a place to stay. And he believed me. He was the first person who did. He helped me take the machine off the prairie and into a warehouse of his. I was the only one who had the key to it. He was my friend." Wolfe put his hands in his pockets. "But I only stayed there for six months, again. Then I had to move forward. And it landed me in 2142. In that same warehouse. I tracked down one of Robert's descendants: Eddie Conrad. Robert had passed word down about me. Eddie hired me right away—taught me to race bikes in an arena. I won a lot of races for him. He was an enterpriser, Eddie. Dangerous that way. We weren't really friends. I didn't tell him where the machine was. But he needed me around so...And it kept food on my table. And I listened. But I still didn't hear anything about my time traveler." He sighed. "After six months, I traveled again. To 2234. Found the next Conrad: Ethan. Worked as a bouncer at several of his clubs on the east coast. Kept my ear to the ground the whole time, but people still thought the time travel thing was ridiculous. Next time, it landed me in 2326—and this Conrad, David, was a good man. Used his family's resources to fight human trafficking. I helped him as an advisor and right-hand-man. Another six months, though, I had to leave. I still hadn't heard anything, and the machine was going to leave without me if I didn't get on." His tone changed. "It wasn't until 2418, the very next stop, that I got my first scent of a trail. I found the next Conrad: Peter. Started working for him in his illegal night clubs. I didn't like it, but I could hear the chatter from there. Pretty soon I started sensing trouble around my employer. I rode a bike to escort him places. Built it myself. Light, fast, smooth engine. Somebody came at him, out in the street. I had to lay out my bike to take them out. Tore open my whole side."

Kestrel swallowed, remembering the long scar on his back. Wolfe's face hardened.

"That's when I found out it was meant to be a double hit. Somebody had paid *Conrad* to kill *me*, but he'd been waiting for some reason. Got cold feet. So the person who bribed him decided to kill us both in one go. Conrad told me the name of the man: William Jakiv. And I told *Conrad* that he owed me his life, and I *would* come to collect someday." Wolfe's brow darkened. "After I healed, I searched every avenue I knew. But there was no such person on the planet named William Jakiv. That's when I realized I'd found him."

Wolfe finally glanced at Kestrel. "The next time I traveled, Conrad's warehouses weren't there anymore. They'd been built over by the KCSP. So I landed in your back room, stepped out and..." He almost smiled again. "I saw you. And you were the *first* person to look me in the eye and tell me that time-travel was possible. Now all I have to do is find Jakiv and force him to send me back, before the time he arrived. I'll get Ada away from the house, and when they show up neither of us will be there. And she'll be alive again."

Kestrel just sat there. Looking up at him. Holding both his medals limply in one hand.

"You don't wear a wedding ring."

They were the wrong words. So many others spun and whirled and tumbled through her mind, but these were the only ones that just fell out of her mouth.

He looked at her. His gaze flickered.

"I...Couldn't wear one on the farm," he answered. "Ada wears one, though." He swallowed. "Wore." He shifted again, his expression turning earnest. "Look, Kestrel..."

The sound of her name, in his voice, sent a thrill through her whole body. And it *hurt*.

She squirmed, trying to bite it back, but it grew. She had to turn away from him. He stopped.

Bzz.

Kestrel twitched. Wolfe sucked his breath and faced the door. He slowly pulled his hands out of his pockets.

"*This is the Intergalactic Space Force*," a mechanical voice came through the door. "*Jack Johnson, you are under arrest for violation of Time Travel Restrictions. Both of you, put your hands on your heads and stay where you are. Any disobedient movement from either of you will be considered an attempt to escape—we are authorized to use deadly force. You have until the count of ten. One...Two...Three...*"

Kestrel stood up, feeling like she was balancing on the edge of a precipice. Wolfe stared at the door. Icily-calm. Settled.

"What are you going to do?" Kestrel demanded, reaching up and gripping the hair on the back of her head with both hands.

"*Six...seven...*"

"I know who he is now, and where he is," Wolfe murmured. "I'll find my way back."

"Nine... Ten."

The door flew open.

Kestrel clamped down on her hair.

Five tall, broad, numbered security androids rumbled in like tanks, leveling their cannon-like weapons at Wolfe. His eyes blazed—but Kestrel saw it instantly in his stance: he was still weak. Pale. And had no strength to resist.

He lifted his hands to his head.

"Jack Johnson, fall in between units one and two," the lead android commanded, his red eyes blinking. Wolfe stayed where he was. His jaw clenched. Finally, he stepped forward, and allowed them to surround him. Kestrel couldn't do anything but watch.

"Keep pace with us or we will stun you," the leader warned. Wolfe didn't answer. They moved toward the door...

Wolfe glanced over his shoulder. Captured Kestrel's gaze.

"Thanks for sticking with me, Brown Eyes," he said. "Left hand pocket."

Tall androids blocked her view. They forced him out through the door. It shut behind them. And the edges of his medals bit into Kestrel's palm.

SIXTEEN

Quiet fell. Kestrel stood as she was for a full five minutes before absently lowering her hands. The medals jingled together in her right palm. She stared down at them.

She pressed her hand over her mouth and closed her eyes. Then, she squeezed them shut as a terrible shudder ran from the top of her spine to her heels, and pain jabbed every corner of her ribcage. She tried to suck in a breath, but the center of her breastbone panged, as if it was fractured, and every muscle turned to stone.

"That's where I met Adelaide. I thought she was the prettiest thing I'd ever seen. Hair like sunshine...She and I both hated city life, even though she'd been born there. We wanted some fresh air. Different scenery. So we got married and headed west. Bought a claim in Kansas..."

Kestrel's left hand fumbled for the back of the chair. She leaned against it, her legs turning to water as she closed her right hand.

"Now all I have to do is find Jakiv and force him to send me back, before the time he arrived. I'll get Ada away from that place, and when they show up neither of us will be there. And she'll be alive again."

Kestrel opened her eyes as tears fell and burned her face. She gasped, and it tore through her lungs.

She slowly leaned sideways and sat heavily on the armrest of the chair. Bowing her head, heedless of her tears, she watched through blurred vision as her thumb wandered back and forth across both medals.

And finally, for the first time ever, she addressed the only other entity on the ship able to answer her honestly.

"Cabin Computer 301," she said, her voice quaking. "What is your designation?"

"Hello, April Johnson," a calm female voice answered as a green light blinked to life over the door. *"My name is Kith."*

"Hello, Kith," Kestrel said, clearing her throat and closing her eyes again. "Sorry we've neglected you."

"*No need for apologies, April Johnson,*" she replied. "*I am here at your service.*"

Kestrel drew in another careful breath. She shivered, then blinked her eyes open.

"Can you answer a few questions for me?"

"*Certainly, April Johnson.*"

Kestrel weakly held up the medals.

"What medals are these? What age are they?"

"*Scanning,*" Kith told her. A moment later, she spoke. "*The star-shaped medal, surrounded by a laurel wreath, is the Medal of Honor in its oldest format. First initiated by President Abraham Lincoln of the United States during the American Civil War. Issued for conspicuous heroism and gallantry under fire. This particular medal dates to circa 1860's. The other is a Purple Heart, issued for wounding or death sustained on the field of battle in the service of the United States Military. This particular medal dates to circa 1960's.*"

Kestrel steadied herself as she put her hand down.

"Thank you, Kith. A few more questions."

"*Certainly, April Johnson.*"

"Was there ever an American Civil War Medal of Honor recipient named..." She swallowed hard, then made herself go on. "Named Jack Wolfe?"

"*Searching...*" Kith said. "*Affirmative. Would you like the details?*"

Kestrel's brow knotted.

"Yes. Please."

"*Please direct your attention to your entertainment console.*"

Kestrel stepped toward it as the room's lights darkened and a floating screen popped up from the console.

It showed a large black-and-white picture of a group of men standing outside sagging cloth tents. They all wore weather-beaten, dark wool uniforms with high collars and bright buttons. Hats sat crookedly on all their heads. One row of men squatted on the ground. Another row stood behind them. And one man stood taller than all the rest.

"*This man, highlighted for you,*" Kith said, brightening the tallest man and dimming the others. He stood with his arms folded, a very long gun cradled carelessly between them. He lifted his chin at the camera. He had a close-shaven mustache and beard and a hard set to his mouth—but Kestrel would recognize those flashing eyes anywhere.

"*Lieutenant John Angus Wolfe, known as Jack the Giant, of the First Massachusetts Cavalry. Shot in the battle of Cedar Creek while saving the lives of four men whose horses had been killed by cannon fire. While wounded, he rode directly into enemy fire and, by rifle, pistol and saber, eliminated the Confederate soldiers manning three cannons, providing his unit with the opportunity to capture vital ground.*"

"Any further information?" Kestrel whispered, stepping as close as she could, unblinking.

"*Yes. After cessation of hostilities, he married Adelaide Barnes in Boston, Massachusetts, bought a claim in eastern Kansas and traveled west with her. No other record of this man exists beyond that point.*"

"Nothing?"

"*No, April Johnson,*" Kith said. "*No record of children, purchases of any kind, employment, census results or obituaries in that century.*"

"Wait—so there's record of him in *another* century?" Kestrel clarified.

"*Yes, April Johnson.*"

The picture changed to a color photo of a young, blonde man in a very antique suit, ducking into a vehicle—and just behind him bent Wolfe's tall, powerful form. He wore his leather jacket, now.

"*In the year 2050. A bodyguard to Robert Conrad, successful businessman and landowner.*" The picture changed again—to one of Wolfe straddling a lean but very classic motorcycle as a pit-stop man handed him a helmet. "*Again in the year 2142, as a driver employed by an Edward Conrad, owner of BlitzBikes International Racing—a company that soon branched into weapon making. Again in 2234, as part of a security detail in seven different night clubs, all owned by an Ethan Conrad, entertainment tycoon.*" In this picture, Wolfe stood with several other burly men in the shadows of a crowded bar.

"*Again in 2326,*" Kith went on. "*As advisor to David Conrad, and co-founder of Project Unfettered, an anti-human-trafficking organization.*"

In *this* picture, Wolfe wore much finer clothes—sleeker, more expensive, black—as he stood, hands in pockets, next to a shorter, earnest-faced young man at a mirror-topped table. Wolfe's head tilted thoughtfully, and he watched the other young man.

"*The latest information about him dates to 2418 when he entered the intensive care unit of Hospital B-864 in Atlanta, Georgia following a near-fatal vehicle collision involving two motorcycles and two multi-passenger vehicles.*

He underwent surgery, stabilized, then disappeared without checking out."

Kestrel did nothing for a moment—then pressed both hands to the sides of her head. For a very long time she stayed motionless, the last picture glowing in front of her. Her eyes unfocused as the room faded into the background.

"*Will you be needing me further, April Johnson?*"

Kestrel's head came up.

Her eyes narrowed.

"One more question..." she decided. "What did Jack say to me before he left?"

"*His last phrase?*"

"Yes."

"'*Thanks for sticking with me, Brown Eyes,*'" Kith quoted. "'*Left hand pocket.*'"

"Left hand pocket..." Kestrel mused. She turned around, hunting...

The sleeve of his leather jacket stuck out from under his bed.

Kestrel stared at it—then put the medals on the chair, hurried to his bed, knelt and tugged it out. His book bumbled onto the floor, but she hardly noticed. She wrestled the heavy coat around, found the left side pocket and stuffed her hand into it.

Nothing. Not even lint.

She opened the coat up, groping for an inside pocket. There wasn't one. Gritting her teeth, she stuck her hand into the outside left pocket again and pulled it inside out.

She blinked.

Two ink-written words stained the lining.

Diary dots

"Diary dots..." she whispered. Her head came around—her attention fell on the book. She dropped the coat and snatched it up. She opened the cover and turned past the first blank page, and arrived at the initial Shakespearian sonnet.

Let me not to the marriage of true minds
Admit impediments. Love is not love
Which alters when it alteration finds,

Or bends with the remover to remove:
O no! it is an ever-fixed mark
That looks on tempests and is never shaken;
It is the star to every wandering bark,
Whose worth's unknown, although his height be taken.
Love's not Time's fool, though rosy lips and cheeks
Within his bending sickle's compass come:
Love alters not with his brief hours and weeks,
But bears it out even to the edge of doom.
  If this be error and upon me proved,
  I never writ, nor no man ever loved.
    - William Shakespeare

She slowed, reading the words much more carefully this time...
And caught sight of something she hadn't before.
Dots. Light dots, made with graphite.
"There's marks underneath certain letters," she said aloud.
"*Perhaps it is a cryptogram,*" Kith suggested. "*A code in which certain letters in a selected work of unrelated—*"
"I know, I've read *Sherlock Holmes*," Kestrel waved her off, staring at the letters marked out by the dots. "Put these letters up on a screen for me," she instructed, getting up and walking back over toward the entertainment console. "And bring up the lights."
"*Yes, April Johnson.*"
The lights came up, and Kestrel scanned the lines painstakingly, careful not to miss a single mark, and told her findings to Kith. When she came to the end of the sonnet, she lifted her eyes to the screen.

stationlevelone
threesickslawsonbrandandwilliam

"Station level one," Kestrel read under her breath. "Three sicks...Six! The number six! There wasn't an X, so he had to use the 'sick' in the word 'sickle'...Three- six-Lawson-Brand-and-William."
She stared. Then, her heart began to speed up. She flipped to the next sonnet.

No, Time, thou shalt not boast that I do change:
Thy pyramids built up with newer might
To me are nothing novel, nothing strange;
They are but dressings of a former sight.
Our dates are brief, and therefore we admire
What thou dost foist upon us that is old,
And rather make them born to our desire
Than think that we before have heard them told.
Thy registers and thee I both defy,
Not wondering at the present nor the past,
For thy records and what we see doth lie,
Made more or less by thy continual haste.
  This I do vow and this shall ever be;
  I will be true, despite thy scythe and thee.
        "Okay, are you ready, Kith?"
        "*Certainly.*"
        Kestrel read the next letters she found.

        levelto
        tentheodorefourten

        "Level to...To what? Oh—level *two*. There wasn't a W. Okay, Level two: ten-Theodore-four-ten."
        She paused—and suspicions broke loose in her head. Quickly, she turned to the next poem...

        Her golden hair in ringlets fair,
        her eyes like diamonds shining
        Her slender waist, her heavenly face,
        that leaves my heart still pining

        Ye gods above oh hear my prayer
        to my beauteous fair to find me
        And send me safely back again,
        to the girl I left behind me.'"

"'The bee shall honey taste no more,
the dove become a ranger
The falling waters cease to roar,
ere I shall seek to change her

The vows we made to heav'n above
shall ever cheer and bind me
In constancy to her I love,
the girl I left behind me.

Nothing. Only ink. Not a single graphite mark. Kestrel hesitated. Was that the end of the code? Biting her lip, she turned the page...

Job, chapter three. 'Let the day perish wherein I was born, and the night in which it was said, There is a man child conceived. Let that day be darkness; let not God regard it from above, neither let the light shine upon it. Let darkness and the shadow of death be upon it; let the blackness of the day terrify it.'

'Let the stars of the twilight thereof be dark; let it look for light, but have none; neither let it see the dawning of the day: Because it shut not up the doors of my mother's womb, nor hid sorrow from mine eyes.'

'For now should I have laid still and been quiet, I should have slept:...'
'Wherefore is light given to him that is in misery, and life unto the bitter in soul; Which long for death, but it cometh not; and dig for it more than for hid treasures; Which rejoice exceedingly, and are glad, when they can find the grave? Why is light given to a man whose way is hid, and whom God hath hedged in?'
'For the thing which I greatly feared is come upon me.'

"Here's more, Kith!" she called, and read them out one at a time.

three
seveneightshadowstareighttwo
goonbrowneyes
findem

"Three," she said. "Seven-eight-shadow-star-eight-two." Kestrel stopped. Then, slowly, she read out the last part. "Go on, Brown Eyes. Find 'em."

Her fingers closed around the edges of the book as the pieces silently clicked together in her mind.

Station, level one, two and three. Sequences of words and numbers.

The Gain Station levels.

And their access codes.

Kestrel sank down into the nearest chair, staring up at the letters on the screen but seeing none of them. Her fingers closed around the medals.

Wolfe had found the codes. Sometime between their initial meeting and their second, he had bribed, overheard or beaten the information out of someone, and then hidden the codes in such a way that only a person who knew what she was looking for would be able to find them.

He had given her exactly what she needed to enter the Gain Station's restricted levels and start the search for her family.

And he was telling her to go on without him.

Kestrel slid the medals in between the pages, closed the book, and sat back in the chair, her thoughts twisting and winding off into the silence.

SEVENTEEN

4:15

The low *click* of the clock at the base of the entertainment console made her blink. Kestrel drew a deep breath, flexed her fingers...

And lifted her head.

She stood up. She lifted the back of her loose shirt and stuck the book into the tight waistband of her pants, then pulled her shirt down to cover it. Then, she unfastened her AdLink bracelet and set it on the armrest.

"Kith," she said, straightening. "Are you able to go mobile?"

"*Yes, April Johnson,*" Kith answered. "*My mobile format is plugged into the opposite side of the entertainment console.*"

Kestrel moved around the console, found and unlatched a little black square from its charging stand. She flipped it open and glanced at the screen.

KITH MOBILE

"Good," Kestrel nodded, shutting it, reaching up and snapping it securely to her lapel. "You there?"

"*Right here,*" came Kith's clear voice from the little box.

"I'm assuming you're programmed with a layout of the ship," Kestrel said, striding toward the door.

"*I am.*"

"Please give me directions as we go," Kestrel instructed as the door slid open and she left the cabin. "First, I need to get to the arcade as quickly as possible."

"*Certainly. Turn left and take the Express Lift on your right.*"

Kestrel found it—framed in bright green lights—entered the lift and watched the doors shut.

"*This will take you on a diagonal route,*" Kith explained. "*And will drop you out fifty meters from the arcade. Please hold on.*"

Kestrel gripped the cold railing, and the lift shot off—sideways. She gritted her teeth and held on as the g-force pressed on her stomach. In a matter of seconds, the lift stopped and the doors opened. She strode out into the white hallway, veered right and didn't break stride until she arrived at the main desk.

"Hello," the young man greeted her. "What package are you interested in today?"

"Just the shooting range," Kestrel answered, not looking at him but assessing the sparse crowd inside the colorful arcade.

"Okay, I need your card."

Kestrel handed it to him. He scanned it, then handed it back, along with a wrist band.

"Thanks," she said, immediately heading toward the shooting gallery. She stuffed the bracelet into her pocket as she swept through the door. She looked back to make sure the door had shut, then cast a glance through the rest of the gallery. Mercifully, it was empty. She took the wrist band out of her pocket, tossed it on the floor, then turned toward the wall of weapons.

For a moment, she eyed the K95 pistol. Then she remembered the broken safety. Folding her arms, she spoke up.

"K98 and K90 to ground level."

Two mechanical arms moved. Two handguns lowered to her, and she snatched them up, their weight clicking in her hands. She stuffed them both into the back waistband of her pants, covered them with her shirt, then faced the gallery.

There.

She strode to a console, hopped up on top of it and jumped over into the target area.

Lights started blinking, and she sensed the game's computer about to give her a warning—

She reached the emergency alarm lever, grabbed it and flipped it.

The lights turned red. A deafening howl blared through the room.

"Emergency. All gamers, please proceed to front entrance. Emergency. All gamers please proceed to front entrance."

Kestrel swung around, eyes narrowed. Then, on the left side of the row of targets, she spotted it. A door marked *Personnel Only.*

She ran across the lanes toward it, shoved through it, and heard it click shut behind her. She had entered a white stairwell—and she began to hurry down a black flight of stairs.

"April Johnson, you have accessed a restricted passageway," Kith warned.

"It's okay—I'm just trying to find my lost AdLink bracelet."

"You left it in the cabin."

"No, the other one," Kestrel corrected, her boots pounding on the hard metal of the landing as she swung around and darted down more stairs. "The other one I purchased. Can you give me directions from here?"

"*Go back to the main commerce corridor and take lift—*"

"No, Kith, from *here*," Kestrel snapped. "From where I am *right* now."

"*Very well. Continue descending these stairs until you reach a door marked Sub-3. It is several levels down.*"

"Okay," Kestrel said. "What are these staircases used for?"

"*Maintenance,*" Kith answered. "*And emergency travel from level to level in case of fire or hull breach.*"

Kestrel didn't answer. She just kept hurrying downward, never tiring, paying close attention to the numbers on each door as she came to each landing.

Finally, she arrived at the door marked SUB-3—and the walls turned from white to blue. She stopped on that landing, pressed her back into a cold corner, and pulled out the K98.

She eyeballed the side of it, setting her jaw, then reached into her pocket and pulled out her credit card. She pressed the corner of it into one of the minute screws on the handle of the gun and rapidly twisted it. That screw came loose, and she brought it up and clamped it between her teeth. She loosed the next screw, then the next. She put her card back and popped the panel off. She canted her head, frowning at the colorful knot of inside workings.

"Dusty," she muttered through the three screws in her mouth.

"*Tampering with arcade equipment is illegal, April Johnson,*" Kith admonished.

"Shut up."

Kestrel glanced up one set of stairs, then down the other. No one was coming. She pulled out her card again, stuck it into a very thin space between wires, and shut her eyes, feeling her way...

Click.

"Yesh," she exulted, trying not to spit out the screws. Then, she replaced the panel, put the screws back in place and tightened them one at a time. She then flipped the safety and stuck the gun back into her waistband. She pulled out the K90 and quickly repeated the same process, though this gun was even dustier inside. She clicked that one's safety on, put it in her waistband, and pulled the K98 back out. It felt better in her hand, more like the K96. Then, she took several steps away from the door, turned and assessed it.

"Does this door open on this side, Kith?" Kestrel asked.

"*Not without a pass key.*"

"Thought so." Kestrel glanced down at the settings wheel on her handgun and spun it—and now, it engaged with sharp *clicking* sounds, instead of spinning freely. She thought for a second, selected one, then aimed at the door and fired.

A blast of blue lightning spat from the gun and zapped through the doorframe. The door groaned, and sagged halfway open.

"*April Johnson—*" Kith cried.

"Sorry, Kith," Kestrel tugged the mobile device off her collar. "You're getting annoying." And she hurled it at the wall. It shattered and fell to the floor. Kestrel spun on her heel and pushed her way through the half-open door, her gun aimed loosely out in front of her. She took smooth steps, glancing up and down the blue, sterile hallways, ignoring her hammering heart.

"Just like the second level of *Ortheus*," she whispered to herself. "No different, no different..."

A yellow sign hanging from the ceiling ahead of her caught her eye.

LEVEL THREE DETENTION
FIREARM REQUIRED PAST THIS POINT

"Oh, great," Kestrel muttered.

Movement.

She threw herself to the left, into a deep doorway, as two men clad in black crossed corridors in front of her. She pressed her left shoulder against the wall and froze, listening. Their voices faded. She leaned gingerly out, easing just one eye around the corner...

Gone.

She slipped out of cover, whispering further down the hall, careful to keep her gun pointed at a forty-five degree down angle, just like in the game.

Though, in the game, her feet never sounded this loud. The air didn't smell like caustic cleaners. And her heart never pounded this hard.

The corridor ahead of her ended in a T. She slowed down, then leaned slowly forward, turning her head back and forth.

A short hallway, stretching about fifty meters in both directions. She eased out, her hands sweaty on her weapon. She stepped carefully. Almost all of the cell doors stood open, empty. Only one door in the entire hallway was shut. She hesitated, then crept up to it.

A small window looked in on the cell. She stopped in front of the door, leaned up, and looked through.

"Hey!"

Her head jerked to the left.

A guard not thirty meters away pointed at her.

"Who are you?" he demanded, starting toward her. "What are you doing here?"

Kestrel raised her gun, aimed and fired.

The blue stunning blast hit him, enveloped him.

Dropped him to the ground.

Without stopping to think, Kestrel stepped back from the door, spun the settings wheel with her thumb—

Sighted and blasted the lock.

Orange flame flashed. The door shuddered and squeaked open. She stepped forward and kicked it aside.

Jack Wolfe stood inside the cell, backed up against the far wall. He had clearly leaped up from his pallet—it lay skewed. He stared at her for a moment, utterly stunned.

"*Kestrel?*"

"Thanks for the codes," Kestrel panted, pulling his book out and holding it up, trying not to look at him. "But you're not getting out of our deal *that* easily."

EIGHTEEN

"How did you do this?" Wolfe demanded, striding toward her and taking the book from her. He did exactly what she had—stuffed it in the back of his jeans—without taking his attention from her for an instant.

"I actually have no idea," Kestrel admitted breathlessly, nervously facing the door. "Guess I've watched too many 4-D's and played too many games."

"Do you understand what it is you're doing?" he pressed, coming even closer to her. She put her hand on the doorframe, listening for the guards...

"You could ruin your life—you're breaking someone out of *jail*—"

"Did you know time-travel was illegal?" Kestrel countered, turning back to him. His eyes, even brighter in this light, focused down on her.

"No—"

"You just got in and let the machine take you, right?"

"Yes..."

"And you didn't *start* in this century—you just came forward from another one."

"Yes."

"Then you didn't break the law," Kestrel finished, looking right up at him now. "Jakiv did, when he sent those men to *your* time. Which means he is an intergalactic criminal, not a scientific benefactor." Kestrel turned around and glanced out the door again. "My money's on the odds that this is a frame-up."

"What do you mean?" Wolfe hissed into the back of her head.

"He tried to kill you at least once before," Kestrel answered, her grip tightening on her gun. "Why wouldn't he try to take you down again?"

Wolfe fell silent. Kestrel braced herself to re-enter the hallway...

"Why are you doing this for me?"

Kestrel paused. Everything inside her twisted. Wolfe's voice lowered.

"You could have taken those codes, gotten on a transport without a hitch and snuck into the lower levels of the station without anybody being the wiser. And you can obviously handle yourself—you don't need me." His voice became a whisper. "Come on, Kestrel. Answer me."

She halfway turned, and lifted her gaze to his. She didn't say anything—couldn't. He searched her.

His gaze settled on hers.

He swallowed.

"C'mon," Kestrel said roughly, pulling out the other weapon, switching it to stun, and handing it to him. "Might need this."

"Kestrel—"

"Look, we get caught now, that's it for both of us," she snapped. "I'd rather not. So let's go."

His jaw tightened. He nodded.

"Fine. Where are we going?"

"To get transport off this thing," she muttered, holding her gun out and stepping into the hall.

"They won't let us on the shuttles."

She lifted an eyebrow at him.

"Wasn't even thinking of that."

Alarms screeched. Flashing blue lights shattered the air.

"That took long enough," Wolfe muttered, hefting his gun and striding out beside her. With her free hand, Kestrel dug in her pocket and pulled out all of her cards—the blue ID, the red Travel Permission, the purple Liquor Line Passport, the orange meal plan and the gold credit—bent and stuffed them in the front pocket of the stunned officer.

"What are you doing?" Wolfe wondered.

"They can track those," she said. "Do you have yours with you?"

"They're back in the room."

"Good," Kestrel nodded. "Take off the AdLink bracelet."

Wolfe did, and handed it to her. She bent and put it with the cards—

Three armed guards wheeled around the corner. Shouted. Lifted their weapons—

In tandem, Kestrel and Wolfe fired. Wolfe took down two, Kestrel the other. They charged forward, hopped over the fallen officers and broke into a run.

"*Security breach. Initiating lockdown.*"

A metal door far in front of them buzzed, and began to lower from the ceiling. Kestrel lengthened her strides, built her speed, Wolfe pounding beside her—

They dove. Skidded through underneath. Rolled.

The door *clanged* shut behind them.

Wolfe winced, then lay over on his back and coughed.

"You okay?" Kestrel gasped, reaching out to grip his arm.

"Fine," he answered, touching her hand. "C'mon."

Together they scrambled to their feet. They hurried forward, trying to get their bearings. Both of them stuffed their guns in their waistbands again, hiding them with their shirts.

"Okay, where are we?" Wolfe huffed, pressing the back of his hand to his mouth for a moment as they swung into a wider, more populated hall. Kestrel didn't make eye-contact with anybody—all of the other people walking back and forth were dressed like ship's crew and officers. And so far, none of them paid them any attention.

"Sub level three," Kestrel answered, straightening her shirt. "Three levels below the lobby."

"Any lifts?"

"Let's try the stairs," Kestrel advised, eyeing another one of those doors marked *Personnel Only*. She pushed through it, Wolfe followed, and again she found herself in that blue hallway. She charged up the stairs two at a time, Wolfe on her heels.

Up, up, up they climbed, their feet pounding, their hands sliding up the metal banisters. They finally reached the landing for LEVEL 1 and Kestrel halted. Wolfe breathed heavily as he pulled up next to her.

"You okay?" she asked again.

"You mean for a man who was dead a couple days ago?" he said, resting his hands on his hips. "Don't worry about me. I'll keep up with you."

"All right," Kestrel murmured, fighting back her anxiety as she aimed at the door, turned the dial on her gun and fired. This door sagged too, and she shoved it out of the way as she squeezed through. Wolfe followed, grunting.

"Lobby level," Wolfe noted as they strode across dark carpet through the much busier hallway, headed toward the swimming pool section. "We'd better—"

Alarms sounded. Red lights in the ceiling began whirling and flashing.

"*Security breach. Shuttle transport will now lock down. There will be no travel from the ship to the station or the planet's surface. All passengers return to your cabins. Any passengers loitering outside the cabin areas will be arrested. This is not a drill.*"

"How do they expect to canvas the entire ship?" Wolfe wondered as they passed the swimming pool—where startled parents scrambled to pull their kids out of the water—and made their way toward a far corridor. "They don't have enough staff to—"

A loud *clank* rang out behind them.

Kestrel stopped and spun—Wolfe did the same.

"They have those," Kestrel muttered.

And five broad-shouldered, wheeled security androids, their silver surfaces gleaming and their red eyes flashing, wheeled swiftly around the reception desk. They focused—and aimed their cannon arms straight at Wolfe and Kestrel.

"Run!" Kestrel yelled. And they turned and pelted down the hallway.

"*Halt!*" one of the androids called. "*We will be forced to stun you!*"

"That would be bad," Wolfe said through his teeth as they reeled around a corner. Kestrel leaped out of the way of an old man, who yelped and spilled his coffee everywhere.

A blue blast careened into the wall right next to her.

She flinched left and stumbled into Wolfe. He caught her, grabbed her arm to keep her from falling. She threw a glance behind them—

The androids raced after them, smooth as skaters on ice, their engines thrumming.

And they were gaining.

"Will the guns work on them?" Wolfe gasped.

"Yeah—probably—"

"Grab my hand," Wolfe ordered. "You look back and shoot."

Her eyes flashed at him as they skidded around a corner.

"But—"

"I'd never steer you wrong." He grabbed her left hand and held on tight. "Go on—shoot!"

Kestrel gripped his hand hard, yanked her gun out of her waistband, flicked the dial, and, trusting Wolfe not to run her into anything, looked back over her shoulder and raised her arm even as she ran at full speed.

She sighted. Her gun bounced with her gait. She gritted her teeth...

Fired. Fired again. And again.

The yellow blasts shattered the walls, the doorframes.

One bit into an android. Punched a sharp hole in its midsection.

It lurched to a stop and fell on its face.

The others fired at her.

"Duck!" Kestrel yelled. She stumbled as she dipped down, feeling Wolfe do the same.

Blue lightning lashed the air where their heads had been.

They staggered back to an upright position, Wolfe jerking her arm. She fired backward again, nicking one android's head. It spun sideways.

Flashing in front of them.

Kestrel faced forward—

Three security androids belted out across their path.

Wolfe leveled his gun at them and fired.

Pang-pang-pang.

They dropped like deer. Wolfe never broke stride—he pulled Kestrel with him—

They leaped high over the fallen droids, thudding halfway to their knees on the other side—

"Go, go!" Wolfe grabbed her by the elbow now and shoved her forward.

The androids chasing them crashed spectacularly into the fallen ones.

Their weapons went off—lightning sprayed.

Wolfe pushed her into a ducking position and pressed his hand to the back of her head. They bobbed around yet another corner.

"C'mon," Kestrel snatched at his hand, tugged it and let go—

And almost tripped. She stared ahead of her at a wide door.

HANGAR BAY
PRIVATE VEHICLE STORAGE ONLY

"How...How did you know...?" Kestrel gasped. Wolfe grimly kept walking.

"Is there another option?"

Kestrel didn't have time to answer. Wolfe fired at the door panel, then shoved his fingers into the small gap and wrenched the door open.

They rushed out into the huge, silver-floored hangar bay, the fluorescent white lights overhead sending glitters and shimmers all across the smooth metal surfaces of the sleek ships. Their feet clanged against the panels.

"I can't fly any of these," Kestrel realized as they swept down the line.

"I've only ever flown an old T289—it was only a two-passenger thirty speed with sub-light engines and two shield levels—"

"Like that?" Wolfe pointed. Kestrel swallowed.

Ahead of them perched a classic red T300—just a few years younger than the one Kestrel had learned on as a teenager. Two parallel wings on both sides, a graceful back fin and a narrow nose, contrasted by a blocky front spacescreen. It had a few dings in the paint, but the lines looked good. Kestrel grimaced.

"This is *really* expensive..."

"Then let's not wreck it," Wolfe advised, charging up to its flank. Kestrel took three deep breaths as she ducked under the belly next to him. She found the red lever, and flipped it.

The ramp groaned deeply, then eased down. Lights up in the cabin clicked on. All of a sudden, Kestrel's skin went clammy.

"We're stealing a spaceship."

"This was your idea," Wolfe reminded her.

"Maybe a bad idea."

"We'll try to return it," Wolfe said, then gestured to the ramp. "After you."

Biting her cheek, Kestrel climbed up the ramp, feeling his footsteps *clunk* as he followed. The ramp lifted shut before they had fully entered, and Kestrel, glancing around the brown-and-white leather interior, turned left and dipped into the cockpit.

"Really," she tried, her voice quivering as she gripped the shoulder of the pilot's chair. "I've only logged a total of maybe five hours of real spaceflight. I—"

"That's more than me," Wolfe cut her off, slipping through and thudding down into the copilot's seat. "How do you work these restraints?" He reached to his right and started tugging on the straps. Kestrel gripped the chair harder. He stopped, and looked up at her.

"You're not going to make *me* fly this, are you?"

Kestrel couldn't answer.

"Look, they're still coming," he said. "And like you said—if they catch us now, that's it for both of us."

Kestrel gritted her teeth, and nodded. She edged forward, stepped sideways and sat down in the pilot's seat, scanning the controls.

Very clean. A dark metallic dashboard, clearly marked buttons, easy-to-grip throttle. She reached out and punched a button—the restraints reached out of their own accord and wrapped around them.

"Of course," Wolfe muttered. The lights on the board flashed on. The cabin lights dimmed. Kestrel took a deep breath, then flipped the five switches that powered up the engine. The ship groggily began to hum.

"How long?" Wolfe asked.

"Probably thirty seconds."

"We've got less than that."

Kestrel's head came up.

Outside the spacescreen, where the two of them had broken into the hanger, six more androids barreled through. Their red eyes now shining infrared-searching beams, they began darting between the ships, searching...

"As soon as the engines come on they'll know where we are..." Kestrel gritted.

"As soon as they come on we'll be out of here," Wolfe corrected.

"Really?" Kestrel said. "Because I still haven't figured out how to get the hangar doors open."

"We'll have to shoot them."

"This ship doesn't have weapons!" Kestrel cried. "It's...It's a glorified *car!*"

"I said *we.*" Wolfe hefted his gun and set it in his lap. Kestrel looked blankly at him.

"What?"

With an energetic thrum, the ship powered up.

Life vibrated through every beam. And every android looked straight at them.

"Oh...*no,*" Kestrel winced.

"Go," Wolfe commanded.

Kestrel punched the thrusters.

With a thunderous blast, the ship lifted off the floor. The nearest android toppled backward. Kestrel gripped the controls as they levitated, rising up higher than the roofs of the other ships. Carefully, she turned the T300 toward the hangar bay door...

Zap. Zap. Zap.

The whole vehicle shimmied.

"I think they're shooting at us," she noted as she accelerated forward, ever-so-slightly. "And I'm *really* close to the ceiling..."

"Is there an upper hatch?" Wolfe asked.

"What—Why?"

"Answer me."

"Yes—"

"Open it."

"Jack—"

"Ask me later," he said, pressing his restraint release and getting up. "And whatever you do, don't hit the roof."

Kestrel shakily clicked the switch for the upper hatch, then grabbed the controls with both hands again. She heard the hatch pop open and hiss. Wolfe charged aft. His boots clanged on the ladder as he ascended.

The broad hangar door waited ahead. The *zaps* stopped as she accelerated.

"Jack," Kestrel winced. "If you're planning on shooting the controls—"

"That's what I'm planning," he called back at the top of his voice.

"*Space* will open up in front of us," Kestrel shouted. "A *vacuum*. It'll suck at you and everything in this whole hanger—and *then* an emergency blast door will probably slam down over the opening—"

"So I'll shoot and jump down, and you'll gun it and make it out before the door comes down," Wolfe answered.

"Yeah. Sure!" Kestrel rolled her eyes, breaking into a cold sweat. The door loomed.

"Ready?" Wolfe asked.

"Why not?"

"Here goes!"

Kestrel bit down.

Brilliant yellow bolts lanced out from the top of their ship and peppered the controls on the right side of the door.

As if it was spring-loaded, the hangar door snapped open.

Kestrel hit the throttle.

The ship shot forward, even as all the other ships in the hangar began skidding toward the gaping hole.

Wind sucked her backward.

Her eyes went wide. Had the hatch—

They blasted out of the cruiser and into vast, black, open space.

The emergency door slammed down behind them, clipping their tail.

The ship's whole frame rattled.

A deafening clang battered the interior.

Wolfe crashed to the floor.

Kestrel twisted in her chair.

"Are you all right?" she cried, her pulse jarring through her ribcage.

Wolfe groaned, turned over onto his side, then heaved himself to his feet.

"Lost my gun," he muttered, brushing his hair away from his forehead as he came through and sat heavily down in the other chair. He fought to catch his breath as the restraints wrapped around him. He stared out front.

"So they'll be after us now," he assumed.

"Most likely they'll contact the planet and the station," Kestrel answered, absently clicking the shields on, as she always did in *Ortheus*. "Send out space security details to escort us to the surface. Or they could just—"

A white flash consumed the spacescreen.

The whole ship rocked.

Wolfe grabbed her arm.

"What was that?" Kestrel rasped. She reached out and snapped on her rear screens—

Then yanked the controls to the left.

The ship spun.

A huge, wicked green bolt seared the space where they had just been and knifed toward the planet.

"The *Exception!*" Kestrel yelped, righting them. "It's shooting at us!" She sucked in a breath. "If I hadn't just put up the shields—"

"Go, go, go," Wolfe urged.

Swallowing the rest of that horrifying thought, Kestrel opened up the throttle, and the little ship lunged forward, blazing straight toward the space between the huge, Saturn-shaped Gain station—with all its tangled metallic members and twinkling lights—and the half-green-half-red planet of Alpha.

"They're trying to kill us," Kestrel realized—then flinched back as the area all around them exploded with laser fire.

"You were right," Wolfe murmured, gripping the armrests. "It's him."

Kestrel glanced at him, her stomach sinking...

BOOM.

Her teeth rattled. Her vision blurred.

She shook herself, her hands clenching the controls—even as she felt them slipping. She blinked her vision clear, cast a look at her readings...

"We've been hit," she muttered. "It broke through part of the shield, cut into our port side engine."

"What does that mean?" Wolfe squeezed his armrests harder as the ship bucked again.

"It means we can't turn toward the Gain Station," Kestrel answered, pushing the ship's speed. "And the harder we accelerate, the more we'll turn toward the planet."

"And if we *don't* accelerate?"

"The next shot will blow us apart."

Alpha's green side loomed in front of them. Kestrel could make out the shapes of the swirling clouds, the large bodies of water...

They picked up speed.

"We're going faster," she noted. "The planet's gravity is pulling us."

"They've stopped shooting," Wolfe glanced behind them.

"A cruiser can't handle a very shallow orbit," Kestrel adjusted her sweaty hands. "They don't want to risk—"

A red light flashed on and a shrill alarm cracked the air.

"What's that?" Wolfe demanded.

"The port engine's gone," Kestrel slapped her hand down and cut its power. "I'll have to maneuver with just the starboard engine and the thrusters—"

"Can you land that way?"

"Don't know," Kestrel confessed, trembling. "Never tried it."

Alpha filled the whole spacescreen. They rocketed toward it, Kestrel pressing back into her seat. Gray wisps began flashing across the screen.

"We're in the atmosphere," she gasped. "And I...I can't—Wait."

She pushed forward, against her restraints, and frantically searched the board.

"There might be a...an autopilot landing switch..."

"Where?" Wolfe gritted.

"I don't know—look for it!" she urged.

The ship began to rattle—and list dangerously to the left.

"There?" Wolfe pointed to a blue button in the middle of the console.

"Yes!" Kestrel cried. "Yes, yes!" she reached forward and pressed it hard.

"*Engage autopilot landing?*" the masculine computer asked.

"*Emergency* autopilot landing," Kestrel emphasized.

"*Understood. The autopilot has engaged,*" the computer said. The controls instantly pulled out of Kestrel's hands and moved on their own.

"*However,*" the computer went on. "*With a missing port engine, possibility of ejection is sixty percent.*"

"Ejection?" Wolfe repeated.

"Understood," Kestrel answered the computer, then leaned back and clenched down on her own armrests.

The ship's flight smoothed, tilting to begin a gradual arc. But Kestrel felt the port side shivering, as if it might shear off at any moment...

The wisps outside the spacescreen gathered body, until they became billowing fog that obscured the entire spacescreen. Kestrel squeezed her eyes shut and pushed her feet down on the floor with all her strength. Her heart pounded erratically, but she couldn't hear it over the roar of metallic friction vibrating through the whole cabin.

G-force crushed her chest. The rattling worsened to a cacophony, like clattering pots and pans...

A strong hand found hers. Fingers wound through hers.

Clenched so hard she thought her bones would break.

A siren wailed.

"*Ejection necessary. Brace yourselves.*"

SNAP.

Wolfe's hand ripped out of her grasp.

A *buzz* as a shield snapped up around her—

The roof exploded.

She shot up, out, whirling, spinning...

Light, dark, light, dark—

Green, blue, green, blue—

Falling...

Black. All black.

Silence.

Then nothing more.

NINETEEN

Buzzing.

Distant, persistent buzzing.

A stench. Poisonous smoke. Rough air.

Heat.

A pang, somewhere down low. Knee? No, further down...

Kestrel's eyes snapped open and her first conscious breath threatened to tear her in half.

She blinked several times before her vision cleared. Her hands fluttered.

She lay over on her left side, strapped to the same chair. The side of her face rubbed against red dirt. Clouds of dust rose all around her, the air stank, the restraints cut like sandpaper into her skin...

And her left foot was pinned under the chair.

She bit back a howling scream and grabbed at her knee, trying to pull her leg free of the heavy chair—as slithering agony clawed its way up her limb. The seat rocked, but though she tugged with everything in her, her restraints pinned her.

Tears leaked out. She bit her cheek, struggling to keep breathing, to think...

She gulped.

Had she heard something? Her skull buzzed so badly...

Her head came up. Her throat closed.

She *had* heard something.

Scrambling. Or—footsteps.

"*Kestrel!*"

"Jack!" she croaked. "Jack, I'm—"

He landed in front of her. He crashed to his knees, the legs of his jeans charred, his gray shirt torn and dirty. Black smears covered his face and arms, but she'd never seen his eyes so bright as when he smiled down at her.

"Hey, Brown Eyes," he said unsteadily. "Hang on, hang on a second—we'll get you out, here…" He fumbled with the right side of the seat…

The restraints snapped loose.

He caught her. Wrapped his arms all around her, keeping her leg from wrenching. Then, he sat back and kicked the chair.

It rolled noisily off her leg. She scrabbled at his shirt and took fistfuls, strangling on a cry but not letting it loose.

"You all right?" he asked, quickly shifting her and helping her sit up.

"I'm…in one piece," she said numbly, holding onto him. "That's good, right?"

"Is your foot broken?"

"Don't know. Never had one," she muttered, her vision fading in and out. "I mean, a broken one…"

"We're too close to the crash," Wolfe said. "Need to get out of the open."

Kestrel couldn't think of any reason for or against that, so she just nodded. Without asking, Wolfe dug underneath her shoulders and knees and hefted her up. Her left arm reflexively circled his neck, her hand gripping his shirt. He clambered to his feet, raising more dust, breathing hard and casting around. He cleared his throat, then faced forward again.

"I'm just gonna pick a direction," he muttered. His strong arms tightened around her, and he started off, limping slightly. Kestrel closed her eyes, pressed her forehead to his throat, and focused on beating back the throbbing pain in her foot.

He trudged over a good stretch of uneven ground, jostling her, and then Kestrel felt the air clear. She opened her eyes.

Short, gnarled, thick-trunked trees crowded around them, their skinny leaves providing a shady canopy. They smelled vaguely like pine, but sweeter. Wolfe's boots crunched through the underbrush. He paused, looked around again, then moved on in a slightly different direction. He kept hiking, saying nothing. Kestrel just held on. And breathed.

She breathed *him*.

Gone was that scent of toxic smoke—tobacco and tar. Now, he smelled like shave cream, and the shampoo in the *Exception*'s showers. A tinge of isopropyl alcohol from the hospital. Spilled ship chemicals from the wreck.

She breathed deeper.

Dirt. Ashes. The beaten leather of that old jacket. And the faint, but unmistakable and familiar scent of gunpowder.

A piercing, penetrating ache wound its way through her chest and slid like poison through all her veins. She tried to hold her breath.

After a long time, a change registered in her consciousness. She lifted her head off his shoulder.

"What's that?"

"Water," he answered. Moments later, they rounded a huge tree and stopped on the bank of a gurgling, stone-bed creek. Beyond it stood a rocky shore, and what looked like a dark canyon wall, with several portions hollowed out by wind long ago. The twisted trees overhung the entire grotto, making it seem like they stood inside a huge green tent.

"Perfect," Wolfe declared, stepped forward and sloshed through the stream. The stones slithered beneath his boots—Kestrel felt his gait slip as he walked. He set her down on the other side on top of a large rock. She winced as he pulled away from her, then he glanced up at her face.

"May I have a look at your foot?"

"Sure," she gritted, gingerly adjusting her position on the rock. He crouched down in the gushing water in front of her, gently took hold of her left foot, unfastened her boot and slowly pulled it off. Kestrel sucked in her breath through her teeth, feeling sick.

"Easy, easy," he soothed, tossing the boot up on her side of the bank.

He peeled off her long sock, then let her heel rest on his knee. Kestrel risked a glance down at her foot. Red, and already swollen. Carefully, Wolfe took both hands and pressed his fingertips to her ankle, feeling along her bones, exploring...

She twitched.

"Right there, huh?" he mused, holding her foot still and feeling around next to her inside ankle bone. The skin tightened around his eyes as he considered.

"Well...It doesn't *feel* broken..."

"Yes, it does," Kestrel muttered.

"I'll bet it does," he acknowledged. "But I think you've just bruised a bone. I hope so."

Kestrel smiled ruefully.

"Now, this water is *very* cold," Wolfe said. "So I'm going to lower your foot down into it and let it soak, okay? It'll keep the swelling down."

"Okay."

"Okay, here goes." Wolfe scooted back, sloshing, and eased her foot down into the water. Kestrel's eyes went wide.

"It's *freezing,*" she whispered.

"I told you," he said, smirking. But he didn't let her foot up, and didn't let go until it was submerged past her ankle.

"Sit here for a second," he instructed, standing up. Water poured off his jeans. "I'm going to go look around up here."

Kestrel gritted her teeth as the icy water flowed over her foot, adding needling surface pain to the much deeper, sharper sensation inside.

In the back of her hearing, Wolfe clattered around in the rocks, occasionally talking to himself, or clearing his throat...

The water began to numb her whole foot. Which made her want to scream—until it abruptly faded to nothing. She glanced up, past the canopy of leaves.

The sky had gotten darker.

She shivered—then shivered harder. She hugged herself.

Two sharp *snaps* brought her head around. Wolfe strode back toward her, holding two broken sticks in his hand.

"These ought to work for a splint..." he said, stepping into the water again.

"No, no, no," Kestrel held up a hand, then pulled her foot out of the water and scooted around to face him on the bank. "Don't get back into that water. It's too cold."

"Thanks," he said, then knelt down in front of her again. "Mind if I use your sock?"

"Go ahead."

He set the sticks down, picked up her sock and tore it lengthwise. He snatched the sticks up again, holding the pieces of sock in his teeth.

"I need you..." he said through the strips. "...to hold these on either side of your ankle." He pressed the sticks to her leg. Kestrel bent forward and took hold of them. He took one of the sock pieces from his teeth and started wrapping it around and around her foot, then back around her ankle, then over the top, then around and around the sticks. He secured one end, then tied the loose end to the next strip. He wound that around the sticks, synching it firmly, then tied it down. It still hurt. A lot. But Kestrel ignored it.

"What now?" she asked as Wolfe sat back on his heels.

"First rule of survival," he said, wiping off his hands on his shirt. "Find

195

water. We've done a good job of that—so the next things are shelter, warmth, food."

"Any ideas?" Kestrel asked, shifting her weight since she couldn't tug on the splint. He glanced back over his shoulder.

"There's a little hollow up there," he said. "I'll carry you—"

"No."

He stopped. Studied her face.

"I'm fine," she insisted. "I can make it."

He hesitated, then nodded.

"Okay. It's right up here."

He got to his feet, then held out his left hand to her.

Her heart contracted.

She ignored his hand, pushed off of the rock, and hopped up on her right foot.

"I've had a sprain before," she said. "This isn't a big deal."

He watched her, confused. Then, he swallowed and ducked his head.

"Right. Um...It's just up here."

He walked slowly beside her as she hopped forward, determined not to reach out to him, to touch him at all. She caught hold of some rough, tall rocks and pushed herself up the slight hill, to a flatter place beneath an overhang. Panting, she stopped at the edge of it, assessing the partial cave in front of them.

"Okay," she sighed, more to herself than anyone, hopped forward, turned and eased down onto the dirt, then leaned back against the rock wall. Carefully, she stretched her left leg out in front of her, then forced herself to begin breathing evenly.

Wolfe stood in front of her, watching her movements.

"So," Kestrel managed, keeping her head down. "We've got water and shelter. Warmth is the next part, right?"

He cleared his throat.

"Right. I'll go look for some kindling."

He turned and started back down, toward the trees. Kestrel watched him go, grinding her teeth, her forehead tensing. She laid her head back against the rock and closed her eyes.

Kestrel stared absently into the soft, bright flickering of the open flames. The sky had darkened all around them, and the forest lay hushed, black and still.

A while ago, Wolfe had returned with kindling, and he had started a fire by briskly rubbing a stick against the crackling leaves and grass. He had quickly built it up until it lived on its own. Now, it cast a warm blanket of light over the ground around it, and scattered all manner of shadows onto the roof of the cave. Each time Kestrel breathed, the scent of earth, ash, must and pine flooded her. She held her arms around herself, trying to keep the cold from the stone at her back from seeping into the rest of her.

On the other side of the fire, Wolfe moved—tossed a bit of bark into the fire. It snapped.

"Hope one of those snares catches soon," he commented. "It's past time for supper."

Kestrel almost smiled, studying the way the leaves curled up and withered in the wake of the flames.

"Are you cold?" he asked. She shrugged one shoulder.

"A little."

He paused.

"I wish I could give you something to make you warmer."

Kestrel took a painful breath.

"You did."

He didn't answer. She looked up at him. He was already watching her, his brows slightly drawn together. The flamelight flickered in his stunning eyes, casting the edges and surfaces of his face in golden contrast. And all at once, she *couldn't* look away.

"So..." she said again. "When you go home...What will you do?"

He blinked.

"When I...When I go home? You mean if we find Jakiv and—"

"Yes," she nodded. He regarded her seriously.

"You still think we will?"

"We're not dead yet," Kestrel reminded him. He smiled ruefully.

"That's true. Well, I..." he sat up and took a thoughtful breath. "I always wanted to be a cattle rancher. I enjoyed the east coast and the country there, and also Missouri, but there's no room for cattle. I also enjoyed riding full-out in a western saddle, and there's no room for that, either." He smiled again, to himself. "I wanted to...To go on adventures, find things nobody else had, build in places nobody'd even thought of yet. Try dozens of new things, see people no white man would see if he just stayed tucked away in some comfortable town someplace." He picked up a stick and scraped the ground by the fire, then stuck the end into the flames. "Not sure I'm really in the right frame of mind for that, anymore," he murmured. He canted his head, watching the stick. "I dunno, I think I'll...I'll build a bigger house this time. Or maybe...Maybe go back home. To my parents' house. See if it's still there. I never went back after they died. I could always rebuild it. It's a big white house, big front porch, lots of land. Could settle down. Breathe for a while." He fell silent, still prodding the edges of the fire. Kestrel swallowed hard.

"You think Adelaide will like that?"

He suddenly frowned, and met her eyes.

"Adelaide?" He stopped, then gathered himself. "I haven't really...Well, I guess when I talk to her... She'll understand. I mean, she wanted to see the West, too—see new things. But after...When I tell her what happened..." He watched the fire.

"Do you look the same?" Kestrel asked.

His head came up again.

"What?"

"I mean," she amended. "Apart from the...the tattoos. And the new scars and everything..."

He stared at her. Then, he shifted and tossed the stick in the flames.

"Sure," he assured her. "I do. I mean, my hair was a little lighter, I think. From being out in the sun. And...Right, the tattoos. And scars." He trailed off.

"And you've probably picked up a little colorful language she's never heard," Kestrel remarked lightly. Wolfe laughed, and met her eyes. She gave him a quick smile back—and it broke. She lowered her head. His laugh stopped in his throat, and she heard him swallow.

"What about you?" Wolfe asked, his voice rough. "What are you going to do? Once you get your family home, I mean."

Kestrel shrugged again.

"Try and find a job," she answered, resting her hands in her lap and rubbing her fingers together. "I was an intern at a museum, but they didn't hire me, and now the shop in the KCSP is gone, so..." She forced another smile at him—but he didn't answer it.

"I'll find something to do," she whispered, looking back down at her hands.

"Well, you might...Might meet somebody," Wolfe ventured. "Get married. Have a few kids—"

"No," Kestrel shook her head, squeezing her hands hard. "No, not my speed."

She sensed his startlement. She shook her head again.

"That just means a lot of...A lot of work and commitment and time. Taking care of somebody." It was getting harder to breathe, harder to think. "I'll get a career, maybe start my own business. I'll rent an apartment in the city and live by myself—it's pretty nice. Don't have to clean up if you don't want to—nobody to impress. Get to come in after work, don't have to talk to anybody, it's quiet..." She couldn't summon much volume. "It's not so bad."

She wiped her eyes, sucked in a bracing breath and heaved it out, then nodded firmly at the fire.

"Maybe I'll get a dog," she whispered. "I've always wanted a dog."

They both fell silent for a long time. A soft wind disturbed the very tops of the trees, and flitted through the tips of the flames.

"Kestrel."

She didn't look up—she didn't dare. But painful thrills shot all through her. She clamped her hands together.

"I haven't told you," he began, his voice low and careful. "How grateful I am to you. You've been so much of a help to me, all along the way. You helped get me to Conrad, through the spaceport, onto the ship—you got me fed and kept me from going crazy when I couldn't sleep at night," he chuckled softly. "You kept me from having to start all over again—and you saved my life. And I should have said thank you before and I didn't."

"Yes you did," Kestrel murmured. "In the room. Before security took you."

"No, I didn't," he said. "Not really."

Kestrel didn't say anything.

He hesitated.

"Kestrel," he said again.

His deep voice pulled at the center of her chest. She finally lifted her gaze to his. His eyes grew bright, earnest.

"There's something..." he began. He stopped, gathered himself. "I mean, when I was in the hospital, getting that treatment...And then you came and you stayed with me, I..." He stopped again, glanced up, then over his shoulder, as if searching. He turned back to her, but watched the fire. "This is stupid, but something..." He halted, and his hand moved toward his heart. Then it closed, and rested on his knee.

Kestrel's attention sharpened. She held her breath.

He looked at her.

Her heart suspended.

Snap.

Both of them jumped. He turned around, glancing into the black forest.

"That's one of my snares," he grunted, getting up. He halfway turned to her. "Hang on a minute. I'll be right back."

"Okay," Kestrel answered, her heartbeat pounding. He stepped down the little hill, and vanished in the darkness. She listened, hearing him pick his way through the scrub, until the sounds of his footsteps faded away.

Her ankle throbbed more with every pulse. She gritted her teeth against it, trying to concentrate on the movements of the dying flames. Wolfe had been gone for a while—she had no way of knowing how long. She wondered if he'd caught anything. Wondered what he'd been about to say...

A soft sound. Almost a footfall.

A shadow.

Chills raced down her spine. She sat up...

And a man slipped out of the dark.

He wore all black, a tight hood, a vox-box over his mouth, and night-vision goggles that flashed green in the firelight.

Kestrel's blood froze.

He looked just like one of the men who had broken into her house and kidnapped her family.

"Kestrel Evans," he said, his voice monotone and mechanical.

"Who are you?" she demanded.

"We've come to arrest Lieutenant Jack Wolfe," he answered instead. "Please direct us to his location."

Kestrel gritted her teeth. He'd said "we" and "us." Which meant there were more of them all around her—she just couldn't see them.

"He's dead," Kestrel told him. "Died in the crash."

"Are we supposed to believe that you built that splint and this fire yourself?" he countered. Her eyes flashed.

"That's a fairly sexist comment," she growled.

"Tell us where he is."

"I did," Kestrel shot back. "The wreckage is back there—go look for yourself."

"We did," he said. "We found no bodies."

"It isn't my fault you're no good at finding things," Kestrel lifted her chin. "You still haven't told me who you are."

"That isn't my place."

Her eyes narrowed.

"Whose place is it?"

He glanced off, then motioned.

Kestrel stiffened—

A sharp pain darted into her right arm. She yelped and slapped a hand to it—

Then slumped onto her side as everything went dark.

TWENTY

When she breathed, it felt like her ribs were made of stone. Her whole body seemed heavy. Sluggishly, she opened her eyes.

Bright, blurry white lights. She groaned. Tried to shift her sore right arm...

"Oh, oh, easy now..." warned a soft British voice. She blinked several times, then turned her head and forced her vision to focus. A hand came down gently on hers—a hand she had felt before. And she looked up into a blonde haired, blue-eyed, *familiar* face.

"Dr. Anthony?" Kestrel managed.

"How are you feeling?" he asked, studying her. She thought for a moment—then sat up.

"Wait, wait, you'll lose consciousness." He took her shoulders and pushed her back down—but she had enough time to notice that she wore both shoes again.

"My ankle doesn't hurt!" she realized. He smiled.

"The wonders of modern medicine," he said, patting her arm. She glanced around the huge room.

All metal. Tall, vast, and utilitarian. Like a warehouse. Filled with rows of gleaming, blinking machines, large and small. It smelled like cleaning chemicals. She lay on a gurney, firm but not uncomfortable, surrounded by a makeshift medical station.

"Where am I?" she wondered as Dr. Anthony took a couple steps back and sat down on a stool facing her.

"A science base on the surface of Alpha," he answered, lacing his fingers. His white lab coat seemed to glow in this light. She frowned at him.

"Wait," she said. "Why are *you* here? I thought you were the ship's surgeon on the *Exception.*"

"That's the truth," he nodded. "I never lie—a man in my business can't afford to clutter his brain with deceptions and half-truths he has to remember later." He looked at her. "Although, I can't say *you've* been entirely honest with *me*. Have you, Kestrel Evans?"

Kestrel's jaw tightened. He held her gaze.

"My name is Doctor William Anthony Jakiv."

All the heat drained out of Kestrel's face.

"I actually *own* the hospital on board the *Exception*," he went on casually. "As well as several other hospitals on other ships. But this is my home base, you would say." He looked all around. "My fortress. My workbench. My gallery." He smiled again as he addressed her. "And you are a long way from home, are you not?"

Kestrel didn't answer. Her limbs still felt leaden. He cocked his head.

"You're from the Kansas side of Kansas City, Missouri," he told her. "You were passed up for a job at the Museum of Literature Antiquities, and so you worked at the supply shop in the KCSP until it had the misfortune to cross paths with a rather valuable time machine." He spoke slowly, deliberately. "Shortly after which, your family went mysteriously missing in the dead of night."

"It's not a mystery to me," Kestrel gritted. He chuckled.

"No, I'd imagine it's not," he said. "But they're all fine—your mother, father, Marcus and Aidus. They're all here with me. And you can see them."

Kestrel blinked.

"What?"

"You can see them, silly girl," he told her, standing up. "I'll even tell you where they are. They're on level two, room ten, of this very station." He pointed at the ground, then raised his eyebrows. "All you have to do is give me Lieutenant Jack Wolfe."

"I'm not helping *you*," Kestrel snarled.

"Oh, don't worry about it," he said lightly. "You already have."

P

Kestrel walked down a metal-floored aisle between rows of machinery preceded and followed by an armed man wearing black. Her body felt much lighter now, back to normal—except for the occasional chill that raced down to her fingers. Ahead of the guard in front of her walked William Jakiv, purposeful and silent. Once in a while, he glanced to either side of him, his delicate brow furrowed. Kestrel closed her hands into fists.

Finally, they turned a corner...

And passed three tall, cylindrical machines.

Kestrel's steps faltered.

Identical machines.

And all of them just like the one that had exploded in her shop at the spaceport.

The guard behind her pushed her forward. Her thoughts jolted. Jakiv stopped next to a small, circular platform and turned toward her.

"Up here, please." He gestured to it. Kestrel stopped, setting her jaw.

The guard behind her jabbed her with his gun.

She bit her cheek, then stepped up onto the platform. Her footsteps rang. She winced.

The space underneath this platform was hollow.

She carefully turned around, back toward Jakiv...

Snap.

Her feet froze. She gasped and looked down—

A green forcefield enveloped each foot. She tried to lift her right one—it wouldn't budge. Like it had been dried in cement.

Her throat closed.

"Don't mind that," Jakiv soothed, facing the same way she did, toward a door just twenty meters away. He picked up a handheld device. "That's just to keep you out of the way for a moment." He paused, and looked back at her. "Oh, and—one word out of you, and I'll kill him."

Kestrel choked, watching the two guards pass behind her and stand at the ready.

"Sir," a voice emitted from a Grammcom lying on Jakiv's table.

"Yes, Barrymore?" Jakiv asked.

"We have an intruder on level one."

"Excellent," Jakiv said. "He's right on time. Keep me updated."

"Yes, sir."

Jakiv punched three buttons on his handheld device, then waved it past the back of his head. He punched another three buttons, then waved it by his head again. He repeated this process three more times. Then, he set the device down on the table, brushed back his lab coat and put his hands in his trousers pockets.

"Sir, he is attempting to penetrate the security checkpoint," the voice over the Grammcom said again.

"Quicker than I expected," Jakiv remarked. "Give him a little trouble, then let him through."

"Acknowledged."

Kestrel stared at Jakiv. Questions hammered the front of her mind, but she stamped them down, stiffening.

"He's through," came the guard's voice. "He's taken a gun."

"Has he killed anyone?" Jakiv wondered.

"No, sir," came the answer. "But he's stunned three of us."

"Hm." Jakiv paused a moment, then spoke up. "Make sure he finds his way in here."

"Yes, sir."

Kestrel's heartbeat took off, shuddering against her breastbone. She battled to regulate her breath, to keep from shaking...

"Sir, he is fifty meters from your door."

"We're ready in here," Jakiv replied. "Let him come in."

Kestrel's fists quivered.

Jakiv lowered his head, staring at the door—and went completely still.

Sparks shot from the doorframe.

The door groaned and gapped open.

A left hand shot through, shoved the door out of the way—

Jack Wolfe charged through, his broad chest heaving, his skin and clothes dirty and burnt. His boots thundered on the metal flooring as his long strides closed the distance in a matter of seconds. A heavy pistol clicked in his scuffed hand as he raised it, and aimed right at William Jakiv.

"You let her go, Doc," Wolfe snarled, his eyes blazing as he drew to a halt. "Or God help me, I will kill you."

"I appreciate your anxiety," Jakiv replied, standing just as he was. "You've just had men shooting at you, after all."

Wolfe hefted his gun, his mouth hardening. Jakiv raised his eyebrows.

"I know what you're thinking," he halfway smiled. "You're thinking, 'I'm just going to blast this poor devil through the brains and have done with it.' But if that *is* your decision, I feel obligated to warn you about the consequences."

Wolfe's eyes narrowed. Jakiv went on.

"You see, I have several sensors implanted in the back of my head," he lifted his hand out of his pocket and pointed at his skull. "I can program them at will. At the moment, if something should happen to my vital signs—any penetration of any foreign object or energy into any part of my body—the door underneath your friend Miss Evans here will open up." Jakiv glanced over at her, and lifted an eyebrow. "And I am actually not sure what it opens up *into*. I believe it may be a vent into an elevator shaft we haven't finished. Whatever it is, it's a long drop." He faced Wolfe again. "Also, all the security in the base will be alerted—and *those* machines next to you will all violently self-destruct."

Wolfe's eyes reflexively followed where Jakiv pointed—

And he caught sight of the cylindrical machines.

He stared at them, shifting his weight, flexing his fingers on his uplifted gun.

He swallowed.

"I see you recognize them," Jakiv noted. "Perhaps now we can talk. Like *rational* men. Not the way we spoke when we first met."

Wolfe's head came around. Kestrel flooded with confusion.

Wolfe's jaw clenched.

"You're Jakiv," he hissed. "You're William Jakiv."

"It's a pleasure, Lieutenant," Jakiv inclined his head, then put a hand to his heart. "An honor, truthfully. I've never been in the presence of such a distinguished and selfless hero in my life." Jakiv regarded him openly, his blue eyes bright. "A Medal of Honor recipient in the American Civil War, a Purple Heart recipient in the Vietnam police action." He shook his head. "As I said—I am honored."

Wolfe kept his gun pointed where it was.

"What do you want from me?" he asked roughly.

"I want what you want," Jakiv answered. "To send you back to your wife."

Kestrel's fists clenched harder. Wolfe said nothing—he waited.

"I know exactly what happened," Jakiv went on, softly holding Wolfe's gaze. "I was there. I was one of the landing party when we arrived at your homestead. It was our first Time expedition—the very first leap into my great exploration: The Paradox Initiative." The words lifted into the air as he spoke them—and he raised his chin as his expression sparked. "The plan to insert new threads into the great weaving that is Time." The spark faded, replaced by sadness. "We had no idea we would intrude upon your settlement," he murmured earnestly. "You must believe me. We thought we would be landing somewhere in the middle of the vast and untamed West. Not your backyard."

"But you did," Wolfe shot back.

"I know," Jakiv nodded. "And there was a misunderstanding, and a terrible accident—"

"It wasn't an accident," Wolfe cut in. "Your man deliberately fired on my house—"

"After you'd shot and killed several others," Jakiv finished sharply. "More lives were lost than just your wife's—remember that."

Wolfe's expression snarled and his grip tightened on his gun.

"I'm not here to squabble over details—details that are burned into *both* our memories," Jakiv said, his voice quieting again. "All I ask is that you listen to me for a moment, and consider what I propose."

Wolfe fell silent—then glanced at Kestrel.

Her heart skipped a beat.

"Never fear," Jakiv soothed. "As long as I'm alive, she'll stay where she is."

Wolfe held her gaze for a moment longer, then returned his attention to Jakiv.

"Talk fast."

"Very well," Jakiv nodded—but when he spoke, he did so calmly. Deliberately. "Several years ago, when I was studying molecular biology and genetics, I met and fell in love with a young woman named Marianne. She illuminated my mind, my soul—she inspired me to achieve great things." Jakiv's slight smile faded. "Not three years after we were married, Marianne was diagnosed with a rare, fatal disease." He lifted his eyebrows. "You can imagine my instant desperation."

Wolfe's gaze flickered. Kestrel honed in on Jakiv's every word.

"I researched the disease thoroughly, and discovered that the use of human cloning would provide a cure." Jakiv leaned back against the table, and turned his attention to the floor. "I brought to bear every ounce of influence and money and power I could muster—but nothing I did or said could convince the government to legalize human cloning for medical purposes. Then, when I realized I was failing in every *legal* arena, I attempted *illegal* methods—but I had exhausted my funds. I failed." He paused. He rubbed his fingers together. "She died in my arms."

Wolfe's gun faltered.

Kestrel shivered.

"And the last thing I said to her," Jakiv murmured. "Was a vow to make this right." He lifted his head. Met Wolfe's eyes. "And so I began a new avenue of study. I proposed plans for hospitals and health centers on interstellar cruisers, and began an entire chain. These provided the funding and clout I needed to buy a portion of the Gain Station, and build this laboratory here. And I began, quietly at first, then with more momentum, to explore the possibilities of Time Travel."

Wolfe's eyes narrowed to slits. Jakiv held up a finger.

"Again, I know what you're thinking," he said. "Why go back in time just to watch my wife die all over again? And you're right—that would be useless. And it would also be useless to the others all over the galaxy dying from this disease. So *this* is where *you* come in, John Angus Wolfe."

"What do you mean?" Wolfe demanded. Jakiv's aspect hardened.

"An organization called Project Unfettered, an anti-human-trafficking movement, proved to be a massive obstacle to my efforts in saving my wife," he said. "It has adopted the anti-cloning position, and it receives much of its funding from a vast business empire owned by a young man named Ian Conrad."

Kestrel started. Ian Conrad—the man who had pulled strings to get them on board the *Exception*—

"After my debacle with you, I decided a more subtle approach would be wise," Jakiv continued. "One that could not be traced. So I sent men back in time to kill one of Ethan Conrad's prominent ancestors. Kill the ancestor, and you eliminate the problem descendant." He paused. A gleam entered his eye. "And this is when I uncovered an important piece in the ever-unfolding puzzle: Time is not a single line. And time-*travel* is *not* hopping back and forth along that single line, but rather it is a weaving of oneself back and forth along *several* lines, creating a new pattern of explored possibility. Therefore, alternate timelines are created, and some can be tied off and finished and made inaccessible by other weavers as the pattern continues to be created. Loops can be formed, overlaps and crossings. And when my missing time machine's thread and yours encountered each other, your thread pulled free, and the machine wove you into various pieces of the grand weaving as it automatically brought itself back to its original time—inserting your brilliant thread into some of the darkest patterns of history." Jakiv fell silent a moment. "And so, when I set out to kill Conrad's ancestor, your thread had already twined around his. The dark thread that followed Ian Conrad all the way back to his grandfather *without* your influence had been tied off and made untouchable to me—I couldn't weave with it anymore," Jakiv explained, gesturing carefully. "If I had *not* accidentally given you the means to time travel in the first place, I could have woven my own thread around Conrad's and killed him without interference. But the bright thread was already there." Jakiv smiled. "And so he lived."

"You tried to have me killed," Wolfe accused. Jakiv nodded.

"Yes, at first," he acknowledged, shrugging. "I'll admit that I panicked. I thought you would damage space-time beyond repair. That was before I truly understood the principle I have just explained to you."

"What does this have to do with me *now?*" Wolfe pressed.

"When you survived the hit, I realized I was not dealing with an ordinary man," Jakiv said. "And the more I found out about you, the more I realized that *you* were the warrior I wanted—*needed*— to complete the Initiative."

"And what's that?" Wolfe asked.

Jakiv smiled.

Kestrel's blood congealed.

"Here is my proposal," Jakiv lay his palms open. "There is a man in the senate at this moment named Jason Talbott. He is fifty-five years old. When he entered law school at age nineteen, he began building an army of supporters that never stopped growing. He has been the driving force behind all anti-cloning legislation, and he blocks it to this day. Just five years ago, months before Marianne contracted the disease, Talbott joined with Ian Conrad's Project Unfettered and his power doubled. The Medicinal Cloning Movement has no chance at success with him in power."

"What do you want me to do?" Wolfe asked. Jakiv regarded him plainly.

"I want you to kill him."

Wolfe's breathing unsteadied.

"I'll send you back to the night before he went to law school," Jakiv explained. "He will be eighteen—a legal man. You needn't shoot or stab him in the back. You may turn him around, let him see you. Tell him what you're doing. You may even give him a weapon if it appeals more to your sense of honor. I don't care—as long as you succeed." His voice grew hard. "And you *must* succeed. If Jason Talbott dies before he even enters school, his anti-cloning army shan't rally. It shan't *exist*. And Conrad's underground resistance will not be able to gain enough influence in the government to stop the Medical Cloning Movement—not without exposing all of their own illegal activities. Human cloning *will* pull through without Jason Talbott. I am absolutely confident of that."

"You want me to kill a boy," Wolfe clarified. "Before he's even a threat to you or anyone else."

"Exactly," Jakiv nodded. "And I will hold Miss Evans and her family here as collateral while you're busy. Once you're finished, I will have the machine programmed to travel back to my home, at this very time." He pointed at the ground. "You will enter it and find me. I am recording this conversation, and it is transferring into the memory banks of one of these machines as we speak. You will show me that recording, and if my wife is alive and well, then we shall have an accord. Then, I will send you back on a one-way journey to perhaps three or four hours *before* our machines ever arrived on your homestead." Jakiv's voice gained warmth—he almost smiled. "You will find your wife *alive*. Your livestock, your possessions intact." He gestured animatedly. "And in order to succeed completely, you must find yourself—your *former*—self, what I call your Foundation Existence, and kill him."

Wolfe stared at him.

"What?"

"That particular step is *absolutely* necessary," Jakiv assured him. "Unless you simply wish to divert him and your wife from the impending danger—in which case, afterward, you would have to give up your wife to your former self, or *share* her with him. And I can assure you, your Foundation Existence is an entirely different man from the man you are now, and *neither* of you will be interested in that arrangement. You would end up forcing your wife to choose between you."

Kestrel watched Wolfe go pale.

"That's what I assumed," Jakiv nodded. "You will probably want to shoot him in the back, from a great distance, if you can. You will not want to fight him hand-to-hand. He may kill *you* instead. Once you've shot him, hide his body. Take your wife and your animals away from that place for a while. The machine will deactivate on its own. When you're able to come back to that place, dismantle the machine and smelt it, so it will not cause you any problems in the future." Jakiv grinned. "Once you have done that, and prevented your Foundation Existence's first time travel, you will have made a loop in time's weaving, and you will tie back into your original thread. You will live in the thread you were meant to live in, you will have your land and your house and your dreams back. You will have the woman you love back. And I will have *mine* back. Or rather..." His voice quieted. "Neither of us will have lost them at all."

Wolfe stayed silent for a very long time. Kestrel couldn't move, couldn't breathe.

"What about..." Wolfe began, his voice unsteady. "What about Kestrel?"

Jakiv glanced at her.

"This little thing?" He turned back to Wolfe. "If you do everything I said, you will create an entirely new thread: one in which cloning is legal so my wife will live, but your initial time travel never occurs. Miss Evans will go on with her life as it would have been without your intrusion. She'll never know you at all."

A chasm opened in Kestrel's heart.

Wolfe met her eyes.

His gun hand drifted down. He drew in a long, strained breath, and considered Jakiv.

"Let her go," he said. "Then we can talk."

"I'm afraid not," Jakiv answered regretfully. "She'll stay exactly where she is until the machine's door closes behind you." He halfway smiled. "It's safer for her, you know."

Kestrel fought to twist her foot—but it didn't budge. Wolfe never shifted his attention from Jakiv.

"How am I supposed to know if you're telling the truth about all this?" Wolfe asked.

Jakiv held out his hands.

"Why would I lie?" he asked, then pointed to himself. "I *need* you, Wolfe. I drove you *to* me. I caused the self-destruction of your time machine so you couldn't get away from me. I sent my men to Miss Evans' house, knowing you had tracked her down, *knowing* that if I took her parents you would ally yourself with her and therefore have help getting to me. And I sent those men after you in the tunnels to gauge you, to see if your skills were still up to par— and they were!

"You're the reason I boarded the *Exception*—I knew that, because of the outlawed weapons discharged on your house, that you'd contract Viridi Carcinoma, and I refused to let you die of that. I paid for all your treatment, oversaw your progress myself. And I tell you all this now because no one else is so suited to be my soldier through time. I *cannot* risk sending you off without your knowing what will and will not happen, and what *has* happened. It would be ridiculously dangerous." He leveled a look at Wolfe. "I am telling the truth, Lieutenant. I am too desperate and too certain to do anything else."

"So the guys I saved in 'Nam," Wolfe said slowly. "They'll die. Because I won't be there."

"In the new timeline, yes," Jakiv confirmed.

"And I...I helped *start* Project Unfettered," Wolfe said. "That won't even exist."

Jakiv didn't answer, but he arched an eyebrow and glanced down. Wolfe's left hand closed to a fist.

"And Kestrel..."

Hot tears trailed down Kestrel's cheeks.

"It won't *matter*," Jakiv insisted, recapturing Wolfe's attention. "You will be long dead before Vietnam or cloning or any of that ever occurs to anyone. It will be distant and irrelevant to you. Moving pictures will be ridiculous, flight will be madness and spacetravel will be fantasy. And you can live the life you were *meant* to live. Simple. Quiet. Finally at peace." Jakiv searched him. "Don't you *want* that?"

Wolfe heaved a deep, shaking sigh, and lowered his gun all the way. He stared at Jakiv a moment, his eyebrows drawn together. Then, he turned toward the Time Machines.

Jakiv stood away from the table, intent on Wolfe.

"Just do as I ask," he murmured, his voice fervent and fiery. "And you can fix *everything*. You can right the terrible wrong turn we've *both* taken." He took a small step closer. "You've already done so much, *sacrificed* so very much, to get back to your home. And you are mere inches away from it, Jack. *Inches.*" He edged even nearer. "Just one more detour. One more simple task—and it will all be over." His voice deepened with certainty. "I know your heart, Jack. I know what you're willing to do to *finally* get what you want—what you deserve. In fact...you've already made up your mind. Am I right?"

Jakiv held out his right hand to Wolfe.

Wolfe sighed again—as if a needle were being pushed through his flesh. His brow twisted.

Kestrel's chest hollowed out.

Wolfe stared at the machine before him for a long, breathless moment.

"Yes," he finally whispered. "I have."

And he turned, lifted his handgun, sighted—

And shot Jakiv through the head.

TWENTY-ONE

Kestrel had no time to register.

Jakiv toppled—

The floor beneath her feet disappeared.

She plunged.

Blackness swallowed her.

No breath made it past her throat to scream. She flailed, reaching up, to the sides—

Her hands hit metal. Screeched as her skin slapped the smooth surface. Wind rushed through her hair and clothes.

She sensed the tube curve—

Her knees banged into the bend, then her hands, elbows and head.

She skidded downward, on a steep, slick slide. She kicked out, trying to slow down—

Glimpsed a flash of light ahead...

The tube forked!

She twisted, shoving to keep from crashing into the center—

She knocked most of her body out of the way—the side of her head clipped it—

She yelped. Pain seared through her skull.

Kept sliding, gathering speed...

She shook her head, trying to clear it...

She rolled over, sliding on her stomach, and made herself stretch her arms out in front of her...

The slide leveled out.

Her feet slammed into a sheet of metal—

Broke through it.

Her lower half shot out into abyss.

She dug her fingers into the slide—

Flew out over *nothingness*—

Her fingers caught a lip. Jerked her to a halt in mid air.

Her body *fell*...

Swung wildly forward. She squeezed the lip with all her might...

Wrestled control of her momentum...

And dangled by her fingertips over a limitless void.

"*Gah!*"

Her sharp gasp echoed tenfold. She bared her teeth as she tipped her head forward to see down.

The vent she had kicked loose fluttered like a leaf as it tumbled into the depths of a bottomless circular shaft. A line of square blue lights on the wall behind her marked the descent.

The muscles in her arms screamed. She grunted again, firming her hold—the sound hissed like a whisper in a cathedral. She glanced up.

The smaller shaft she had come out of wasn't very big—maybe four feet by four feet. If she could heave herself back up into it, she'd have to crawl back up the vent...But she remembered how steeply she had fallen. And without tools of any kind...

Her chest constricted and she gasped. It would be better than falling, though—

She looked down again.

One of those blue lights glowed right in front of her.

And beneath it stood a door-shaped indentation.

"I believe it may be a vent into an elevator shaft we haven't finished. Whatever it is, it's a long drop..."

Kestrel braced herself, then painfully slid her hands toward the right, until she met the edge of the vent. She eyed the side of the door—found the emergency button.

She swung her legs back, then forward—

Stretched her right foot toward the button—

Missed.

Swung back...

Her sweaty fingers slipped...

She kicked the button.

It lit up.

She swung backward, her hands nearly coming loose...

The door slid open.

She threw her lower body forward—

Let go.

She flew through the open door into a white hallway—

Crashed all over the floor and rolled.

Panting, icy shivers racing all over her skin, she fought a wave of faintness and clambered to her feet. She brushed a strand of hair out of her face and took a look around.

A long, all-white hallway. Like a hospital. It smelled like antiseptic, too.

And the noise of running footsteps battered all up and down the corridor.

Kestrel glanced to her left to see a dozen people, all dressed in lab coats like Dr. Jakiv, carrying tablets and racing pell-mell back and forth, in and out of the rooms, shouting to each other. She hesitated, listening.

"I don't know—something's combusted in the main lab—" one yelled.

"Combusted?" a woman cried, spilling her coffee.

"Exploded, okay? Didn't you hear that boom?"

"I thought it was in one of the test tanks—"

"No, it's in the *main* lab! Where Dr. Jakiv is!"

"What's the order?"

"Evacuate!" called an older man with a beard as he hurried away. "Erase the memory banks and sound the alarm! Seal all the toxic containment chambers and open all the doors! We don't want anybody to get trapped down here!"

"Yes, sir!" a younger man said, and darted off.

Moments later, red lights flashed on everywhere and a repeating ascending howl reverberated through the halls. The next instant, every single door sprang open, and more people poured out from them, wide-eyed, toting small machines and dragging wires—none of them even looked at Kestrel.

Her heartbeat stuttered.

An explosion right where *Jakiv* was...?

BOOM.

The walls rattled. Beakers in the neighboring rooms rattled. The scientists shrieked and barked more orders. And they fled.

Her legs going weak, Kestrel turned and hurried down the hallway, fighting not to call out...

She skidded to a stop. Frowned at the sign above a doorway.

LEVEL TWO
GENETICS

Her attention darted to the door next to it. It read "2."

"Level two, room ten," Kestrel gasped, suddenly remembering. She broke into a run.

Numbers flashed by on either side, ascending as she went. And then—

"Room ten!" she realized...

And stopped.

Her mother, father and two brothers stood right inside the open doorway.

As if they had just jumped to their feet, but had halted, uncertain, on the threshold. They wore the same clothes she remembered from the last time she'd seen them: casual, loose-fitting, after-work clothes. Her brothers' hair looked unkempt, her dad hadn't shaved, and her mom's hair hung loose.

They stared at her, their eyes wide.

"Mom!" Kestrel yelped, her chest bursting—

And threw herself into her mother's arms.

"Oh, *sweetheart!*" her mom cried as her dad and brothers broke into wild exclamations and crowded desperately in to touch her. "Oh, are you okay?"

For a breathless moment, Kestrel collapsed into her mother's soft, familiar form, submerging in her warmth, the safety of her embrace.

Then, when she drew another breath of that antiseptic scent, Kestrel forced her mind back to reality.

"Yeah, yeah, I'm fine!" Kestrel answered, drawing back and ignoring the tears on her cheeks. She searched their faces—all of their bright eyes. "Are you? Are you guys okay?"

"Are you *sure* you're fine?" her dad fiercely took hold of her shoulders. "Your head is bleeding!"

"Where *were* you?" Marcus demanded.

"How did you find us?" Aidus cut in.

"We have to go," Kestrel drew back out of her dad's strong arms but gripped his shirt sleeve. "There are explosions going on upstairs, people are evacuating—" She swiped her tears away with her sleeve so she could see clearly. "We've got to find Jack—"

"Who's Jack?" her mom asked. Kestrel tugged on her parents, pulling them out of the room.

"He's the one who helped me get here," she explained. "But it was a

217

trap for him—Dr. Jakiv set a trap for *him*, and now I'm afraid he's—"

BOOM.

Kestrel looked up. The light fixtures shivered.

"That sounded close," Aidus muttered. Kestrel turned on her brothers.

"Do you guys know the layout of this place?"

"Yeah, they've walked us back and forth a hundred times," Marcus answered.

"How do we get to the main floor?" Kestrel asked.

Aidus raised his eyebrows.

"You mean where all the *explosions* are coming from?"

"*Yes,*" Kestrel shot back.

"We've been there a few times," her mom said. "When Dr. Jakiv was asking us questions."

"Know the way?" Kestrel wondered.

"I do," Aidus said. "Come on."

And he and Marcus jogged forward, in step. Kestrel and her parents instantly followed.

They darted down a handful of abandoned hallways and around several corners, which made Kestrel's head spin. Then Aidus shoved through a door.

"Figure we'd better not use the lifts!" he said as he began leaping up the winding staircase, his feet pounding. The rest of the family barreled up after him single file, never hesitating, hauling on the railing to help them climb.

They raced upward, occasionally feeling the whole building shudder. Kestrel bit down, battering back any stray thoughts except for *step, step, step, step, step...*

"Main level!" Aidus called down. Kestrel paused, glanced back at her dad who was last, then hurried on up. Aidus flung the door open and leaped out—

Marcus jerked backward, her mom ran into him—

Kestrel slammed into her mother's back.

Aidus swore.

"Don't move."

A different voice.

Kestrel's heart stopped.

She slipped in past her mom, peered over Marcus' shoulder...

Jack Wolfe stood outside the door.

And he held a gun point-blank at the side of Aidus' golden head.

His clothes were torn, part of his hair had burned away, blisters rose on his left forearm, and bright blood trickled down his forehead. He breathed raggedly, his gray eyes vibrant and deadly.

"You work here?" Wolfe growled, his face vicious and terrible.

Aidus twitched. Wolfe pressed the gun into his head.

"There's a shaft that opens up into this level, where the Time Machines are," Wolfe bared his teeth. "But forks midway down. Where does the other pipe lead?"

"Jack?" Kestrel whispered.

Wolfe's head came around.

Kestrel pushed out past Marcus, but gripped her brother's elbow.

Wolfe stared at her.

She stared back.

He transformed.

His gun went slack. His expression sharpened and softened all in the same instant—and his eyes gained a sudden brilliance she'd never seen. His eyebrows pulled together. He opened his mouth and pulled in a breath that seemed to hurt every length of his frame.

Kestrel's heart panged so hard that literal pain shot to the ends of her fingers.

"What is going on?" Marcus hissed.

"This is...This is Jack," Kestrel choked, unable to take her eyes from Wolfe. "Jack, this is my mother and father, and my brothers Marcus and Aidus."

"It's an honor," Wolfe breathed, his gaze flickering, never looking away from her. "Beg your pardon."

BOOM.

The walls shook—Kestrel *saw* it. And the floor vibrated up through her bones.

"We've got to go," her dad decided. "You guys remember where the hangar is?"

"Yes, I do," Marcus nodded, eyeing Wolfe coldly.

"Let's go then," Kestrel's mom urged, grabbing her husband and Aidus with both hands and tugging. Marcus skirted Wolfe, looking him up and down, then hurried on down the corridor. Kestrel stayed where she was, rooted to the floor.

"Kestrel—" Wolfe tried, gulping.

"Wolfe!"

Wolfe spun around—Kestrel's dad motioned to him.

"You've got the gun—we want you in front!" her dad ordered.

"Yes, sir," Wolfe nodded quickly, glanced back at Kestrel, then ran to catch up. Kestrel convinced her legs to move. She began to run, right on her mom and Aidus' heels. All together, they careered through the corridors, never encountering anyone—but the whole place now constantly trembled. As if the ceiling might fall down at any second.

"Right up here!" Marcus called—and Kestrel caught sight of the glowing signs marked "Hangar Bay."

CRASH.

Kestrel tripped, threw her hands out and caught herself on the wall, twisted back to see—

The walls collapsed. Cement and drywall smashed onto the floor. Wires sprang loose, sparks sprayed. The back of the corridor went black.

"Come on!" her mom shouted. Kestrel regained her footing and ran harder, pumping her arms as Marcus and Wolfe led the way. They burst through the wide doorway, gasping and searching.

Dust fell from the high ceiling. Sunlight glared in from the huge open bay off to their right.

Only one ship remained in the entire vast hangar:

A white, streamlined multi-passenger ship unlike any Kestrel had ever seen. It had no markings, no numbers. It was gorgeous and lethal-looking.

"That has to be Jakiv's," she panted.

"Why hasn't *he* left already?" Aidus wanted to know as they trotted toward it.

"He's dead," Kestrel answered.

Up ahead, Wolfe turned, and met her eyes for an instant.

The ceiling cracked.

A thunderous groan traveled through the whole hangar.

"Run!" her dad yelled.

They lunged forward—

Rocks tumbled from overhead and *smashed* all over the paving. Aidus grabbed Kestrel's shirt sleeve and tugged her forward—the six of them bolted toward the ship, Marcus skidded underneath it and slapped the ramp release...

The floor shook. A large piece of air-cooling machinery tumbled from the ceiling and shattered all over the cement, splattering metal and glass.

"Go on!" her mom commanded, and they all charged up the ramp. It started shutting before they all had gotten in—Kestrel's foot almost caught. It slammed shut and sealed.

Her brothers immediately and wordlessly swung through the red interior toward the cockpit. Kestrel followed, her parents and Wolfe on her heels.

Her brothers sat down, Marcus in the pilot's seat, Aidus in the copilot's, and began firing up the engines. They barked information back and forth as they flipped dozens of switches. The console lights flared to life, and the engine beneath them began to hum.

The ceiling outside kept crumbling. Kestrel winced as rocks tumbled down, and dust obscured the view of the bay.

"Can we get shields up yet?" her dad asked, pressing up by her shoulder.

"Yup," Aidus answered, and punched his thumb down on a big red button. "There we go. Up and running."

"Does this ship have weapons?" her mom asked, crowding up next to her dad. "We might have to shoot our way out of here..."

"Yes, actually," Marcus replied. "Here and here. But we're up already—that was quick."

"Go, then," her dad said.

"Rightoh," Marcus gritted, grabbed the controls and fired the thrusters. The ship lifted up as debris showered across the bow.

"Careful..." Kestrel warned, wincing.

"Oh, relax," Marcus retorted. " *We* can actually *fly*, remember."

And the ship shot forward. Kestrel grabbed the back of Marcus' chair to keep from falling into her dad. A rock broke loose in front of them, plummeted—

Missed them by inches.

The ship burst out into the sunlight, screamed over the tops of the trees—

And swooped into a heart-stopping climb.

The gravity machine kicked in.

The g-force eased, and Kestrel stood without having to hold on. The ship leveled out. Marcus turned in his seat and winked at her.

"That's how you do *that*," he said. She made a face at him, reached forward and flicked his ear. He laughed.

"Hey, Kes—we're gonna need our subspace scanners," Aidus interrupted.

"Okay..." Kestrel raised her eyebrows.

"Not sure, but we *might* get shot at out here," Aidus went on. "And right now our scanners are off."

Kestrel's stomach jumped.

"They're probably manual," Marcus assumed. "Back there. Somewhere. Go look and turn them on, will you?"

"Okay," Kestrel said quickly, turned and slipped past her parents and into the tiny corridor.

"Kestrel—"

She jerked to a stop, whirled—

Wolfe stood *right* there, still panting. His eyes captured hers.

Her heart thundered. She smelled him again—earth and gunpowder... She turned away.

"I've got to find the switch for the scanners." She hurried down the little hall toward the cabins, searching the walls...

"Kestrel, I'm sorry," he gasped as he followed her. "I tried to catch you—"

Kestrel found a console. Flipped the door open, scanned the buttons...

"I dove in after you, when everything exploded," he said in a rush. "I almost had you—I felt your hair go through my hand—"

Kestrel's fingertips trailed down the buttons, even as her heart banged against her ribs. She battled to make her eyes focus.

"I hit a fork in the tunnel," he went on, stepping even closer to her. "I fell through the ceiling into one of the hallways. I had no idea where you were, what happened to you—"

Kestrel found the button. Pressed it with all her strength. Slammed the panel shut.

"Found it, the sensors are on—" she gasped, starting back toward the cockpit.

He seized her arm. Hard.

She spun to face him.

His eyes burned.

"Are you okay?"

"Yes," she panted, nodding. "Yes, I'm fine."

He halted. His gray gaze sliced right through her.

And suddenly he grabbed her shoulders and yanked her to him—

And his warm mouth collided with hers.

He slid his hands down and bound his arms around her waist, crushing her to his chest, kissing her lips rapidly, repeatedly, fiery and desperate —

And her hands came up, took fistfuls of his hair, and she kissed him back.

Heat flooded her body. Their mouths moved together in a wild fever—unfamiliar and floundering. He pulled back for an instant—both of them gasped—then he pressed back in, deep and strong, his arms shivering.

Salt on her tongue.

His lips broke from hers. He sucked in a breath. Kestrel's eyes opened—she stared back up at him. His long lashes were wet, as were his cheeks—his eyes vivid as the morning sky. He panted hard, his gaze locking with hers.

His head dropped. Kestrel swallowed, fighting tears of her own. Together they just stood, breathing shakily.

Finally, Wolfe drew himself up. He cleared his throat, let her slide out of his arms, and swiped at his face. He turned away, and stepped back toward the cockpit.

"Let's go home."

The ship didn't even shiver as Marcus touched down in the gleaming, bustling hangar bay of the Darrow Station. Kestrel stood behind her brother as he flipped the switches and started post-flight. She sighed, her whole body aching, and rubbed her eyes.

They'd flown all the rest of the day at top speed, all the while discussing what they ought to do once they got here. Kestrel had explained everything that had happened after their kidnapping: that she'd traveled on the cruiser using a false identity—an identity that, as far as anybody on the *Exception* knew, had crashed and died on Alpha. Therefore, her dad decided that they ought to ditch this ship in the hangar of Darrow and get public transport back to Earth from here, using all their *real* identities. Her mother and brothers had agreed. Her dad could make a few calls, recite a few security codes, and get copies of their ID cards sent to them. Kestrel had found no reason to argue with any of it—it was a relief to just let them handle everything. In fact, the relief of simply hearing their *voices,* seeing their *faces,* being able to *touch* them, often threatened to overwhelm her.

But during all those hours of intense discussion, Wolfe had secluded himself in a rear cabin, and hadn't spoken to her once.

Now, Kestrel straightened as she heard the exit ramp pop open back there. The gears groaned as it lowered to the hangar floor. Her dad and mom crawled up into the cockpit, smiling.

"We're here," her mom said, rubbing Aidus gently on the head. "Want to go get something to eat?"

"I'm starving to death," Aidus commented, sitting back heavily in his chair. "Have we gotten to eat *anything* except that hospital paste for the past two weeks?"

"I'm going to commence blocking these past two weeks from my memory," Marcus answered. "Like they never even happened."

Kestrel felt a sudden twinge in the center of her chest. She glanced at her mom.

"I'd better go get Jack."

Her parents glanced at each other.

"Honey, we've been wondering..." her mom began.

"We wanted to ask you about him," her dad finished. "Who is he? Where did he come from, exactly?"

Her family waited. Kestrel smiled softly.

"It's actually..." she said quietly. "A very good story."

Her parents' eyebrows went up.

"But it's also really long," she added. "And he can probably tell you better than I can."

Still smiling to herself, Kestrel ignored the concern in her mom and dad's eyes, slipped between their shoulders and strode carefully down the very narrow hallway toward the cabins. She passed the first two doors, which stood open, then paused in front of the third, which was closed. She pressed the buzzer next to it.

"Jack," she called. "We've landed. We're getting off."

Nothing.

She waited a beat. Pressed on the buzzer again.

"Jack? Are you okay?"

No answer.

She pressed the door release. The door slid smoothly open.

The bed was made. The bathroom door hung open. The cabin was empty.

Her legs went weak.

"Jack?" She pulled back and charged aft, plunging into the luggage compartment. It was empty. So was the little white kitchenette.

"Mom!" she yelped. "Dad! Have you seen Jack?"

"Isn't he in that back cabin?" her mom shouted back.

"No!" Kestrel's throat choked shut as she hurried toward the front again. "Jack!"

She stopped. Stared at the open ramp.

The busy bustle of the hangar bay rose up to greet her.

"*Jack!*" She raced down the ramp. Her boots pounded on the metal floor as the cool air of the huge, bright hangar rushed through her clothes and hair.

She stumbled to a halt, gaze darting back and forth, searching through the milling crowds of new arrivals and crewmembers. Lighted consoles blinked, carts hummed as they toted luggage back and forth, people laughed and talked. Crowds of people. None of them familiar.

"Jack!" she shouted, heedless of the people who turned to gape at her. "Lieutenant Wolfe!" Her hands clenched into fists. She heard her family come hurrying down the ramp behind her, but she started away from them, toward the crowds...

"*Jack!*" she cried, taking a fistful of the front of her shirt. She waited.

But he didn't appear. And he didn't answer.

He was gone.

TWENTY-TWO

Two Months Later

"Honey?" her mom called from the back door. "You'd better come in. Looks like it's going to rain."

"Okay, give me a second," Kestrel answered. She adjusted the way she was kneeling on the blue towel, secured her grip on her hand shovel and kept digging, deepening the hole in the rich, black earth. The metal scraped and grunted, and dirt got all over her already-stained yellow dress. She didn't notice.

A moist gust of wind blew through the courtyard, cooling the July heat even as the sky darkened. The leaves of the center tree rustled wildly, as did all the rosebushes around the perimeter.

Kestrel finished her hole, then eased the very last purple petunia down into it. She swept the spare dirt all around its base and smiled.

"This rain will be *perfect* for all of you," she told it. "And I don't even have to turn on the sprinklers."

She sat back, resting her muddy hands on her knees, and glanced around the courtyard.

A month ago, she and her mom had dug up all the flagstones around the wall, filled the empty space with rich soil and planted climbing roses, morning glories and ivy, all of which had just taken off with new shoots and blooms. Then, Kestrel and her best friend Anny had taken charge of planting all kinds of other flowers in the beds—including several different colors of roses—and when they'd produced, the two girls had started selling them to the neighbors. Everyone loved them—the roses had a *smell*. So different from the forced blooms at the stores, and infinitely better than the 3D Gramcomm message roses.

Now, a dark shadow fell over the whole garden, and the contrary wind whirled through the courtyard. Large drops of cold water splattered onto the stones—two struck Kestrel's arms. She looked up.

Dark, weighty clouds loomed, churning. Lightning darted around inside them. She took a deep breath of the wind, which hung heavy with the scent of rain. Thunder rolled. She stood up, admiring the shape of the mighty clouds. There was nothing like a summer thunderstorm in Kansas.

"Kestrel!" her mom called out the back window.

"I'm coming," she answered, dusting her hands off on her skirt and striding bare-footed back toward the house, just as the storm broke loose and the rain began to pour.

"It's only seven o'clock and look how dark it is outside," Marcus commented, strolling toward the big window that faced the back yard. Rain gushed across the stones as thunder growled overhead. Kestrel, her arms full, paused next to him, gazing out into the storm. The rest of the house lay in darkness and silence.

"I hate it when the power goes out," Aidus grumbled, flopping down in a chair. "There's nothing to do."

"You two have no imagination," Kestrel determined as she set her things down on her "new" antique secretary desk next to the window. She eased down into the squeaky chair in front of it as she opened the desk and began to arrange.

"What's that stuff?" Marcus asked.

"Treasures," Kestrel answered as she set a candlestick and candle on the top of the desk. Then, she very gently laid two leather-bound books down on the desk, pulled out a tiny box of matches and struck one. Her brothers started.

Flickering golden light blazed to life above Kestrel's hand, and she quickly held it to the wick of the candle. The white candle cheerfully accepted the flame, and glowed inwardly, as if pleased.

"Where did you get those?" Aidus wondered, getting up and coming closer.

"My professor, Dr. Stanley," she answered. "He gave them to me for my birthday." Kestrel picked up the top book, gingerly opened the front cover, and began to read by the firelight. Her brothers stood there.

"*Well?*" Marcus folded his arms. "Don't keep it all to yourself!"

Kestrel smiled.

"'*Rip Van Winkle,*' by Washington Irving," she said. " '*Whoever has made a voyage up the Hudson must remember the Catskill Mountains. They are a dismembered branch of the great Appalachian family, and are seen away to the west of the river, swelling up to a noble height and lording it over the surrounding country....*'"

Kestrel sat alone in her dark bedroom in front of her dresser. The power had been restored, but she didn't tell Ajax to turn on the lights or any music at all. That solitary candle still burned, casting little light and deep shadow across her as she gazed at her reflection. She brushed her long chestnut hair slowly, methodically, enjoying the feel of the brush pulling through her locks. Sighing, she absently ran her eyes across the surfaces in front of her, noting the subtle changes.

Bits of lace softened the edges of the mirror. An old silver bowl held potpourri that smelled of pumpkin pie. A stack of precious blank paper waited off to the left, guarded by a single antique pen. To the right lay the papers that bore her diligent efforts at handwriting, spotted with ink and sometimes marred by wandering lines. But she was getting better. And over on her nightstand sat her three most cherished treasures: books. Jane Austen's *Persuasion*, Washington Irving's *Rip Van Winkle*, and another entitled *Dear Sarah: Love Letters from the Battlefields of the American Civil War.*

She finished, set her brush down, and gently braided her hair, then tied it off. She reached out, her fingertips toying with the edges of the blank paper.

"Honey?"

She looked up. Her mom leaned in her door and smiled. Kestrel answered it.

"Something came for you from the Missouri Society for the Preservation of Antiquities or—something," her mom said. Kestrel's brow furrowed.

"Something *came?*"

Her mom nodded, stepped in and held a piece of paper out to her. Kestrel stared at it.

"Is that...an *envelope?*"

"I don't know—looks like it!" her mom laughed. Kestrel took it with both hands, afraid it would rip, and glanced across the words. It had been hand-written.

Biting her lip and hating to do it, Kestrel carefully tore the envelope open and pulled out the card inside.

"What is it?" her mom asked.

"'Dear Miss Evans,'" Kestrel read. "'Upon the recommendation of your professor, Dr. Stanley, at the Missouri University of Linguistics and Literature, you are hereby invited to a picnic and ice-cream social at the historical Haggerty Mansion in St. Louis. This event will take place at three o'clock in the afternoon, Sunday July 24th. Please wear semi-formal summer attire suitable for outdoors. RSVP by electronic message to Dr. Helen Hildibrand, Co-Chair of the Missouri Society for the Preservation of Antiquities.'"

"That sounds like fun!" her mother exclaimed. "I know what a picnic is, but what's an ice-cream social?"

"Something they used to do all the time in ancient days, just to get together," Kestrel answered, re-reading it. "It's a nice idea."

"I've heard of the Haggerty Mansion," her mom added. "It's beautiful. A big, white house with a huge front porch with pillars and everything. Very, *very* old. You'll love it."

"Dad and I were going to do some job hunting for me that weekend..." Kestrel murmured.

"Job hunt while you're eating ice cream!" her mom countered. "Dr. Stanley got you invited to this—it must mean that he thinks there's an opportunity there for you. I *know* the Haggerty Mansion is a museum. Maybe he wants you to meet someone there!"

Kestrel studied the card.

"Maybe."

"Go to bed," her mom urged. "It's late."

"Okay," Kestrel murmured.

"I love you."

Kestrel looked up at her mom.

"I love you, too."

"G'night, sweetie."

"Goodnight."

Kestrel leaned her elbow on the sill of the train window, watching the bright green countryside flow past outside. She wore a light blue, knee-length dress with soft, ruffled short sleeves and a sash, and white sandals. She'd washed her hair this morning and let it air dry, then pinned sections of it up, letting other strands curl gently around her shoulders and down her back.

The train wound through the forested hills, speeding smoothly toward St. Louis. Kestrel watched the landscape change subtly—the hills rose higher and the valleys reached deeper, and once, swinging out across a suspended bridge, she caught sight of the great, old river.

Finally, the train pulled into the station. She got off with the other passengers, slipping her purse strap over her shoulder and making her way outside. Within moments she was able to hail a little black cab. She slipped into the single back seat as the door slid shut behind her.

"Haggerty Mansion," she said to the android driver.

"*Fifteen minute duration,*" the android answered.

"That's fine," Kestrel replied, and the cab took off. It sped noiselessly through the busy streets, then peeled off down a two-lane road flanked on both sides by tall trees. The sunlight flickered through their branches as she passed. The road dipped and wove, and at last pulled up to a towering stone wall and a black, iron gate. A smiling older man dressed in black and wearing a brimmed hat, who had been standing by the gate, drew up to the window. Kestrel pressed a button and the window rolled up and out of the way.

"I'm sorry, no vehicles with engines are permitted past this point."

Kestrel blinked.

"All right—So I can get out here?"

"Yes, madam," he answered cheerfully. Kestrel pulled out her credit card and slipped it into the payment slot in the cab, then got out. The android said nothing. The door shut. The man in black offered her his arm.

"Welcome to Haggerty Mansion," he said. "I assume you're here for the ice cream social?"

"I am," Kestrel smiled back. "I've been looking forward to it."

"Who invited you?" he asked.

"My former professor, Dr. Stanley."

"Of course! He was supposed to be here today, but I'm afraid he's under the weather."

"Oh. That's too bad," Kestrel said, genuinely disappointed.

"Don't worry," the man assured her, pushing one of the iron gates open. "Dr. Hildibrand will make you feel right at home."

They stepped through, and Kestrel gazed ahead at a broad, weathered lane, hugged on either side by towering oaks.

"Just follow this road here a little way and you'll come to the Lawn," the man instructed. "You're about half an hour early, but Dr. Hildibrand will be there to meet you!"

"Thank you," Kestrel nodded to him, adjusted her purse and started forward.

The air smelled like freshly-cut grass, and as she walked she caught other scents: water from sprinklers. Wildflowers. Pine. The bright sunshine shone down through the oak leaves in cookie-cutter patterns, and the gentle breeze set those patterns dancing across the path in front of her. She reached the end of the lane and drew to a stop, gazing.

A broad lawn, completely canopied by heaven-reaching trees, had been mown down evenly, and dozens of white metal sets of circular tables and chairs filled it. Brilliant flower arrangements stood on each table, along with elegant place-settings and decoratively-folded cloth napkins. Waiters dressed in sharp white swept between these tables, making adjustments and adding touches. Kestrel smiled.

"Miss Evans?"

She straightened, and turned toward the sound of the voice.

A green-eyed, red-headed woman slightly older than her mother smiled at her from beside one of the great trees. She wore an elegant, ankle-length white dress, her hair pinned up in a graceful bun.

"Yes, that's me," Kestrel answered pleasantly. The woman strode up to her and offered her hand, which Kestrel took.

"I'm Dr. Hildibrand, the one who sent you the invitation."

"Very nice to meet you," Kestrel inclined her head.

"I'm so happy you could come!" Hildibrand said earnestly. "So few young people nowadays take an interest in these kinds of events."

"I wouldn't miss it," Kestrel assured her. "I studied history all through school, and my mom told me how beautiful this mansion was."

"Oh, yes, it is *gorgeous*," Hildibrand said. "Unfortunately, the guests of *this* event can't actually enter the house—it's having some renovation done to the plumbing—but since you're early, please feel free to explore the grounds! The house is up that way," Hildibrand turned and pointed toward her right. "And past it, on the side, you'll see a very old, bent-over pear tree, and that's where the family cemetery is. We're very proud of that," she turned a smile back toward Kestrel. "Just a couple months ago, an excavation was begun—a very delicate one, since we didn't want to disturb anybody!—to dig up the headstones that had sunk into the ground! They're all above ground now, clean and straight. You have to go take a look! We'll ring a bell when the social starts."

"Thank you, I will!" Kestrel said, and started off the way Hildibrand had pointed.

She made her way up a slight hill, following a path through a patch of wild rosebushes. When she reached the top of the hill, she passed through a gap in a knee-high stone wall, ducked under a wide, low-hanging oak branch...

And stepped into full sunshine.

A great, wide stretch of vibrant meadow greeted her, dotted with wildflowers. The full, sweet scent that she'd caught earlier—cut grass—flooded her, and she had to stop just to drink it in. She turned to her left...

Framed, sheltered and shaded by two more enormous oaks stood a three-story white mansion. A tall, pillared front porch dominated the first level, a balcony graced the second, and stately black shutters decorated the many tall, four-paned windows. Three chimneys crowned the roof, and ivy crawled up one side of the house. A black iron-wrought lantern hung down from the roof of the porch to light the grand front door, which was painted red. A swing and white wicker furniture waited in inviting circles in the corners of the porch. Kestrel stood looking at it for longer than she knew.

Finally, her feet drew her around to the side of the house, through a long wooden arbor draped in vines, and toward a walled portion of the yard: the cemetery.

It had been planted on a very gentle hill, the headstones facing away from the house, mostly in the unadulterated sunlight. A gnarled old pear tree, half-dead, guarded the little gate in the short wall. Kestrel stepped under the shade of the pear, pushed aside the creaking white gate, and slipped in amongst the headstones.

A soft breeze touched her as her feet swished through the grass. The intricately-carved headstones had indeed been raised from depths—Kestrel could see the fresh earth around each one. But Hildibrand had been correct: the restorers had cleaned and polished every single one. They looked almost new.

Kestrel let her purse slide off her shoulder, and she set it by the first headstone: a pale one bearing a lamb and the brief dates of a baby girl named Elinor. Canting her head, Kestrel wandered down the line of tombs, tracing the names and dates with her eyes, sometimes letting her fingertips drift across the leaf or cross designs.

They were extremely old, all of them. But she noticed as she walked that they were getting newer. She stepped to the row closest to the house and worked her way toward the left, absently murmuring the names to herself.

"Sullivan Haggerty, Mary May Haggerty, Elmer Haggerty, Astoria Elder Haggerty, Angus Haggerty, Margaret Haggerty-Wolfe..." Kestrel stopped.

A very tall tombstone, beautifully carved with roses.

Kestrel whispered the words to herself.

"Margaret Haggerty-Wolfe, Wife of John Wolfe..." She looked to the left of Margaret's stone. "John Wolfe."

Her attention darted back and forth between the dates.

Husband and wife had both died the very same day.

Her heart skipped a beat. The wind whispered through the pear tree.

And she heard something.

Soft plucking. Notes.

Like humming, through a wooden chest.

Notes—harp-like, but richer, more rugged. Gentler.

A guitar.

And she recognized the song.

A soft, slow, steady version of *Leaning on the Everlasting Arms.*

Her heart stopped altogether.

She turned toward the pear tree...

A young man sat on the ground, leaning back against the old trunk, an acoustic guitar in his lap. He wore a loose-fitting white shirt, rolled up to the elbows; jeans, and brown, beaten boots. His handsome head bent, attending to the instrument, his solemn brow furrowed, his hair falling across his forehead. His right hand fingers played expertly across the guitar strings, while the fingertips of his left easily changed chords. And the tattoo on the inside of his left arm stood out against his skin.

Kestrel pressed her right hand to her chest. She listened.

He played the whole song, the notes drifting through the summer air and pulsing through her blood. It slowed. He lifted his hand off the strings, and sat still for an eternal moment.

He turned his head.

He looked at her.

A vivid, gray gaze.

He didn't say anything. Kestrel stood right where she was, trying to keep breathing.

He set his guitar carefully down on the ground to his left, leaning it against the tree, and slowly got to his feet. He dusted his jeans off, stepped through the gate, and walked up to her side. She pressed her hand harder against her chest—every heartbeat hurt.

He hooked his thumbs in his back pockets and faced the tombstones. His shadow fell across her—he was so broad-shouldered and tall...

"That's my mother and father," he said, his deep voice resounding through her whole frame. "This property is hers—she inherited it. The house, the grounds, the orchard out back—everything. That's why there's all these Haggertys buried here."

Kestrel tore her gaze from his profile to look at the tombstones.

"I played hide-and-seek here when I was little," he went on. "With my cousins. It was especially scary when the sun was going down." He nodded to the pair of headstones next to John and Margaret. "Astoria and Angus, those are my mother's parents. That's where I get my middle name. And the ones next to them are my great-grandparents, and so on—their children, too."

He stared back at his parents' graves, falling silent. Kestrel could look nowhere but at him.

He took a breath.

"C'mon," he said—reached down with his right hand, and took hold of her left.

She gasped, thrilling pain jolting through her. He glanced up, past the low wall, and absently entwined their fingers and secured his hold. Then, he turned and drew her out of the cemetery, beneath the pear tree and past his guitar, then up toward the great front lawn.

"This is an excellent place for baseball," he said, gesturing to the wide open space. "Have you ever played?"

"I...No," Kestrel whispered, reveling in the feeling of his warm hand.

"Got to change that," he decided, turning toward the house. Together, they crossed the gravel drive, their feet crunching on the rocks, and stepped up the front walk.

"After I told Robert Conrad who I was, and he believed me, he bought this entire property, restored it and put it in a trust," Wolfe said, striding up the porch steps. "He made it a museum, and paid for its upkeep. He also retrieved a bit of *my* inheritance and put in a savings account to accrue interest. A portion of all his descendants' fortunes went to maintaining all this. It could only transfer *out* of the trust by someone who bears my signature and retina scan." Wolfe paused a moment, smiling distantly. "Robert was always trying to get me to stop hunting, to settle down. Stay put. I never quit arguing with him. But he was never a man to take no for an answer." With that, he twisted the knob and opened the door, then drew her inside.

They stepped into a broad, towering white entryway, dominated by a sweeping staircase, and peaked by a crystal chandelier.

"I'm not going to take it away from the Society for Antiquities," Wolfe said, his voice echoing as he pulled her to the left and through another door. "But I'm going to close off the upper floors to the public."

They entered a lovely morning room, complete with a baby grand piano, open windows and soft yellow furniture. Wolfe kept hold of her fingers.

"This was my mother's favorite room. She always entertained in here," he said.

"It's very pretty," Kestrel managed honestly. He glanced down at her. "You like it?"

"I do," she nodded. He softened.

He took her out into the drawing room, across it, and into a dark-wood study—

Packed with antique books. Kestrel instantly felt light-headed.

"I've never seen this many..." she breathed. A trace of a smile crossed Wolfe's lips.

"I lived in here during the winter," he told her, gesturing to a green chair in the corner by a short table and lamp. "And that was my father's desk," he pointed to a broad, ebony desk that probably weighed a thousand pounds.

"It's impressive," Kestrel said, running her free hand across its smooth surface.

"I am...Well, I can't believe it survived," Wolfe said, his voice unsteady. Kestrel looked up at him, but he was glancing around the room.

He rubbed his thumb against the back of her hand, then took her out of the study and toward the staircase. They climbed up it wordlessly, Kestrel sliding her hand along the banister. At the top, they entered a long, bright hallway hung with portraits—most of which featured children sitting amongst flowers. Their footsteps creaked on the wooden flooring.

"This was a guest bedroom," Wolfe pointed to a door to her right. "Another guest bedroom; *my* room," he said, stepping up and pushing the door out of the way. He shook his head. "They told me there was a leak and the ceiling fell in and ruined everything—it doesn't look anything like it did."

Kestrel took a look. Dark wood, blue walls, a twin-sized bed, a chest of drawers and a masculine vanity mirror. All very plain.

"*This*, on the other hand," Wolfe pulled her out of that room and on down the hall. "Has managed to stay almost the same." They paused in front of great double doors at the end of the corridor. He pushed them both open.

Red carpet. A king-sized bed half hung with embroidered drapes. Lace curtains hanging at the two windows. Two impressive wardrobes; a woman's vanity set and a man's, at opposite ends of the room. Wolfe did not pull Kestrel inside.

"This is the master bedroom," he said. "What do you think of it?"

She glanced up at him. He was watching her. Very carefully. She swallowed, her face heating up, and determined to give an honest assessment.

"Well..." she said. "I love the window seats. And the curtains are gorgeous."

"Anything you would change?"

She hesitated. Looked up at him again.

"Really?" she asked.

He waited.

"Um...I'm not sure I like the red carpet," Kestrel ventured. "Maybe something more neutral? I think it would match the rest of the room, and the house, better."

He considered the chamber. Nodded firmly. Squeezed her hand, turned her and led her further up the stairs.

He showed her the nursery on the third floor, where he told her he'd fallen over his toys that he'd refused to pick up, and broken his arm. He also showed her the servants' quarters, which he noted were now used to store Christmas decorations. Then he took her all the way back downstairs, and they trailed through the grand maroon-colored parlor, the lavish dining room, the enormous ballroom, the pink breakfast room and the state-of-the-art kitchen. He told her all about the new plumbing, and the heating and air conditioning system that had been put in just a few years ago—put in *very* carefully, so as not to ruin any of the walls or flooring. Then he drew her back outside, into the summer heat, and they strolled around toward the back of the mansion, hand in hand.

"*We* didn't have a vine on the side of the house," Wolfe noted. "Mother didn't like the idea—she thought it'd start climbing in through the windows."

Kestrel laughed.

"*I* like it."

"Yeah," Wolfe smiled up at the twining plant. "I do too."

They passed around the back corner of the house, and Kestrel caught sight of a rear building she hadn't seen before: a majestic, old, white stable. The two walked underneath the shady arms of another live oak, listening to the birds tweeting in its upper reaches.

"There's only one horse here right now," Wolfe told her as they reentered the sunshine and their feet brushed through the wildflowers. "She's semi-retired, and pulls a buggy for tourists. I'd like to get more horses, maybe two or three young ones to ride. Have you ever ridden?"

"Just a blastbike," Kestrel answered.

"Nothing alike," he chuckled, shaking his head. "I'll take you to auction. You can pick one out."

"A horse?" Kestrel's heart jumped. He looked at her.

"Would you like one?"

She suddenly grinned.

"*Yes*," she nodded. "I...Yes, I would."

They reached the stables, and he gave her a tour of the whole thing, telling her all about his great black horse named Captain that he'd bred, raised and broken himself—then ridden him into and lost him to the war. His mother had had a strawberry mare, his father a big bay. And when he'd been very little, he'd had a gray pony named Swift. Kestrel watched him as he spoke, as he gestured. With every word, she saw weight lift from him, and his scars seemed to fade. And he never let go of her hand.

Finally, he tucked her arm under his and pressed her hand to his chest, and escorted her back past the house and down the hill into the trees, toward the picnic lawn.

Dozens of people sat at the tables, all dressed in bright colors, eating and talking. But Wolfe led her past them, toward the shaded lane.

"Oh, good! You found her!"

They turned and saw Dr. Hildibrand clasp her hands together in pleasure. She smiled at them.

"Yes, thank you Miss Helen," Wolfe inclined his head to her. "Have a good afternoon."

"We will, thank you," she promised.

"Where are *we* going?" Kestrel asked quietly as they strode away from the party and back up the road she'd walked in on. His eyes gained a tinge of sadness.

"I have to show you something."

Kestrel frowned, but didn't press him. They strolled the rest of the way without saying anything, gently swinging their linked hands. When they reached the gate, Wolfe smiled at the older man waiting outside.

"Hello, Mr. Charles."

"Hello, Mr. Wolfe," Charles replied. "Here's your taxi for you."

"Thank you," Wolfe nodded, and drew Kestrel up to the side of a two-passenger taxi that stood waiting. Kestrel's curiosity flared from the mere embers it was before, but she didn't say anything—she had to let go of Wolfe to get inside. He bent down and slid in after her, shut the door, and immediately picked up her hand again, her right one this time. He focused straight ahead, even as he absently rubbed his fingertips across her palm and up and down her fingers.

The android had apparently been pre-programmed—the taxi sped off, back down the winding road, and up to the train station again. They got out, walked through the bustle and out onto the platform. Wolfe dug in his pocket, slid a card through a reader, and the train doors opened. They climbed onboard the comfortable car, and Kestrel chose a pair of seats. They sat down, and he laid an arm around her shoulders.

For the hundredth time, Kestrel glanced up at his face—but for the first time, she sensed something within him, something that wrestled deep inside him. It wasn't that he wished to show her affection by putting his arm around her. Instead, it was as if he couldn't resist the impulse. As if he couldn't bear it if she was not touching him.

She eased against his side, feeling his hand rest on her arm. But the tension remained in his chest even as the train lurched out of the station.

They rode for a very long time. Kestrel watched the country flit by outside, gradually flattening. The train stopped at The Hub in Kansas City, but they didn't get off. The speed train continued west, and the land calmed, the forests faded back, and the sky opened up. Finally, the train hit a small town called Valley Falls, Kansas, and Wolfe stood up, pulling Kestrel with him. They got off the train, moved through the station, and again stepped out into the late afternoon sunshine.

It smelled different here. The air was filled with the scent of sun-baked grass. They caught another cab, climbed in, and Wolfe leaned forward.

"320 Jefferson, please," he said.

"*The farm, sir?*" the android asked.

"Yes."

The cab drove off, and they left the station behind.

As soon as they left the limits of the town, Kestrel's attention wandered over the light green hills of waving grass, the gentle valleys filled with shimmering cottonwoods, and the herds of brown, grazing cattle. The sky had altered completely, gained a towering depth, a piercing, pure blue that she didn't remember seeing in a very long time.

They turned, and headed down a perfectly straight road, Kestrel counting the gleaming silver fence posts as they went. Finally, they drew to a stop by a tall, iron ranch gate. Wolfe slipped his credit card into the reader, and they got out.

"Wait for us," Wolfe instructed the android. "We won't be long."

"*Yes, sir.*"

Together, Wolfe and Kestrel strode through the gate, and up to a massive blue farm house, flanked by two great industrial barns and three mighty silos. Two dogs came barreling out, barking—Wolfe didn't break stride. The dogs jumped all around them, panting excitedly. Wolfe reached down once and tousled the black lab's ears. Kestrel petted the head of an Irish setter, who then glued her shoulder to Kestrel's right leg and looked up at her adoringly, her tongue lolling. Kestrel laughed.

"Jack, boy!"

Kestrel looked up to see a middle-aged, bearded man standing out on the porch, wearing jeans, boots and a work shirt. Gregarious smile-lines marked his face.

"Mr. Carter," Wolfe greeted him, raising a hand. "How are you?"

"Good!" Carter answered. "Just came in for supper! Why don't you join us?"

Startled, Kestrel glanced back and forth between the two men. Wolfe shook his head.

"We'd love to, but we can't stay long." Wolfe motioned to Kestrel. "Kestrel, this is Aaron Carter. Mr. Carter, this is Miss Kestrel Evans."

"Nice to meet you," Carter said, coming down off his porch toward them. "When Jack here told me what was on my property, I couldn't believe it—but he got those archaeologists in here and wouldn't you know it?" He put his hands in his pockets. "I'm glad, though. Now that poor girl can get the rest she deserves."

Wolfe quietly smiled, and lowered his head. Kestrel watched them carefully.

"So you're here to show her that site, huh?" Carter squinted at Wolfe. Wolfe nodded.

"Yeah, if it isn't any trouble."

"No trouble!" Carter cried. "You go right ahead. And I don't care what you say, stop in and get a drink of something before you head back. It's close to a hundred degrees out here."

"Thank you," Wolfe said again.

"I'd better get inside—my wife's going to holler at me," Carter winked. "Nice to meet you, again, Miss Evans."

"Nice to meet you, too," Kestrel answered. Carter charged back up his porch steps, pulled the door open and went back inside.

"This way," Wolfe tugged slightly on her hand, and together they rounded one of the silos. Thick grass waited for them, and a narrow path cut through it. Wolfe had to lead, still gripping her fingers. The dogs didn't pay any attention to the path—they bounced headlong through the weeds, sending the buzzing grasshoppers flying. They continued down a slight hill, to a thicket of trees. Kestrel heard water gurgling as they entered the shade.

They stopped at the edge of a wide, shallow, sandy-bottomed creek—completely clear, singing softly. The dogs ploughed into it, splashing recklessly, and lowered their mouths to take sloppy drinks. Kestrel hesitated—

Wolfe pulled her closer, bent and picked her up. She gasped and held on tight as he stepped up to his knees into the creek, and carried her across to the other side. He sloshed up onto the bank and set her down lightly.

"Thank you."

"Your dress and shoes are too pretty to ruin," he murmured, lacing their fingers again. Kestrel blushed, and the two of them followed the path up the bank to the top of a little hill...

They crested it. Stopped.

Kestrel stilled.

Out there, on the edge of a golden field that stretched to the end of the earth, stood a solitary tombstone.

Carved out of pale limestone in the shape of a Celtic cross, it waited, unmoving, a stark contrast to the waving wheat behind it.

Wolfe's hand tightened hard on Kestrel's. She answered the pressure.

For a long while, neither of them moved. Then, slowly, Wolfe stepped forward. Kestrel stayed beside him. Their feet crunched on dry grass, then on dirt that had been heaved up recently and smoothed. A mound of earth, much darker and full of clay, lay before the cross. And as they drew near, Kestrel could read the name carved on the crossbar.

ADELAIDE BARNES-WOLFE

They stood in front of the grave for several minutes, saying nothing, Wolfe rubbing his thumb back and forth, back and forth on Kestrel's hand.

"I made that. The cross," he muttered, halfway pointing to it.

"It's beautiful," Kestrel whispered.

"Wish I could get some more stone," he cleared his throat. "Bill should have one, too."

"Bill?" Kestrel canted her head.

"My dog. Was in the house, sleeping," Wolfe smiled crookedly as his eyes shone. "Worthless mutt."

Kestrel smiled, and it hurt. Wolfe gazed at the wheat.

"She died six-hundred forty-four years ago," Wolfe whispered. "But to me it feels like it's just been three." He drew himself up and pulled in a breath. "I told myself for so long that I could go back, fix everything. But I know now I can't. I never could have."

Kestrel watched him, her heart throbbing.

"What I would have had to do—what I would have *become*..." He stared distantly at the cross. "And...I would have lost you."

Kestrel swallowed. He paused, his jaw tightening. Then, he stepped around in front of her, turning his back on the grave. She didn't move.

He pressed both her hands to his chest and held them there, gazing earnestly down at her.

"You know," he murmured, suddenly unsteady. "That night at the pub, when you stepped on my feet..." he paused, expression flickering. "I never stood a chance, after that."

Kestrel couldn't keep her eyes off him. And beneath her fingers, she could feel his great heart pounding wildly.

She slipped her left hand loose of his gentle grip, reached slowly up and touched his face. Ran her fingertips across his cheekbone, his eyebrow—the long scar on his forehead. Wolfe's eyelids fluttered closed. She brought her other hand up to caress a strand of his hair away from his brow. His hands slid down to rest in the crooks of her elbows. Gently, she traced the scar on his right cheek, then the corners of his mouth, his soft lips. Then, she stroked her fingers through the hair on the sides of his head, and drew him down to her.

He gave way. His eyes stayed shut. Kestrel leaned up toward him, standing on tiptoe...

Her nose brushed his. His breathing quickened.

Her lips found his again.

She kissed him. He breathed deeply, his desperation gone. She pressed deeper—and he instantly answered.

His hands slid up to cradle her neck, and he tasted her mouth deliberately, longingly. He lowered his arms and wrapped her up—lifting her off the ground, and Kestrel could do nothing but hold onto him and drown in the earthy scent of him.

He slowly bent. Her feet touched the ground again, and his fingers

242

wound through her hair.

One last aching kiss lingered on their lips, and he finally drew back. But he kept hold of her head, and looked straight into her eyes.

And, for the first time in ages, his gaze sparkled.

He kissed her forehead—fervently pressed his mouth against her skin. Then, he pulled her close and held her to him, sighing. She encircled his waist and embraced him tightly, burying her face in his chest. And that knotted tension in his body melted, and vanished.

"You think your parents would mind if you brought me home for dinner?" he finally asked, his deep voice rumbling through her head. She grinned into his shirt.

"Not if you take off your muddy shoes at the door."

He chuckled, which sent pleasure tingling all through her body. He turned from her, just enough to wrap an arm around her waist and guide her back toward the creek.

"Why do you want to come home for dinner?" she asked as they stopped on the bank.

"I think your brothers may hate me," he said, scooping her up easily. "And there's something I need to ask your father."

She considered him, mystified, but he only smiled secretively and carried her back across the water and set her down. They strode out of the shade, back up the path, but this time Wolfe walked through the grass, so he could keep beside Kestrel. She smiled, and leaned her head against his arm.

"You know, that night I stepped on your feet at the pub..." she remarked as she reached down and entwined their fingers. "...I never had a chance, either."

And her heart swelled as she watched Jack tilt his face toward the sunshine, close his eyes, and smile.

The End

Other novels by
Alydia Rackham

Christmas Parcel

Bauldr's Tears: A Retelling of Loki's Fate

Scales: A Fresh Telling of Beauty and the Beast

Linnet and the Prince

The Last Constantin

The Oxford Street Coffee House

The Beowulf Seeker

The Riddle Walker

www.alydiarackham.webs.com
alydia.rackham@facebook.com

On Patreon:
https://www.patreon.com/AlydiaRackham?ty=h

Made in the USA
Lexington, KY
11 July 2017